CAMPFIRE CATASTROPHE

AMI DIANE

Copyright

For all of humanity during a dark night. May the sun rise on us again.

CHAPTER ONE

ELLA BARTON STOOD in a clearing in the middle of the Keystone Forest. She inhaled the scent of pine, fir, spruce, and dirt, trying very hard to ignore the litany of curses floating over from a nearby tent.

"Yep, nothing like the great outdoors."

Flo planted her hands on her hips and aimed a well-placed kick at the tent. Her under-developed muscles caused the green canvas to do nothing more than flutter. "I'm just gonna set it on fire."

"Yes, that'll make for a great sleeping experience."

The tent hung limply, listing to one side. Flo stooped over a stake and wrestled with the rope. Before Ella could finish saying, "You're doing it wrong," the rope had already coiled tightly around Flo's arm in a python grip.

Flo's face turned a dangerous shade of red, and her foul mouth released another chorus of expletives that would've made a trucker blush. Ella smiled at their audience: six kids, ranging in age from eight to sixteen. They stood gaping at Flo in her tower of hair and thick, coke-bottle glasses.

"Don't worry, kids. She has this condition called Tourette syndrome." Ella's smile remained fixed as she said through gritted teeth, "Hey, Bride of Frankenstein. Take a break. You're scaring the kids."

"This rope's knotted…" Flo grunted, then let out a frustrated growl. The next utterances out of her mouth were words even Ella, a linguist, had never heard.

Ella had to speak loudly to drown her out. "Hey, kids, why don't you go play in the forest or something? I think I saw a pinecone over there. Should be fun to toss around."

"Horatio doesn't want them wandering off," Wink called out beside a perfectly erect tent.

"What the—when did you put that up?" Last Ella had looked, the diner owner had been unfurling the canvas. "Hey, Flo. See that?" Ella pointed. "That's what it's supposed to look like."

"Eat my knickers, Poodle Head." The rope cutting off circulation to her arm had, somehow, extended to her legs, ensnaring them, as well.

"If you're going to insult me, do it right. The phrase is, 'eat my shorts'. And that's such an outdated burn, I regret telling it to you. What is this, the 1990s? Hey, Flo, Bart Simpson called, and he wants his catch phrase back." Since no one laughed, she made her own rimshot sound effect.

The army green canvas of Wink's tent rippled in a gentle breeze, proudly, as if to show off how unlike Flo's tent it was. This was a proper tent. Even Chester, darting about the diner owner's feet, chittered his approval before ducking inside.

For the occasion, Wink had dressed the squirrel in a scout uniform, reminiscent of the ones worn by Boy Scouts and the surrounding Firefly troop. As to her own attire, Wink had chosen a particularly loud velour tracksuit, one she'd promised Ella she'd never wear again.

Ella wondered if there was a covert way to "accidentally" throw the outfit into the campfire later. At least hunters could spot that fluorescent green fabric prancing through the woods from miles away.

Having finished a full circle around Wink's tent, surveying it, Ella rubbed her hands together, eager to finish setting up. "Alright, where's the rest of it?"

"The rest of what?" Wink asked.

"You know, the rest of the camping gear? Blow-up mattress, portable heater, travel toilet, chairs, bbq…" Her voice trailed off at the confused expressions aimed her way. "No?" She did her best to hide her disappointment, shrugging. "Looks like we're roughing it. What about my tent?"

Wink continued to stare at her. "What do you mean?"

Ella indicated Wink's fully formed tent, then Flo's drooping one—which now resembled a melted candle. "I thought you said you were bringing one for me since I don't have my own camping gear."

"Yes, this is it." Wink inclined her head towards the standing tent.

"Well, that was sweet of you to put it up for me. I'll help you with y—"

"We're sharing."

It took a moment for Ella to process this statement. Then she poked her head inside the confined space. "But where will you sleep?"

"In there."

"Where's the rest of it?"

"That's it."

She looked from her boss to the tiny, simple tent, the entirety of which could be summed up into three parts: canvas, rope, and tent pegs.

One of Wink's eyebrows arched. "It's either this or you share with Daniel Boone over there."

"I'd rather hug a velociraptor."

At the Keystone inn, Ella's bedroom was across the hall from Flo's, and she was well acquainted with the fact that the woman's snoring rattled windows.

"Fair warning," Flo said, her hand now turning a funny purple shade from the lack of circulation, "I sleep in my birthday suit."

"Well, thanks for the nightmares." Ella dismissed the issue with a wave. "It's fine. I'll share with Wink. Remind me some time to introduce you to the wonders of *glamping*. Now that's the kind of camping I like."

Nearby, Horatio—cook at Grandma's Kitchen and, as it turned out, troop leader of the Fireflies—instructed the kids on how to set up their tents. The Firefly troop, according to the lengthy history he'd told her despite her insistence that she didn't care, had started some years back at Keystone's church as a means to teach kids survival skills. Given that they lived in a town that saw all manner of life and environments, Ella thought the intention of the troop a great idea.

When he'd enlisted her and the other one and a half adults' help, he'd said the troop had been planning the trip for some time, but they'd had to postpone when Keystone Village had been overrun by dinosaurs. That and the giant mosquitos. It turned out, parents weren't overly fond of sending their children off into the woods to be maimed and contract malaria.

She stared into the forest. The daylight was waning, creating longer, deeper shadows along the forest floor. The surrounding woods hid the landscape of Keystone Village's new location: another forest of deciduous trees and low mountains. It blended nicely with the surrounding native Colorado plant life.

The weather of the current clime was mild, raining occasionally, the temperatures warranting sweatshirts and light sweaters. The best part, however, was that it lacked certain man-eating reptiles.

Suddenly, the bough of a pine bobbed up and down while the others around it remained still. "Uh, random question, but when was the last dinosaur spotted?"

"Yesterday." Wink's mouth cracked into a wide grin. "I'm kidding. You should see your face."

"Hilarious. So, the woods were combed thoroughly?"

"Sure," came Wink's absent reply. She slid a compact mirror from her tracksuit and checked her reflection, fluffing her pink hairdo.

"Meaning not at all?"

"Meaning the Murphy brothers were in charge of that."

"I don't know what that means."

Near the ground, Flo spoke up. She'd managed to free her hand, but only because she'd attacked the rope with her pocket knife. The rest of her arm and her leg were still hope-lessly ensnared. "Them boys are namby-pambies. Scared of their own shadows, if you ask me. I doubt they so much as stepped foot in the forest."

"Why'd they volunteer then?"

Flo grunted, extricating her forearm. "You were at the meetin'. No one else wanted the job."

"Plus," Wink added, stowing the compact mirror in her backpack, "they probably thought it'd impress some of the female population."

"That's—holy 1990s MTV music video. Wink, your pants read 'Hers' across the butt."

Wink grinned. "Isn't it darling? I have the matching set that reads *His*, but I can't get Stewart to wear it."

"What a shame." Ella made a mental note to thank the grocery store merchant, along with applauding his sense of good taste.

Once all the tents were set up in a circle and Flo's resembled a lean-to, the troop gathered in the center and prepared a fire, stacking kindling in a teepee shape with Ella and Wink offering unhelpful tips. Flo opted to watch, suspiciously attentive. Once the kindling was ready to be lit, Horatio turned to ask the troop for matches. As he did, there was a soft *whoosh* from the fire pit behind him.

Flames devoured the wood and shot high above their heads. Ella grabbed the nearest Firefly—a young girl with freckles and red hair—and yanked her back. The heat blasted her skin, her face instantly prickling with sweat. Others dove for cover, crying out—except for an older boy who shouted, "Neat!"

Wink held her arms out protectively, shielding others.

"What happened?" Horatio shrieked in a thick Italian accent.

Flo, firelight dancing in her eyes in a way that suggested the woman needed to see a psychiatrist, held aloft a canteen of water and a small jar of white powder. "Sorry, did you wanna do the honors?"

Ella rose to her knees, helped the young red-headed girl up, and glanced at her watch. "Under an hour, and she's nearly singed off her eyebrows. And after they just grew back, too. That has to be a record."

"Not a record," Wink corrected. "There was that one time she blew up a stump, then caused a small fire in my car on the way to the hospital."

Flo scowled. "I told you, I don't know how the pin fell outta my stun grenade."

Horatio's face turned varying shades of red before settling on a light flush. He sputtered several words in Italian.

Ella whispered theatrically to Flo, "I'd be happy to interpret that for you. Spoiler: it involves your mother."

"I turned my back for one moment, Florence!" Horatio seethed, finally finding English. He breathed heavily through his nostrils, visibly struggling to curb his true feelings in light of their audience. "What did you do?"

Flo sifted the jar of powder back and forth. "Will said it was calcium oxide something or other. Anyway, he called it... quicklime, I think?" She gave a small shrug with her generous shoulders. "Whatever it is, it's amazing. Ignites when water touches it."

"Quicklime..." Ella said softly, more to herself. The word sparked a distant memory from a high school history class. "Wait, isn't that what the Byzantines used for Greek fire? Will gave you Greek fire?" Her voice grew shrill. "Fan-freaking-tastic. I was just thinking, 'Hey, Ella, you know what this camp-out is missing? A forest fire. Yeah, that's what we need.'"

She was going to have a serious talk with the inventor about enabling Flo's love of incendiary devices and propellents.

Once the fire had dwindled from a height of The Depths of Hell to something that wouldn't make Smokey Bear cry—and Flo's quicklime had been confiscated—the troop timidly gathered around the fire once again. The patch of sky over the clearing was streaked in pinks and purples that bled into a deep blue, the surrounding trees obscuring what promised to be a brilliant sunset.

Ella left the fire to retrieve a sweatshirt and found Wink unpacking a cooler, one of the few camping accouterments she'd brought.

"I'm hungry."

"How do you do, Hungry? I'm Wink."

"Wow. Great dad joke."

Wink's brows furrowed. "What's a dad joke?"

"Only the greatest type of joke ever." Ella leaned over the cooler to peer inside, but Wink shooed her away.

"You ate before we left."

"Yeah, but that was—" Ella checked her watch "—two hours ago."

"You ate half a pie, child."

"And your point...?"

Really, the woman should be impressed rather than chastise her. Also, when she burped, it still tasted of apple and cinnamon. And how could that be a bad thing?

Since the town lacked the mainstay ingredient to make s'mores (chocolate), Wink had come up with an innovative treat involving a muffin pan, biscuit dough, and vanilla pudding. Supposedly, it tasted like eclairs sans chocolate, but Ella had her doubts. Not for the first time did she lament the fact that the town's greenhouses didn't grow cacao beans.

While Wink and Flo portioned out bits of dough, using the cooler as a makeshift table, Ella instructed the six Fireflies on how to assemble the treat.

"Right. So, it's pretty straightforward, really. Take a ball of dough, flatten it to about a half an inch in thickness, then lay it over the underside of this muffin tin. Make sure you remember which one's yours." She added the last instruction when a young boy with badges and cow-licked hair named Sam rooted his finger inside a nostril.

She continued her instructions, explaining how the dough baked into a bowl for them to scoop vanilla pudding into.

"I also brought strawberry jam, frosting, and whipped cream," Wink added. Just then, Chester climbed her leg like a tree, scrambled up her back, and perched on her shoulder.

Ella nodded. "Yes, if you want cavities, add all the things Grandma Wink just mentioned."

After Wink gave a subtle nod that they were ready, Ella held up a hand, then brought it down as if starting a race. A breeze bristled her clothes as the hooligans swept past her in a mad dash. Their energy would heighten once the sugar rush kicked in, but after that would come the glorious sugar crash—a rollercoaster ride she was all too familiar with after many Halloweens and, more recently, working in the diner.

Wink handed a ball of dough to a young boy with dirt freckles splashed across his cheeks, saying to Ella, "Aren't you forgetting something?"

"Hmm? Oh, yeah." In her announcer voice, she added, "Also, if Flo over there says anything offensive—more than you've already heard—come see either Wink or me. Wait, no. On second thought, scratch what I just said. We'd have too many complaints. Just come get us if she gets to the point you feel endangered." Ella ended her speech with a satisfied nod.

"That's not what I meant," Wink said, "but I'm glad you warned them all the same."

Flo scowled. "Keep talkin', Poodle Head. I know where you eat, and I know where to find some laxatives. Take from that what you will."

Ella winced.

The kids raced off to the bonfire, dough and muffin tin in hand. They gathered around the dancing flames, and Horatio searched for a spot to rest the muffin tin where it wouldn't be completely engulfed by fire.

Ella, Wink, and Flo remained at the cooler, watching the chaos.

"Ah, nothing like a good bonfire." Ella's finger drifted towards the pudding bowl before Wink slapped her hand aside.

Soon, darkness descended, causing the temperature to drop. In jackets, sweaters, and blankets, they huddled together on the logs while Wink began a ghost story. Her voice drifted through the cool air, weaving with the popping of the fire. Chester snoozed on her lap, his tail twitching.

The faces of the troop glowed in the amber light, their eyes riveted on Grandma Wink as she told her tale of the ghost of a Tyrannosaurus rex coming to take revenge on the towns-people who'd killed it. Even the preteens listened raptly, though they tried to hide their interest.

Just outside the reach of the light, Flo hunched over, hidden in shadows. Ella couldn't see what she was doing but heard the disconcerting noise of clinking metal.

What fresh hell is this?

With a sigh, Ella discreetly abandoned the warm circle for the cold darkness. Flo remained hunched over, oblivious to Ella's presence behind her. She hovered over the woman, watching her cotton candy hair wobble about, hiding whatever dangerous or illicit activity she was up to.

"Whatcha doing?" Ella whispered in Flo's ear.

The senior citizen jumped, a surprisingly feminine yelp escaping her. "Poodle Head, you can't sneak up on me like that. Not unless you want a blast from The Hammer."

"The Hammer? Is that what you're calling your right hook? Because I have to tell you, the wind from your farts is stronger."

Flo's wrinkled hands held up a familiar weapon that looked like a potato gun on steroids with an ominous glow at the end of the metallic cylinder. Her plasma cannon. Experience and Sal's apartment window could attest to the fact that it shot plasma balls capable of wreaking havoc and singing eyebrows.

Maybe it was a trick of the weedy firelight, but the boarder's hands seemed to tremble under its weight. She tapped a finger on the optical sight mounted on top. "I added this last night."

"Good, maybe now you can actually hit your targets. Also, in no way, shape, or form does that resemble a hammer."

"I'm glad you asked—"

"I didn't."

"Thanks for taking an interest, Poodle Head."

"I'm not. I just wanted to know what it was I was confiscating." Before the old broad could so much as protest or move an arthritic joint, Ella wrenched the weapon away.

"Hey!"

"You'll get this back at the end of the campout tomorrow."

As Ella hefted the plasma cannon onto her shoulder to stow it in hers and Wink's tent, Flo produced a hunting knife from some location near her ankle. She leveled Ella with a glare before using the blade to clean dirt from under her fingernails.

By the time Wink finished her story, the kids were yawning. Horatio rose and clapped his hands, saying in a sonorous, accented voice that it was time for them to "punch the hay." This was met by an awkward silence.

"Do you mean, 'hit the hay'?" Ella asked finally.

Nodding, he bounced enthusiastically on the balls of his feet. "Tomorrow, we go hiking."

As the Fireflies shuffled off to their respective tents in pairs, Ella groaned. "Didn't we get enough exercise hiking in with all this gear?"

"What gear?" Wink asked. "You just had your backpack."

"Yes, but half of it was Flo's stuff."

Wink chuckled. "You fell for her backache line, didn't you?"

"What? No, of course not." She had. "I was simply worried about her keeling over dead on us and ruining our trip."

When Ella had spotted Flo the Liar foisting the rest of her supplies off onto Billy, she'd forced her to carry all her gear again, including the rocks she'd discreetly added to the bottom of the woman's backpack.

"I'm with Poodle Head. Why do we need to do any more wandering through the woods?" Flo lounged across a large log near the fire. "What're are we going to see there that we don't see here, hmm? More trees?"

Wink side-eyed her. "The exercise'll be good for you. And El, I thought you went for jogs regularly?"

Ella waved the question aside. "That's different." She wasn't sure how, but it was.

After ensuring the youngsters were tucked into their sleeping bags, Horatio rejoined them by the fire. Ella reveled in the beautiful silence that followed, broken all too soon when one of the tents started giggling.

She held up a hand. "I got this." Without getting up, she announced, "I'll be sending Flo over to anyone who makes noise in the next five minutes." The tent stilled, and the blissful peace returned once again.

"You joke," Flo said, "but I got a gas canister in my bag that'll put them right to sleep."

"You're great with kids, you know that?"

They stayed up for a while longer, the night stretching out, joined by a dusting of stars overhead. Wink and Flo fell into one of their usual arguments about who would bring the better dish to the potluck the next day while Ella taught Horatio new American Sign Language signs for various items around them.

His son, who'd just had his second birthday, was deaf. Since there wasn't a Deaf culture in the isolated town, she was doing her best to create one for him at home, as well as showing the cook how important it was for Jack to have full access to ASL. Once they'd covered the obvious vocabulary of FIRE and TENT and FOREST, she refreshed him on the grammatical structure of the language.

"Remember, ASL has a different syntax than English. It goes topic followed by comment or subject-verb-object, if you will. And if there's an adjective, it proceeds the noun or pronoun it modifies, not precedes it, like in English. We'll get deeper into verb tense and negation another time. We'll also discuss how to make a noun from a verb by duplicating the sign, as in SIT versus CHAIR."

His eyes glazed over. "Huh?"

She mentally played back her words, wondering where she'd lost him and at what point she hadn't been clear. A realization struck her. "Oh my gosh, this must be how Will feels when he talks theoretical physics with me."

Ignoring her comment, Horatio announced loudly that he would be punching the hay. After he left, she snuggled into her sweatshirt, listening to the soothing sounds of the forest —nature's sound machine. The croak of frogs. A breeze in the branches overhead. The shrill arguing of geriatric hellions.

When she could no longer keep her eyes open, she stood. The fire had died down to an orange glow with small flickering flames.

"I'm going to punch the hay. Wink, I apologize in advance if I snore. And by 'if' I mean I most definitely will."

Sometime during the night, Ella sat up with a start. At first, she wasn't sure what had awoken her. Her ears strained, listening to Wink's soft breathing beside her. Outside the tent came Flo's percussive snores, sounding like a wrench caught in a garbage disposal. That had to have been what woke her.

She turned over, feeling the cold metal of The Hammer digging into her side. Sleep tugged at her, and she'd just begun to drift off when there came a loud, animalistic scream from the surrounding woods.

She bolted upright again, her breath catching in her throat. The feral scream sounded a second time, putting the hair on the back of her neck at attention.

What *was* that?

She'd never heard a cougar cry in person before, but the noise sounded similar to the mountain lion screams in movies. It didn't come from nearby, but the fact that she could hear it at all made it too close for comfort.

Her hands fumbled for Flo's weapon, and she hugged it to her chest, listening. If the cougar got any closer, she'd take the plasma cannon out for a late-night stroll. Actually, she'd send Flo out with it for a late-night stroll.

It was a long while before sleep caught her again.

CHAPTER TWO

"DID ANYONE ELSE hear that noise last night?" Ella asked over a plate of bacon. They sat around a morning campfire Horatio had coaxed back to life after telling Flo she couldn't use her quicklime. Blank faces met Ella's. "No? Just me? Cool."

"I heard it," a small voice said.

She looked around, her eyes finally locating the source of the voice. The youngest Firefly, the same red-headed girl she'd saved from Flo's inferno—about eight if Ella had to guess—sat one log over.

The Firefly looked up from her scrambled eggs with wide eyes, freckles standing out against pale skin.

"What did you hear, Judy?" Horatio asked, settling down with a ham and cheese omelet and a lemon blueberry scone topped with cream.

"I-I don't know. But it was awful. Sounded like a scream, but... different."

Horatio looked from her to Ella, his brows drawing together.

With a mouth full of bacon, Ella described what she'd heard, then said, "Have there been reports of any cougar in this area? Besides Flo, I mean."

Wink shook her head. Despite having just rolled out of a sleeping bag, the woman's 1950s dark pink coif looked as fresh as if she'd just come from the beauty parlor.

"Maybe it was that hairy, overgrown ape-thing." Flo used her hunting knife to cut into her omelet. On one side of the plate was a collection of red onions excavated from her food.

"That's not a very nice way to describe Leif," Ella said.

"Not the Viking. I was referrin' to... Footman? Big Ape? What's he called?"

"Do you mean Bigfoot?" The boarder was a paranormal enthusiast, but the lore of Bigfoot had only begun gaining ground in the early 1950s.

Flo nodded. Ella crunched into another bacon strip, then paused, considering the idea. This was Keystone Village. If she hadn't faced down dinosaurs a few weeks back, she would've thought the idea of Sasquatch living in the forest crazy. Here, crazy was as relentless as Flo leaving her toenail clippings all over the bathroom floor despite Ella's repeated threats that she'd cut off her toes if she persisted.

"What's that?" One of Wink's delicate fingers pointed at the plate of bacon on Ella's lap. "You were supposed to pass that around to the others."

"What? Really?" She looked around at the Fireflies, all staring hungrily at the pile of bacon. "You guys didn't want any, did you?"

A log over, Horatio waved his fork at her in a warning. Reluctantly, Ella passed the plate off to Judy, but not before snagging one more crispy strip for herself.

The clearing brightened as the morning aged. The scent of smoke mixed with fresh, crisp air hinted at a warm day ahead.

After the food had been stowed in airtight containers, then stuffed into Wink's ancient cooler, they changed clothes and reconvened in the clearing. They would break down the camp when they returned.

Once Horatio ensured the fire had died to embers, he led them into the forest. Wink followed, then came the Fireflies, while Ella and Flo took up the rear. They marched around trees and ducked under branches, dodging an undergrowth of ferns and bushes.

Eventually, they met up with a trail, and walking became easier. Now, they could hike two abreast, which meant Flo jostled Ella's elbow constantly, huffing like a steam engine with pneumonia.

To be fair, the woman was packing considerably more weight than Ella, most of it in the form of the plasma cannon riding atop her shoulder. For once, Ella hadn't objected to Flo arming herself, not after that eery scream the night before. Her eyes darted about on a constant swivel, her mind occupied with the frightening, feral cries heard during the night.

When the group paused for a rest, she pulled out her canteen and sipped. Then she exchanged it for a thermos of fresh coffee she'd poured from the percolator on the fire before leaving. She needed the caffeine boost after lying awake half the night, cuddling Flo's cannon like a body pillow, listening. The flavor of the coffee was dulled, somewhat, by a stuffy nose. Morning smoke from the campfire wasn't doing her seasonal allergies any favors.

What she'd thought was a water break turned out to be a lesson in reading compasses. She joined Wink and Flo on a collection of large rocks and sipped the weak brew, watching.

"See the needle?" Horatio said. "It's pointing to Magnetic North, yes? But because this direction changes so often when Keystone jumps, we kept the town's original orientation. So, the greenhouses are north, and Stewart's and the wind farm are south. Main Street runs north and south. It makes it easier. It's what you would call…"

He glanced at Ella for confirmation of the correct word. "… arbitrary?" She nodded. "Yes, arbitrary," he continued with more confidence. "However, if you were to get lost in our large forest, it might be a problem. It becomes important to know which direction is really north." He held up the compass. "That's why we'll learn this skill."

He rotated on the spot until the red arrow pointed straight at his waist. Around him, the Fireflies mimicked his movements.

"Before I got stranded in this town," he continued, "I knew what hemisphere I lived in, then all I had to do was face the sun at noon, and that was south.

"Now, however, when we don't immediately know what hemisphere we're in, or have to guess the season based on the angle of the sun, it's a lot harder, yes? We rely on the stars more than we used to, much as the navigators of old did. Fortunately, we have some amateur astronomers around."

Flo snorted. "You mean Tate Gingrich?"

"I don't think that's what he uses his telescope for," Wink chimed in.

"What's he use it for?" Judy asked. She was struggling to get the bezel on her compass to turn in her small hands.

Flo leaned towards her, giving what she probably thought was a pleasant smile, but looked more akin to a wolf about to chow down on its next meal. "He points it across the street at Betty—*oof.*" Wink had elbowed her in the ribs.

Holding his compass level, Horatio waved them to look over, ignoring Flo's commentary. "Currently, the town's heading is about two hundred and fifty degrees…"

The topic drifted into "adjusting the declination," and Ella zoned out. She rolled up her sleeves. The exertion from the hike along with the hot coffee and the climbing sun was making her rather warm—not enough to shed her hoodie, though.

A twig snapped behind her. She jumped to her feet and spun, sloshing hot coffee down her hand. A deep breath escaped her lungs when a human figure approached and not some unearthly creature.

Unfortunately, Flo's eyesight wasn't as good as Ella's. With surprising alacrity, the boarder swung her cannon around.

"Flo, no!"

Ella lunged as the plasma cannon let out a *whoosh*. The end lit up electric blue, wind and heat fanning out. Her hair stood on end, and her skin tingled, as did the fillings in her teeth. A blue lighting ball larger than a basketball zipped out.

The recent scope upgrade had improved Flo's aim only marginally. The plasma ball went wide, missing the approaching person by ten feet. It hit a lodgepole pine, and part of the trunk exploded.

Splinters and flaming debris rained down. When the dust cleared, a charred hole was left in the trunk.

The person was on the ground, either having dived for cover or been knocked off his feet by the blast, Ella couldn't be sure.

Lumbering to his feet, he yelled at Flo, his voice carrying over the distance. "What d'you do that for?"

It took Ella a moment to see the shotgun in his hands, aimed at them, and the moment she did, she sprinted for the nearest tree for cover before remembering the six kids behind her.

She jumped back into the middle of the trail, waving frantically. "Wait! There are kids here!"

Slowly, he lowered his weapon. Ella glanced back and hissed at Flo to drop The Hammer. Muttering, the woman reluctantly brought the cannon to rest at her side.

Ella's lungs deflated, and she felt her pulse returning within normal range as the man cautiously approached.

Stupid gun-loving nuts and this crazy town.

She gave a start when she recognized him. "Howard?" she said when he was within earshot.

"Harold," he corrected.

Close enough.

He looked much as he had the last time she'd seen him, right down to the same stained t-shirt and dusty overalls. That day was etched into her memory, mostly because she'd fled his cabin alongside Wink and Flo, running for their lives from a large beast he'd affectionately called Spot. She hadn't gotten a good look at the animal, only glimpsing tan fur and claws as it chased after Wink's car, but that glimpse had been enough to determine that Spot was not—as she'd assumed—a dog.

"What are you folks doing out here?" His face was darkened by a thick carpet of stubble.

"Oh, you know. Taking in a movie. Heading off to work. The usual."

He stared blankly at Ella.

She let out a soft sigh. "Camping." The kids, decked out in their uniforms, jostled listlessly. "Are you hunting?"

"Looking for Spot."

"Spot's lost?" Wink asked.

Harold nodded, his eyes full of concern. "Slipped out a couple nights ago. It's happened before, but he usually comes back."

"Oh, no," Ella said in a flat voice. "That's too bad—wait, Spot's loose in these woods?" Her eyes darted about their surroundings, and she took a step back. "What's the gun for, then?" He clearly loved the animal, so why the weapon?

He brought his shoulders up in a lazy shrug. "Can't be too careful in these woods, here. Folks say they're haunted."

There was a shuffling of feet on the path behind her as the kids gathered closer together.

"Also, I didn't wanna take the chance of running into one of them dinos."

Ella cleared her throat and glanced pointedly at Horatio. "How very prudent of you."

"Not to worry." Flo patted the plasma cannon. "They ain't a match against The Hammer."

Grunting, Harold glanced back at the smoldering tree. "I see that."

"Yes," Wink said, "if anything the size of a barn comes after us, we'll be fine."

"Well..." Ella shifted her weight from foot to foot. "Good luck finding Spot. Not finding him's an option, too. Just saying."

He nodded a farewell and slipped into the forest, abandoning the trail.

In the Keystone Forest, the trees were further apart than what Ella had grown up around, so she could see him walk several yards before a copse of quaking aspen swallowed him. Now, on top of a possible mountain lion, they had to worry about Spot loose in the woods.

Glancing uncertainly at the other adults, she said, "Are we sure it wouldn't be best to just call it a day? We'd only be cutting the trip short by a few hours."

Overhearing this, the kids groaned and protested. Horatio seemed to be reconsidering their hike. Meanwhile, Flo waved her cannon about, some veins in her hand standing out under the strain of lifting it.

"Again, we don't gotta worry as long as I've got this." She smirked. "I'm also packing a landmine, inter-dimensional tripwires, and my ultrasonic slingshot."

Ella turned to Wink. "I thought you went through her stuff before we left."

"You live with her. I thought you'd do it."

A few feet away, Horatio stabbed a finger in Flo's direction. "If anyone gets hurt because of you—*non mi rompere le scatole…*"

Even after he spun and resumed hiking along the trail, a diatribe of Italian continued to pour out of him.

Ella shot Flo a wicked grin. "He's moved on from insulting your mother to your ancestors."

The old broad growled as she hefted the cannon to her shoulder, pointing it in a threatening gesture. "How'd you like to get Hammered?"

Ella blinked. "Sorry, what?"

"It's what am I gonna say when I'm about to shoot a bad guy with The Hammer. Or I'll shoot 'em, then say, 'You just got Hammered.' I haven't decided yet."

"No."

"No, what?"

"Just no."

Clicking her tongue in disgust, Flo turned, probably to look back at the tree she'd maimed, and the monstrosity of a weapon swung into the side of Wink's head. There was a loud *thunk*, followed by Wink yelling, "Dagnabbit!" She slapped the backside of Flo's head before marching off to join the rest of the troop.

Flo called to the woman's back, "It's not like you got much up there to worry about."

Shaking her head, Ella motioned Flo forward. "Come on, Rambo."

* * *

They hiked for what felt like hours, but was, in actuality, only an hour. Ella knew this because she checked her watch every five minutes. Her thermos of coffee had gone dry about a half-hour back, and she'd taken to inventing names for the passing trees—the ones she couldn't readily identify.

On the left was a White Bark one. Ahead on the right was yet another Tall Bushy Old Man, an evergreen that reminded her of an elderly gentleman bowing. She didn't have the energy for creativity with her naming conventions.

When they stopped for another short water break, Horatio pointed out a tree with deep grooves in its bark. It wasn't particularly tall, but it grew in enough of a clearing that its branches, full of frond-shaped leaves beginning to bud, could twist towards the sky.

"This is interesting, kids." The expressions on half of their faces said it was anything but. They'd been good sports so far, engaged, but even a young generation pre-technology had their limits when it came to attention spans. "This is a black walnut tree. It's not native to Colorado."

After screwing the cap back onto her water canteen, Ella sauntered over for a closer look. "How did it get here, I wonder?"

"That's a good question. But as you can see, it's not doing so well."

What leaves had come through did seem to droop. "I'm sure the drastic changes in weather don't help."

"We'll need to tell Gladys, so it can be transplanted," he said, referring to Mrs. Faraday, resident horticulturist and supervisor of the greenhouses. "It releases a… *come si dice* biochimica?"

"Biochemical."

"Yes, that. It could harm these surrounding trees."

Two male Fireflies—Bobby and some kid whose name Ella couldn't recall—began arguing about a rock one of them had found, and Horatio called out louder, "Does anyone know what we use black walnut for?"

Bobby punched the other boy in the shoulder, then said, "For making furniture?"

"That's one thing."

"I can tell you what it *shouldn't* be used for," Ella said. "An ingredient in a gelatin mold." She grimaced at the memory of a particularly awful dinner at the inn, courtesy of one of Rose's infamous dishes. Judging by the expressions on both Wink's and Flo's faces, they recalled the same dish. "And it definitely doesn't go well with trout, artichoke hearts, and strawberries."

Wink raised a veiny hand even though they weren't in class and she probably hadn't seen the inside of one in five decades. "Hair dye. The beauty parlor's used black walnut to dye m—I mean, *some* people's hair, along with lemon juice, henna, coffee, and carrot juice." She reached up and fluffed her large curls.

"I'm sorry, but are you actually pretending you don't dye your hair?" Ella gaped at the very unnatural hair color. "Really?"

The woman's pink bob had changed to a deeper fuchsia in recent weeks, but the locks were still a far cry from the color a person was born with.

The diner owner sniffed and scratched Chester, who rode atop her shoulder like a dutiful parrot. "Jenny recently ran out of the boxed stuff she bought off that delivery driver in Oregon, in that jump you came from." Like most people, she pronounced Ella's home state wrong, saying the last syllable like the word "on."

"She's been using beet juice instead."

Nodding, Ella gave her an *I'm impressed* look.

The short lesson over, Horatio led the march along the trail once again. Ella hollered over the top of bobbing ponytails and mussed hair, "Are we hiking just to torture them, or did you have a particular destination in mind?"

He shot a grin over his shoulder, one full of crooked teeth and mischief. "You'll see. We're almost there."

Periodically, Chester left his perch on Wink's shoulder for the canopy overhead. He chittered before leaping to a trunk, running along branches, then returned to his roost.

"So, this is fun," Ella said. "Not like Disneyland fun or a football game fun, but more like, 'hey, let's all get sweaty and smelly kind of—'" Something big and tan streaked through the forest off to her right. She stopped short, causing Wink to run into her pack.

"El?"

Ella didn't answer, squinting into the forest. Nothing moved. Had she imagined it? Without a word, she resumed her trek. When they'd gone a few more paces, she thought she spotted it again out of the corner of her eye. Judging by Wink's gasp behind her, she'd spotted it too.

"Hey, Flo?" Ella intoned, keeping her voice level so as not to frighten the kids. "Do you have a rocket loaded in that thing?"

The older woman lumbered in front of Ella, the cannon bobbing on her shoulder—her version of a parrot.

"It's not a rocket launcher, Poodle Head. It's a plasma cannon. You don't need rockets for it."

"Whatever. Is it ready to fire?"

Flo seemed to sense the tension because she peeked back at Ella and Wink and gave a stern nod.

"Off to our right," Ella said softly.

Their feet continued to shuffle over the dirt path, branches of leaves and needles pulling at their clothes.

Wink brushed past Ella, murmuring, "I'm going to go warn Horatio."

The diner owner caught up to the man, and their heads bent in hushed conversation. When his head twisted sharply, taking in their surroundings, his expression was grim.

For her part, Ella whistled the tune to a UB40 song as loud as her dry lips would let her and continually glanced behind them. She'd heard of mountain lions sneaking up on people while out jogging, and she wasn't going nearly as fast as that. Worst-case scenario, she could outrun Flo. So that was something at least.

More movement off to the right. Her hand shot out, pointing. "There."

As she said this, a large streak of fur darted out from behind a bush. The predator stalked forward.

Flo spun the cannon around to train her sights on the animal, knocking Ella in the head with a metallic *thunk* as she did.

The pain barely fazed Ella, her eyes wide and focused on the beast. Her mouth hung open. "Son of a preacher man. Is that what I think it is?"

CHAPTER THREE

THE ANIMAL'S FUR was a deep orangish tan, the color of wheat, with light spotting like washed-out leopard print. Powerful, stocky limbs rippled with each step below a thick body. It was big—bigger than a lion. But all she could see were two ridiculously elongated canines. The beast was all muscle and teeth.

"Holy crap, is that—is that a saber-toothed tiger?"

When had the animal gotten stranded on this side of the border? She wasn't up on paleontology and had no clue during what epoch the ginormous cats had roamed the earth.

Then she connected the dots. The streak of tan fur running through the orchard. Harold looking for his lost pet.

"Spot is a freaking saber-toothed tiger? Are you *kidding* me?"

"I don't know why you're upset." Flo adjusted a dial on her weapon as the animal let out a low growl and continued to lumber forward. "I was the one hanging on top of the car with him nipping at my heels while you were snug as a bug inside."

"Yes, but who do you think he would've eaten when he finished with you? Not Wink. She'd probably taste like jerky."

Ahead on the trail, the diner owner had taken charge. "We have to get the kids out of here." Panic edged her voice.

"The caves," Horatio said, his olive skin having gone pale. "That's where we were heading. It's not far."

"We'll create a distraction. You run. Get the kids to safety."

Ella nudged Flo forward. "Welp, it was nice knowing you."

Spot was still yards away, but prowling closer. Ella couldn't help but notice he was the size of a horse.

The two youngest kids, Judy and Bobby, took Horatio's hand as Wink said, "Flo?"

"On it. Get ready to run."

Ella's muscles tensed, her legs coiling. The prehistoric animal was doing the same just a few yards away. Those teeth didn't look natural, like a cruel joke from Mother Nature. Where was the forest's resident Viking when they needed him?

"Wait." She picked up a large limb, roughly the size of a baseball bat. "Okay, now I'm ready."

Flo snorted. "Yes, that'll slow Spot down."

"Hey, maybe use your new sights this time so you actually hit your target." Ella's eyes tore away from those massive fangs to The Hammer as Flo's finger pulled the trigger.

"Now!" Flo yelled.

The troop booked it down the trail, Horatio dragging the two youngest ones by their hands. The ground in front of the saber-toothed tiger exploded in a shower of dirt and mangled ferns and blue electricity.

Spot released a feral scream and took several tentative steps back. As he did Ella noticed his limp, his right front paw covered in crusty blood.

The last of the dirt rained down. Still, the trio lingered, wanting to make certain Spot didn't chase the kids.

Ella's hands were cramping around the limb-turned-bludgeon. She spared a glance down the trail in the direction the troop had fled and let out a breath at seeing it empty. They'd made it.

Wink tilted her head, actually taking a step *closer*. "You have to admit he's kind of cute."

"No," Ella and Flo said at the same time.

Wink made cooing noises at the beast which only resulted in a feral hiss from Spot. She harrumphed.

At a cue from the diner owner, they began walking backward down the dirt path, The Hammer and Ella's wooden club held at the ready.

Spot stalked forward, letting out another cry that sounded like a mix between a roar, an air horn, and a screaming toddler.

"Well, he sounds happy," Ella murmured. "Shoot the ground near him again, Flo."

"I was aiming for his head."

Ella frowned. "If we survive this, we're taking you to an optometrist."

The older woman called Ella several dirty names under her breath.

"Knock it off, you two." Wink had taken Chester off her shoulder and clutched the little guy to her bosom.

"Hey," Ella whispered, "do you think Spot's after Chester? Should we maybe, you know...?" She made a clicking noise with her tongue and jerked her head from Chester to Spot.

"Ella Barton!" Wink cried out, her grip tightening on the squirrel.

"I'm just saying, sacrifices might have to be made."

"I agree with Poodle Head."

Spot stilled and crouched, his pupils dilating, a move Ella recognized all too well from Fluffy when he was about to pounce. It put an end to their "Chester as bait" discussion.

"Any day now, Flo."

The cannon lit up, building with another plasma ball. Lightning tore out of the barrel in a wave of heat and electric blue light at the same moment Spot sprang through the air. He vaulted a log that caught the brunt of the plasma ball. It detonated, wood shrapnel flying out. What remained of the log glowed a Smurf blue.

Ella jogged backward, her blood going cold. Flo had missed. Again.

"Stop!" a voice shouted from the woods.

In the distance, Harold darted amongst trees, heading straight for them. His voice caused Spot to still, the predator's ears twitching. This bought them precious seconds.

"Run!" Ella yelled.

Turning, they sprinted down the trail, running as if they were being chased by a deadly prehistoric animal capable of tearing them from limb to limb. Even Flo kept pace, though she did make a concerning whistling noise with each breath.

The Hammer bounced on Flo's shoulder, and she began to lag behind. Ella's feet slapped over the hardened dirt, running faster than she'd ever run in her life. She overtook Wink before realizing she didn't know where the caves were.

Were they off the trail, or did the trail lead right to them?

She slowed to steal a glance back. Wink, who'd been at Ella's heels, passed her in a heartbeat, taking the lead once again. About five yards behind them, Flo lumbered along, gasping for air. And a few yards behind her was Spot.

Harold was a figure in the distance, trailing after his pet and waving his arms, yelling for them not to shoot.

"Flo, toss me the cannon!"

For once, the woman readily relinquished a weapon. Ella caught it with a grunt and brought it to bear in one smooth move.

"That's the wrong—"

Ella squeezed the trigger. Heat blasted her back as something behind her exploded.

Without turning to assess the damage, she spun the weapon around, aimed, and fired again. She didn't necessarily want to hit Spot, but she did want to make him think twice about eating them.

After another electric blue explosion, the path in front of the predator became a pit, a cloud of dirt, and an expanding debris field.

Ella spun on her heel and passed a smoldering stump that had been a tree moments before. Ahead, Wink was urging them on, smoke rising from her hair.

"Uh, Wink..."

"I know." She glared. "You nearly took off my head."

"My bad."

Wink's mouth turned down slightly at Ella's turn of phrase. They abandoned the trail, darting between trees and bushes, following a narrower path beaten along the forest floor, leading to gray, craggy rocks.

Flo's breath rasped somewhere behind Ella, indicating she was closing the distance. Ella clutched the cannon in case she needed to fire again. Ahead, the foliage cleared, and she spotted the large mouth of a cave, a dark hole standing out against pale limestone.

It took her a breath to realize they were at the base of the eastern Twin Hill. She had only a moment to consider this before she was plunging through the mouth and into a darkness that swallowed her whole.

Once her eyes adjusted, Ella found the Firefly troop huddled together, cowering behind Horatio. Inky blackness extended behind them, suggesting the cave wound deep into the rock.

Flo swiped the cannon back from Ella and stationed herself at the entrance of the cave. Her head swiveled back and forth, scanning their surroundings. There was no sign of the prehistoric predator.

"Here's a question," Ella asked Wink between gulps of air. "Should the woman with the poor eyesight be holding our only weapon?" Her mouth turned down, just now realizing she'd lost her tree branch bludgeon at some point while fleeing through the woods.

"Hmm, good point," Wink said before going to relieve Flo of The Hammer.

Ella opened her mouth to protest and point out that Wink's eyesight wasn't much better, but the two women's ensuing argument drowned out her voice.

Their disagreement bounced around the interior rock, echoing in the expanse behind the troop. Both ladies had their hands on the plasma cannon in a tug of war. Turning to the Fireflies, Ella planted her hands on her hips and attempted a reassuring smile.

"Don't worry. We do this sort of stuff all the time. Just a few weeks ago, we fended off a Tyrannosaurus rex. Twice. So, we're kind of experts—" her words were punctuated by an explosion behind her.

The kids gasped and jumped.

Her smile remained plastered to her face. "Yep, all perfectly normal." When she whipped around to see what in the *Looney Tunes* was going on, she discovered that a bush near the mouth of the cave had become a smoldering, charcoal skeleton.

"See?" Wink spat at Flo.

"You made me do that."

"It's my turn with the cannon."

"I made The Hammer. Why should you get a turn?"

"You didn't make it. Will did, probably after you threatened him."

Striding forward, Ella wrenched the weapon from both of their grips and handed it to Wink.

"Take turns keeping watch…" Her words died on her lips as Flo pulled a familiar-looking slingshot from her backpack.

"Hmm, the charge on the interior battery's low," the boarder muttered to herself.

Ella winced. How had she forgotten the weapons enthusiast was packing more heat?

"Why didn't you give me one of those when we were running for our lives?"

"You woulda preferred to stop, so I could pull out another weapon to make your namby-pamby butt feel better?"

Ella sniffed. "Well, when you put it like that…"

Flo waved the benign-looking slingshot in the air. "I only brought nonlethal weapons in case the kids started acting up."

"In case the kids… nonlethal…" Ella floundered for appropriate words. "First of all, you should be banned from coming within ten feet of children in the future. Second of all, I think there's a charred stump back there in the forest that would disagree with your definition of 'nonlethal'. Crap on a cracker, woman." She sucked in a slow breath, gathering patience. "Wait. Didn't you say you had a landmine?"

Flo ignored her.

With Chester safely tucked into her backpack, Wink surveyed the clearing in front of the cave, unfazed by Flo's disturbing conversation. By this point, the boarder's antics were old hat. Heck, half the time Wink was involved in them.

"Flo," the diner owner said without pulling her gaze away, "didn't you say something about having a tripwire in there? Can you hook it to the landmine?"

"It's inter-dimensional. It'll only capture non-corporeal forms who aren't fully present in this plane of existence."

Wink's pained expression said she was sorry she asked. Ella considered pressing the landmine issue, planting it in front of the cave, but was concerned about the children being so near and Harold's unknown whereabouts outside.

"We need to figure out what to do next." Horatio paced, then joined Wink at the entrance, looking out. "We cannot hide in here forever. I'll hike into town for reinforcements to help escort the children to safety."

Balancing the plasma cannon on one bony shoulder, Wink patted him with her free hand. "Let's not do anything brash. Let's wait here for a spell before considering that."

Horatio shrugged her off and took a bold step beyond the safety of the cave. Then another.

Bushes rustled several yards out, followed by one of Spot's angry growls that would put the fear of God into any human. Horatio backpedaled faster than a celebrity making an offensive remark.

Ella hid behind Wink and The Hammer. "Yeah, no. That's not happening. I agree with Wink. Let's just hang out here for a while. Maybe Harold'll get here and can leash his hellhound." Her eyes roved over the bleak stone cavern walls around them. "It's not too bad in here. Kind of cozy, actually, in a depressing, Batcave sort of way. Now, we just need a rich, handsome man in a suit and gadgets to come rescue us."

Flo leaned against the wall, sonic slingshot in hand, her expression bored. "What're you talking about, Poodle Head?"

"He's a superhero in my time."

"Oh?" Wink risked a look back. "A superhero, you say? Like in the comic books?"

"Yeah, specifically Batman. I thought the whole mention of a Batcave gave it away."

She knew they had no idea who she was referring to, but when she was bored, she liked to educate them on the pop culture of her era in a way that implied they were really missing out.

Behind the troop, the darkness became absolute beyond the terminator of daylight, a demarcation of day and night. Dank, musty air reached her nostrils, and she shivered. It was several degrees cooler in the cave, and the sweat she'd created from the hike and subsequent flight for her life wasn't helping matters.

"Do you know how far this goes back?" she asked Horatio.

"I am not sure, but it's extensive. I've heard of people getting lost in them."

Wink piped up from her sentry position. "It goes deep under the hills. It's got lots of offshoots. Kids wander in here on dares, but most don't venture in too far. Supposedly they're haunted."

Ella looked over at Flo, waiting for her to pick up the paranormal thread of conversation. Instead, however, the woman's mouth was pressed in a firm line, her bug-eyed glasses focused on the depths of darkness at their backs.

"Stay together," the cook cautioned the Fireflies. "Nobody wander off."

Shuffling, they murmured that they would. Several minutes passed, and the kids' palpable fear began to dissipate, quickly turning to boredom. As it turned out, the troop was more resilient than the adults. Soon, the six Fireflies were sitting on the dank sediment that had blown in through the entrance, playing marbles and eating sandwiches from their packs.

"Where's Judy?" Horatio asked abruptly.

Turning her head, Wink said, "She didn't pass me to go outside."

Ella looked up from her phone. She'd been flitting through old photos, a recent habit she'd developed. The passing of the holidays had caused her to grow sentimental. She swallowed the growing throb in her throat at seeing pictures of her parents from last year's Thanksgiving, just before she'd become stranded. Cinnamon sticks, had she really been in Keystone over a year now?

Horatio's hands cupped around his mouth like a megaphone, and he called to the interior of the cave for the young girl. Standing, Ella brushed the damp bottoms of her athletic pants.

"I'll go get her."

"No, I'll go," Flo said abruptly, jumping forward.

Ella frowned and noticed a similar expression from Wink. For Flo to leap at the opportunity to help was odd behavior, and she seemed eager, almost nervous.

"No, really," Ella insisted. "I'll go."

Wink cautioned her to be careful, then said, "Flo, give her your weapon."

"No, you give her yours."

Wink inclined her head at the cannon. "This is clearly better against Spot. Give her your slingshot."

Reluctantly, Flo handed over the slingshot. It looked like it couldn't knock over a flower, but Ella knew better. The sonic slingshot—which used focused beams of ultrasonic sound waves similar to a device used by the military and police— had been her trusty weapon all during the Jurassic occupation in the previous weeks.

She took the proffered weapon with ginger fingers and gripped it tight as she plunged into the darkness. Her phone served as a flashlight, so she could leave the lanterns the Fireflies had brought for cave exploration with them.

Daylight from the mouth of the cave grew dim. Soon, the passage narrowed to five feet wide and made a sharp turn to the right before descending. If she'd thought it was dark before, it was nothing compared to the abyss into which she now plunged.

A glint of metal on the ground caught her attention, and she stopped short. She'd nearly stepped on a bear trap.

Well, that would've ended her nonexistent tap-dancing career. It seemed odd to place a trap this far in, but she didn't know much about the mammals other than they were big and had sharp claws and were against forest fires.

Around the metal jagged jaws, dried blood flaked off in places, too dry to have been Judy's. Also, the trap wasn't sprung. Whoever had reset it hadn't bothered cleaning it.

Gross.

Her mouth turned down as she rose. The need to locate the girl had just turned more urgent. What if there were more traps further in? Or what if Judy had run into a bear?

Silence pressed on Ella's ears, and her senses heightened. She became aware of the smallest movement of air. The echoes of her party grew distant behind her before being snuffed out altogether.

Periodically, she called Judy's name but heard no reply. At each juncture, she scratched an arrow on the wall using a stone she'd found, indicating her route.

The passage opened into a small chamber. Above, long stalactites hung down, and she wove around their sharp points. Why wasn't Judy answering? Was she hurt?

A shuffling sound came from ahead where the chamber narrowed into another passage. Ella's breath caught, and she whispered repeatedly, "Please don't be bats, please don't be bats."

Even with her shorter frame, she had to duck through the opening. As she drew towards the noise, she realized the sound was sniffling, like someone crying. It grew louder the deeper she trekked.

Her fingers cramped from their death-grip on the sonic slingshot. The acoustics in this place were doing a number on her ears. With each turn, she was sure to find the source of the sound only to be met by more mineral formations and shadows.

Frustrated, she called the young girl's name again and ignored the sense of foreboding growing in the pit of her stomach. Then, quite abruptly, the passage opened into a ginormous cavern. It was the size of the entrance hall at the inn, with a vaulted ceiling so high, the meager light from her phone couldn't touch it.

The uneven ground was mottled with waist-high mineral formations, which made walking slow as she picked a path forward. She swept her light back and forth.

More crying. Turning, she saw a lantern. As she drew near, the light coalesced, illuminating a form: Judy.

Ella let out a breath and approached. Her steps faltered. Something was off.

The girl stood frozen, facing away, and she gave no indication she'd heard Ella.

"Judy? Are you hurt?"

A scan of the Firefly showed she was unharmed. But the girl continued to stare forward at a single point, the lantern in her small hand trembling. Her face was pale.

"Judy, what is it? Did you see something?"

It felt like the beginnings of a horror movie, and all Ella could think about was the two of them fleeing. She tucked the slingshot into her waistband and took the girl's hand. It was as cold as ice.

"Come on."

Judy squeaked at the contact, as if coming to from a deep trance, but she allowed Ella to guide her back across the expansive cavern. Walking, Ella swept her light from side to side, taking in more of the chamber's interior and chasing away the shadows. The beam fell on a form lying motionless on the ground.

A body.

Ella sucked in a breath. Judy's hand tightened in hers, and she let out a small whimper.

Ella's light played across the form, revealing Professor Kaufman. Creator of the time device, responsible for the town's constant jumps and subsequent isolation, the reason Ella was separated from her home and family.

He let out a rattling breath.

Jumping, she choked back a scream. The man was still alive.

"See?" she said loudly to no one in particular, her voice echoing around the chamber. "This is why I poke bodies. Everyone thinks I'm crazy, but it's so instances like this don't make me soil my pants."

After taking a steadying breath, she squeezed and released Judy's hand. Then she told her to wait there, stare into the lantern, and hum her favorite song. Leaving her a few feet away, Ella dropped to the cold stony ground beside Dr. Kaufman. "Professor?"

His eyes slowly tracked to her but remained unfocused. He gasped, struggling to breathe, his skin an unnatural pink in the meager light. There wasn't a hint of recognition in his expression upon seeing her. In fact, he seemed to stare right through her.

She searched for the source of his injuries and found a head wound. Her hand came away with blood. Behind her, Judy whimpered again.

"Judy, I need a big favor. It's really important, okay? I need you to keep a lookout. Keep your eyes peeled and don't look over here, can you do that?"

The girl's lips trembled, but she nodded. When Ella was certain Judy was distracted, she focused on the professor again.

His mouth moved in whispers over slightly blue lips, and she bent close.

"He found me."

Ella frowned. "Who found you?"

His eyes were glazed over, his breathing labored. "Don't fix it. He'll use it and change everything."

"Who? Fix what? Do you mean the time device?"

Fear flashed through his eyes, and one hand reached out, trembling. His chest heaved with death rattles.

Despite what he'd done, she grabbed his hand. In this moment, he wasn't the man who'd stranded her, nor the scientist who'd invented the time machine. A fellow human was dying in her arms, and she wasn't about to let him part this world alone.

His hand curled around hers in a weak grip as he released his final breath. Then all was still.

Ella stared for several moments, then cursed softly under her breath. All he'd wanted was to fix the machine so he could save his wife, and now, he'd never get to.

The back of her eyes stung, and emotions roiled around inside her like a tempest, threatening to spill out. But she forced them aside, thinking of Judy. The girl had stayed true to her assignment, her light and face pointed away. Her red hair caught the glow from the lantern in her small hand, making it look like fire.

Judy stood stiff, staring into the darkness at something. Watching.

"Judy? What's wrong?" After resting the professor's hand on his chest, Ella stood.

A noise came from the direction the young Firefly stared, causing a cold sweat to break out over Ella's skin. She heard the shuffle of feet before she saw the shadow. It darted behind a stalagmite.

They weren't alone.

CHAPTER FOUR

ELLA WHIPPED THE slingshot out from her waistband. Her muscles shook as she pulled the tension band. It made a creaking noise that broke the silence. Unlike similar slingshots, Flo's sonic one didn't require a projectile to be loaded into the pocket.

As the figure stepped out and raised something that looked like a club, Ella released the pocket. The rubber tubing snapped forward. This particular exotic weapon of Flo's was anticlimactic—right up until the focused beam of invisible ultrasonic sound waves found its target.

It hit the figure with the force of a tsunami, throwing them into the rock wall. They grunted once, slid down to their haunches, and didn't move.

She and Judy remained frozen, waiting to see if the figure stirred. The light from the lantern barely reached the mysterious figure.

"Huh, I forgot how much of a punch this thing packs. Say what you will about Flo, but she makes a mean weapon, lethal or not. Or rather, Will does since she coerces him into it."

Judy's lower lip trembled. The poor girl would probably have nightmares for months and maybe need therapy after this.

Ella patted the Firefly on the back and assured her they were safe. After retrieving her phone, she asked Judy to aim the light at the shadowy form, freeing up her hands for the slingshot.

"Y-you're going over there?" Judy's voice trembled as she spoke for the first time.

"I'm just getting close enough to see if they or *it* is still a threat."

She wasn't confident what she'd shot was a person. The thing was bipedal, sure, but didn't appear entirely human, full of fur and grizzled hair. She'd never admit it, but she was secretly hoping she'd knocked out a Sasquatch. That was something she could lord over Flo for ages.

Both hands gripped the slingshot as she tiptoed forward, mindful of the uneven ground. Even with her phone's light added to the mix, the slumped figure was hard to make out, but she didn't want to scar Judy any further by asking her to get nearer with the light.

Squinting, Ella held the weapon ready and nudged the figure with her shoe—the only scientifically proper way to ensure someone was dead or unconscious. It didn't move, save for the steady rise and fall of its chest. After several tense seconds of holding her own breath, she relaxed her pull on the sling and wrenched the club from the figure's grip.

Did animals brandish weapons? She thought she remembered reading that a gorilla might use a stick as a weapon or a tool. This instrument appeared to be a bone of some sort and a very large one at that. Part of the top was stained crimson, and bits of rotting meat stunk up the air.

She squatted beside the unconscious figure. This proved to be a mistake as the stench emanating off the—animal?—was enough to curl her nostril hairs.

Trying to distract Judy, she said, "So, what sort of hobbies are you into?"

The girl stared at her.

"You know, hobbies? What do you do for fun when you're not in school?"

Judy shrugged.

Ella kept the one-sided conversation going as she inspected the creature. Its midsection was covered in fur that appeared to have been sewn together, and its feet were shod in shoes made from grass and bark. Bare arms poked out the sides, covered in very human-like flesh. Definitely not a gorilla.

"Do you collect anything, like stamps?"

Judy shrugged again.

When Ella got to the face, her confusion turned to awe. It —he—was covered in facial hair, a scraggly beard that would make a Hells Angel biker jealous. But the prominent brow ridge grabbed her attention, as did the overall unique facial structure.

"What is it?" Judy called out from several feet back.

"A caveman," she whispered. She wasn't an anthropologist, so that umbrella term was the best she could use.

She tore her eyes away finally. They needed to get Chapman, and who knew how long the caveman would remain immobile. Now that the immediate danger had passed, she felt comfortable tucking the slingshot into her waistband.

As much as she wanted to stay and sleuth, her priority was getting Judy back to safety, away from the immobile bodies. However, that didn't stop her from hungrily surveying the rest of the chamber as they edged towards the exit.

Her light lingered on the professor's body, specifically, the small, dark pool of blood around his head. Beyond this, amongst mineral formations and stalagmites, were a slew of items she hadn't noticed before: a bedroll, sleeping bag, food, newspapers, and a myriad of other things—items one accumulated when holed up for a while. So this was where the rat had been hiding. No wonder they hadn't been able to find him.

She averted Judy from looking over at the body, her light sweeping the walls as she did. It revealed a tapestry of primitive paintings of animals, stick figures, and random designs (mostly circles) stretched as far as the pin light reached. Rembrandts they were not, but a thrill shot through her.

Unless Dr. Kaufman had suddenly taken up art and had the skills of a toddler, these were the handiwork of the cave-man. It meant she could identify what epoch he hailed from. This kind of artwork pre-dated written language, and the linguist in her itched at the opportunity to discover what sort of spoken language the caveman used—supposing she hadn't caused any brain damage with Flo's nonlethal weapon.

As she led Judy back through the labyrinth using the marks she'd scratched as guides, her mind was filled with the possibilities of study and what this discovery could do for the field of linguistics. It wasn't until she heard the distant voices of their group that her thoughts turned to the professor, and her heart sank.

How selfish could she be? Keystone Village's main hope, the man who had all of the answers, was now dead, and with him, his secrets. Not only that, but the girl clutching her hand had just had a frightening experience.

Ella again reassured Judy that everything would be all right and that she was safe. She didn't know the status of the

Spot situation, but one way or another, she was going to ensure this girl wouldn't be traumatized further.

"Charms," Judy said suddenly in a small voice.

"As in Lucky Charms, the delicious cereal dentists love?"

"No, charms." She dangled a charm bracelet that hung from her wrist. "I collect them."

Ella squeezed her hand. "One of my friends does, as well."

Then she did what she did best and told jokes. Eventually, the ghost of a smile tugged at the Firefly's mouth.

Ella watched the town doctor and sole coroner, Pauline, inspect Dr. Kaufman's body—or rather, she watched the woman search her myriad of pockets on her trademark jacket, muttering, "Where is it?" over and over. After the coroner pulled a wrench from one pocket and calipers from another, she let out a triumphant "Ah-ha!" as she dangled a pair of gloves in the air.

"Do you think she ever washes that thing?" Ella asked. She'd rarely seen the woman sans coat. "Like, does she empty each pocket before sticking it in the washing machine?" It had more pockets than a closet full of cargo pants. "Also, did she sew *more* on after buying it?" It was hard to believe the design intentional.

"Focus, Ms. Barton." Sheriff Chapman stood before her, his tall, lean frame cutting an imposing form in the dim light.

"Sorry, what was the question?"

"You were telling me how you shot that other man with one of Ms. Henderson's infernal devices." His voice came out in a relaxed drawl, like dripping honey, but it had soured slightly at the mention of Flo's sonic slingshot. A person just meeting him wouldn't have noticed the subtle shift in tone because he showed as much emotion as a rock, but she'd caught it.

"Incapacitated," Ella corrected.

He tipped back his derby hat, considering her with steel-colored eyes. "And where's the weapon now?"

She opened her hands innocently and looked around the cavern. "Huh, that's strange. I must've dropped it in the chaos."

It definitely hadn't been nabbed by Flo earlier.

"I see," he replied in a tone that implied he didn't believe her. "Did he say anything?"

"Who? The caveman? He tried to sell me car insurance." She grinned, then realized the joke was lost on him. Also, a dead body lay a few feet away.

The only reason they were conducting the interview in the cavern was because she'd led them back through the labyrinth and had started talking as soon as they'd arrived. This had been intentional on her part as she'd hoped to get a better look at the professor's bolt-hole and the crime scene.

"Did the *professor* say anything?" Chapman repeated, tugging one end of his handlebar mustache between his fingers, a sign of frustration—or just a tick. She hadn't figured that one out yet.

She took a hesitant breath, about to tell him the professor's final words, but she found she couldn't form them. Shadows danced across his features, cast by the various kerosene lanterns now scattered around the chamber, as he waited for her to answer. She found herself shaking her head.

Before he could ask any further questions, Pauline called him over. He strode away, his spurs echoing their metallic song.

Ella didn't waste a moment. She strolled over to the caveman's paintings on the wall. It was just the three of them in the ginormous cavern at the moment, but who knew how long that would last or at what point he'd kick her out.

A couple of hours earlier, when she and Judy had rejoined the others, Wink and Flo had gone to get help—well, just Wink because, according to her, Flo moved as slow as molasses in winter. On the trail, she'd run into Harold, who'd informed her that Spot had run south and was long gone.

Now safe, Horatio and the Fireflies had hiked out and were reuniting with their families. Meanwhile, the Troublesome Twosome were currently packing up the campsite. The two of them left to their own devices made her anxious, part of her motivation to hurry.

With all this happening, Chapman had sent Jimmy off to deposit the caveman in a jail cell. Her attention returned to the primitive paintings, her eyes lingering—not on the artwork—but strange chinks in the limestone wall.

That's odd.

Reaching out, she brushed her index finger along the striations. Here and there, it appeared rock had been chipped off at different angles. She leaned in until her nose nearly touched a particularly round divot with a darkened starburst pattern shooting out around the circumference. It took her a moment to realize where she'd seen this before: target practicing with Flo.

Pulling out her phone, she recorded a video of the paintings and the odd markings, then she discreetly pointed the lens down, zooming in on the professor's belongings littering the ground. Stacks of canned foods mingled with jars of pickles and preserves. There were crates filled with produce beside recycled glass milk bottles, growlers, and antique moonshine jugs. The last two were filled with a clear liquid she assumed was either water or moonshine.

Near a dingy mat and blankets was a partially eaten piece of bread topped with strawberry jam. Beside this lay the town's bimonthly newspaper, *Keystone Corner*, which—given the village's size—was little more than a newsletter. Her nose wrinkled at the squalor. Then she spotted the revolver next to a yellow-stained pillow.

Well, that explained the pockmarks along the cavern wall. It obviously hadn't scared away the caveman. Also, the professor's aim was apparently on par with Flo's.

She glanced back to be sure Chapman and Pauline weren't watching, and she casually knelt to tie her shoe. As she did, she leaned down and sniffed the barrel of the revolver. Since she didn't want to touch it, this required pressing her cheek to the stony ground.

The gun had a faint metallic, greasy odor with only a hint of burnt gun powder. While sniffing, she tuned in to the conversation behind her. The acoustics of the chamber provided little privacy, despite Chapman and the doctor whispering. They'd been discussing the professor's cause of death.

"I'm not a law enforcement officer," Pauline said abruptly, "but shouldn't she be waiting outside?"

Ella turned in time to see Pauline incline her head in Ella's direction. Traitor. She'd always felt a certain kinship with the woman, given that the coroner hailed from an era Ella had actually been alive in. Also, she knew what a high five was, so that endeared the prickly woman to her.

Chapman's chin dipped in a subtle nod. "Come on, Ms. Barton. I'll walk you out."

"I'm pretty sure I can find my way back."

Despite her protest, the sheriff escorted her all the same.

At the entrance, the afternoon light blinded her, and she was surprised to see three people congregated at the mouth of the cave.

Nearby, Chapman's Appaloosa horse—creatively named Horse—munched on a shrub. His tail flicked, and he let out a soft, bored whinny. Above the horse, Chester sat perched on a branch, watching the large animal, a pinecone gripped in his tiny mouth. His miniature Firefly uniform was unkempt and had definitely seen better days.

"What are you two doing here?" she asked Wink and Flo, sparing a greeting in Jimmy's direction. "Is the camp already packed up?"

Wink nodded. "There wasn't much to pack."

Ella was used to the extravagant camping she'd grown up with, ladened with gear and not the barebones they'd come with on this trip.

"We'll have to borrow a vehicle or wagon to haul out the kids' stuff."

"I'll take care of it," Jimmy said. The innkeeper turned sheriff's deputy wore a slim-fitting uniform that was a slightly different color than Chapman's, probably due to the limited clothing options available.

Ella beamed at him, picking a tree needle from his uniform. "Look at you."

"Doesn't he look just so…" Wink pinched his cheek as if he was a young boy and she was his grandmother. "… grown up?"

"Are you going to grow a mustache now?" Ella asked.

"Why would I?"

"Because—" she looked pointedly in Chapman's direction "—all great lawmen have them."

The sheriff, who'd gone out to check on Horse, said, "I heard that."

"Giving as how we're a few feet away, I'd be concerned if you didn't." She smiled at Jimmy. "So… where'd we land on the 'stache?"

He let out a harassed sigh that told Ella the two older women had already been picking on him prior to her and Chapman showing up.

Without bothering to respond, he spoke to the sheriff. "Found some tracks in the dirt leading up to the cave here.

Several, actually. It's tough to distinguish but looks to be the professor's and some strange shoe. Probably our caveman."

"Did he give you any trouble?"

"He struggled, but I got the impression it's because he doesn't know what's happening." Jimmy ran a hand over his thinning hair. What hair there was, he'd combed into a deep side part and lacquered it with enough pomade to warrant an environmental hazard zone. "Anyway, I found some big animal tracks, but lost them amongst all the others from today."

"He means us," Ella said to Wink and Flo.

Jimmy consulted his notebook. "I already interviewed these two about what happened. They claim—" his gaze flitted to the ladies "—they were chased by a saber-toothed tiger."

Ella murmured out of the side of her mouth, "He had to look at his notes for that?"

Wink made a *tsk-tsk* noise. "Dear me. That doesn't bode well for the deputy, does it?"

Flo was too preoccupied with carving something on the cave wall to join the conversation.

Chapman cleared his throat, quieting them. "I don't reckon it's occurred to you all yet the implication of the professor's death."

Ella exchanged a glance with Wink before the weight of the cave seemed to press down upon her. It had occurred to her, but only at the moment she'd spotted the professor, a thought she'd buried in order to deal with the crisis.

With the professor dead, their chances of getting home had reduced drastically.

"It's all on Will now," Wink whispered.

Ella nodded. "He's not going to like that." And not just because the responsibility of fixing the device was solely on him. He and Dr. Kaufman had been friends—of sorts. Their relationship had severely strained when the professor had bolted, but they still had a history of friendship between them. "Who's going to tell him?"

All eyes turned to her, and her shoulders slumped in defeat. As she opened her mouth, however, the sheriff mounted Horse and gripped the reins. "I'll tell him."

Within moments, he was gone.

Ella glanced over at Flo, whose hair had been progressively deteriorating throughout the whole ordeal and now resembled a tumbleweed, to see how she was taking the news that their biggest chance of returning home was gone. When she did, she discovered Flo had carved a crude word into the wall.

The woman caught Ella staring. "Mind your own business, Poodle Head." The scowl on her face shifted to panic as Jimmy strode past, going deeper into the cave.

"Where are you headin' there, String Bean?"

"To the crime scene. Where else?"

The tension in Flo's face eased, but only marginally. "Whatcha waiting for, then? Don't let me stop you."

"Wasn't going to." Jimmy, who hadn't broken stride, shook his head, muttering about the woman's grasp on reality slipping. He trudged into the darkness, his lantern casting flickering lights along the tunnel. The moment he turned the sharp bend, the light was gone.

Ella rounded on Flo.

"What's up with you?"

"What're you talkin' about?"

"Something's up. You're acting strange. I mean, you're usually nuttier than a bag of trail mix, but this is different."

Flo returned to her carving. "You're imagining things."

CHAPTER FIVE

AFTER ELLA SANK into the clawfoot bathtub and scrubbed off the odor of campfire, musty cave, and death, she changed into clean clothes and descended the grand staircase. She had to straddle a stair claimed by Fluffy, who'd stretched out to his full, furry glory. She paid the pet toll and scratched the monstrous Maine Coon under the chin, listening to him purr as loud as an outboard motor on a boat, before continuing on.

In the kitchen, Rose hummed merrily at the stove. She wore a blue tea-length dress with a Peter Pan collar and a skirt that flared out below her knees. It swayed with each movement like a bell. When she spotted Ella, her lips, ladened with scarlet lipstick, widened in a smile that belonged in a toothpaste commercial.

"Ella, dear. Did you eat lunch?" Her cat-eye glasses reflected the seizure-inducing yellow walls in the 1950s style kitchen—the only room that didn't match the rest of the historic mansion.

"I had some leftover lemon blueberry scones before leaving the campsite. I wanted to help Wink so she wouldn't have to pack them back. It was for a good cause."

Her mouth began watering when she noticed the ground beef sizzling in the skillet and added, "But they didn't fill me up."

"This is for the potluck. I was going to tell you there's leftover meatloaf in the fridge."

Ella thanked her and scavenged inside the refrigerator while the innkeeper remarked on the state of Ella's hair.

"It's better if the curls air dry," Ella explained, taking a bite of cold meatloaf. It would take too long to warm in the oven.

"I don't get why you don't wash your hair in the sink."

Ella blinked. "How's that?"

"In the sink. You said you washed it while taking a bath." Rose's manicured eyebrows furrowed. "So odd. Why not wash it in the sink?"

"B-because that's crazy? Who washes their hair in the sink?"

"Nearly every woman I know."

"But *why*? Why not wash at the same time you scrub your body?"

Rose pondered this. "Because hair doesn't need to be cleaned as often. It gets styled and keeps fresh with product. Besides, it's easier to bend over a sink and wash."

They continued to stare at each other like they were from different planets. Instances like this made Ella feel like Dorothy in the *Wizard of Oz*.

"Right. Well…" She rinsed her dish in the sink and moon-walked backward. "Smell you later. I'm sorry. That's a cheesy way we say farewell to each other in my time."

"Is it really?" Rose said, her voice piqued with interest.

"Yep. Definitely."

"Well, then. Smell you later, dear."

As Ella pushed out the swinging door, she had a satisfied grin on her face. After being chased by a saber-toothed tiger that morning, wandering around a creepy cave, and the professor's death dooming them all to eternal time jumping, her day was finally starting to look up.

A drop of sweat rolled down Ella's forehead, and she swiped it away. This was bad. Very, very bad.

Chaos roared around her. Sal, their newly elected mayor, had just kicked off the potluck. Nearby, a woman swung a baguette like a baton at Gladys. Over at the refreshments table, the town mechanic, Lou, swayed over the punch bowl and dumped the contents of his flask into the red drink, snickering.

Across the way, Patience and Jenny were in a tug of war over an entire pie, the Puritan accusing the hairdresser of being sent by the devil, while Jenny declared the colonial woman's split ends a travesty. Leif, the resident Norseman, used his ax to hack off a turkey leg. With one hand, he gnawed on the hunk of meat, his other arm putting a man in a headlock after he'd approached the stuffed bird.

But Ella had the worst of it. She stared down not one, but *two* young girls. Sally, Ella's blond-haired archnemesis, had brought in a ringer—a brown-haired misfit with braids and a toothy grin.

They stood in front of the dessert table, blockading access to cookies and other pastries. While glaring at Ella, Sally lifted a snickerdoodle to her lips and took a languid bite, making sure to lick her lips.

"She-demon," Ella said. "Hey, I loved your work in *Children of the Corn*. Oh, and you've got a little cookie right here." She pointed at the corner of her mouth.

Sally mirrored her, brushing the spot.

"Not quite. Almost. It's just—it's right there." Ella pointed to the other side of her mouth. After the girl swiped that spot, Ella laughed. "Ha! I got you. There was nothing there."

Sally scowled.

Behind the girls, Keystone residents approached the dessert spread from the other side of the table, converging like vultures. Soon there would be nothing left for Ella but the carcasses of crust and crumbs. And Rose's green gelatin mold. The innkeeper had waffled between lumping it with the sides or the desserts since it contained both sweet and savory.

Time for Ella to call in her own reinforcements. Reaching down, she unclipped her walkie-talkie from the waistband of her yoga pants in a way she hoped was menacing. The clip caught and pulled her pants up, giving her a wedgie.

Cursing, she freed the device and pressed the push-to-talk button. "Night Angel, Bride of Frankenstein. This is Black Orchid. We have a problem."

The device hissed with static before Flo's voice croaked out. "Poodle Head, is that you?"

Ella ground her teeth. "We agreed my handle was Black Orchid."

She searched over the undulating mass of townspeople for her friends. Wink's hair stood out, a flower amongst weeds, near the appetizers. She was using her arm to sweep mini tacos and chips onto her plate while barking commands at Chester, who clung to the top of a screaming woman's head like a bull rider.

"I need help," Ella said. "Sally brought a friend. Now there's two of them." Her gaze flicked to the girl's companion, and she could swear the little child hissed at her.

Static. "Look... we've got... our... own problems." Flo's words came out haltingly, punctuated by grunts.

What was keeping her? They'd rehearsed this part dozens of times.

Wink's voice blared out of the walkie-talkie. "This is Night Angel. Robert's camped out in front of the ribs. Our window's closing. We need to activate Nightwatch. Repeat, activate Nightwatch. Over." After a drawn-out pause, she added, "Bride of Frankenstein, do you copy?"

Flo didn't respond.

"For crying out loud. Flo, that's your cue, dummy. I'm growing old here."

"Growing?" Flo finally responded. "That ship's already sailed." Her comment elicited a static-filled growl from Wink.

Ella listened to them bicker another moment before clipping the walkie-talkie back onto her hip. There would be no rescue. She was on her own against the horror twins. Hopefully, she could still execute her part of the plan.

She rolled up her sleeves. "So, this is the hill I die on."

The heavy duffel bag draped over her shoulder dropped to the floor. With her eyes glued to the hellions, she pulled out an antique film camera with wires and antennas glued to the side.

"El—I mean, Black Orchid," Wink's voice crackled from her hip, "if you can hear me, you should already be geared up and in position. Over."

Quickly, she unclipped the walkie-talkie. "Night vision's ready. We're a go. Over."

No one responded.

She sighed, squeezing the button again. "Numbnuts, did you hear me? I've got your infrared iPhone thingie. Over."

"I-SEC," Flo responded, her tone slightly acerbic.

"That's what I said."

"It stands for Infrared-Sensitive Electron Camera... or something. I wasn't paying attention when Will explained it. Those blue eyes of his—"

"Florence Henderson!" Wink interrupted. "Didn't you hear me? Robert's got his paws on the ribs. I repeat: he's made it to the ribs. By my calculations, we have 7.5 seconds before they're gone."

Wink had been quite proud of the fact that they'd timed the man at the last potluck to get this information, calling it "gathering intel."

The lights flickered out.

The noise of bedlam and wrestling bodies in the church died, proceeded by confused shouting.

"Who turned out the lights?" a nearby voice hollered.

Ella felt herself smirk as she pressed her eye to the camera lens and used it to navigate to the dessert table. The red blotchy forms of townsfolk fumbled about, arms out-stretched.

She skirted two bumbling forms in braids and pigtails, sticking her tongue out at them as she did. Silently, she shoveled slices of pie and other pastries onto a plate. She didn't take more than the three of them could eat—well, not *much* more. She wasn't selfish.

"Hey," a voice called out, "someone check the breaker box."

Her time was nearly up. Any minute now, the lights would be back on. She swept past the two little minions, then stopped, a wicked idea forming.

After hurrying with her plan, she finished and stood, gave a self-satisfied nod, and stole away, her hands ladened with the dessert plate and I-SEC. In the limited periphery provided by the camera lens, she spotted an orangish-red figure near the punch bowl digging through his pockets as he said, "Hold on. I think I have a light."

There was a metallic click, and a small flame flickered in the night vision. Someone bumped into him, and the lighter slipped from his fingers, falling into the punch spiked with Lou's high octane booze.

There was a *whoosh*, and a fireball flared in the night vision camera, blinding her. Several people screamed and dove for cover. A few brave souls jumped into action to put out the flames.

They were still fighting the punch bowl inferno when the lights came back on. As order was restored, movement, more subdued than before, resumed around the room. Either the frenzy had worn off, or the fireball had tamped their spirits.

Sally and her brown-haired twin spotted Ella and the mountain of desserts piled on her plate. Ella winked at them.

Glowering, they took a menacing step forward before falling flat onto their faces, their shoelaces tied to each other like a classic cartoon. The shock on Sally's face shifted to rage, then she burst into tears. Her mother materialized from the crowd, scooping the girl up into her arms. Through crocodile tears and sobs, Sally wailed something in her mother's ear, then pointed at Ella.

The woman glared over, and Ella tensed, waiting for her wrath. Instead, she carried the girl—who was definitely too big to be carried—away, leaving her companion devil spawn to fend for herself.

Sally eyed Ella over her mother's shoulder and returned a wink. Any shred of guilt that had been creeping up over tying their shoelaces together evaporated. That little girl was either a future cult leader or politician.

"Well played, Sally. Well played."

CHAPTER SIX

WITH HER SPOILS of war, Ella hunted down the others, finding Wink, Flo, and Rose at a table near the stage. She sat between her partners in crime to divvy up their food. Amid dividing the apple pie, Stewart joined their table. He sat on the other side of Wink and gave her a peck on the cheek.

After she and Flo dutifully teased Wink about the chaste kiss, Ella surveyed their group. "Where are Will and Jimmy?"

Rose's brows furrowed with concern. "Jimmy's still working. As for Will, I assumed you'd know where your beau was."

"I'm just going to bypass the whole 'beau' comment and say that I know he was working on the time device today, but didn't think he'd be late for the potluck."

The inventor loved the bi-monthly gathering almost as much as she did. Actually, more, since she dreaded having to stand off against Sally. She really needed to discuss reassignment from the dessert table with Wink and Flo.

Stewart sipped from a glass of the spiked punch, grimaced, then set it back on the table, scooting it farther away. A moment later, Flo snatched up the cup and chugged like a frat boy. She finished by smacking her lips, saying, "One of Lou's better mixes, I think."

"You should be studied by science," Ella said.

Digging into her food, she bypassed the ribs for the moment, warming up her stomach with a shortbread cookie. She was two bites in when a young voice spoke near her elbow.

"I hope you like those."

Ella twisted in her chair and found two large doe eyes blinking innocently at her.

"I made them special for you." Sally smiled sweetly, giggled, then skipped away.

The cookie fell from Ella's fingers. "Oh, God. She poisoned me. Wink, if I die tonight, tell Will the Boston Red Sox finally win the World Series again."

Stewart dropped his fork. "They do? The Curse of the Bambino was broken?"

She gave him a distracted nod. "Rose, take care of Fluffy for me, will you?"

"Since he was already the inn's cat, and I was taking care of him long before you got here, sure, dear. I will."

"If you're gonna die, can I have your phone?" Flo stabbed her fork into a thick ribeye steak, causing blood to pool beneath it.

"What? No, that goes to Will. You, I'm haunting until you die because this is entirely your fault."

Flo shrugged, then attacked her steak with a knife.

Conversation resumed despite Ella's impending demise. All things considered, and as many close calls as she'd had in the past year, death by cookie wasn't too bad.

She prodded Wink for her compact mirror until the woman finally relented, rolling her eyes and handing it over. Staring at her reflection, Ella poked her skin and checked her pupils. After a half-hour of this, when nothing so much as a sneeze materialized, she decided Sally was a big fat liar. She returned Wink's mirror to her and dug into her now-cold food with the gusto of one who'd recently cheated death.

As she tucked into a third rib, Wink snapped her fingers as if remembering something. She dug through her purse, pulled out a container, and handed it to Ella.

The moment she opened it, the warm, welcoming aroma of gingerbread—not the hard, cookie kind, but the actual bread—wafted out.

Rose gaped at her. "How could you possibly need *more* food?"

"This isn't because I'm hungry. She's helping me with a recipe. And by that I mean she's making the recipe, and I'm taste-testing it."

Sucking in a slow breath of anticipation, she broke off a hunk and popped it in her mouth. The flavor lingered on her tongue, the bread dissolving. Wink stared expectantly at her.

"Close, but not quite. It needs more... molasses? It's not quite..." She searched for an appropriate adjective. As a linguist, she rarely struggled for the right word, but as someone who only baked if she wanted a kitchen fire, she couldn't give Wink helpful feedback.

Wink patted her forearm before holding out her hand for the container. "It's alright. I'll keep trying."

"Oh, I'm still going to eat this." Ella tucked the container into her duffle bag. The bread may not be the taste of home and Barton Christmases, but that was no excuse to let it go to waste.

As she chowed down on another rib, one of the town's amateur radio hosts Ukulele Joe strode onto the pulpit-turned-stage, carrying his instrument. A murmur of groans rose.

At Ella's side, Flo swore loudly and stuffed her cloth napkin into one ear. Then she stole Ella's and shoved it into her other ear.

"Joke's on you because that's got steak sauce all over it." But her words fell on deaf, cloth-filled ears.

Joe tapped the microphone, causing ear-splitting feedback, like nails on a chalkboard. He plucked and tuned the ukulele until all the strings were flat and off-key before he began strumming.

After a moment of listening and wincing, Ella said, "You know, I think he might be improving."

"He's doing scales." Wink shoved two buttermilk biscuits to her ears.

Ukulele Joe finished with his "scales" and pulled the microphone closer. Ella applauded and whooped loudly, pumping her fist in the air Arsenio Hall style.

She was the only one.

Wink slid down in her seat, while Flo took advantage of Ella's divided attention to steal a bite of her cherry cobbler.

Once people had stopped gawking, Wink hissed, "What're you doing? Don't encourage him."

"He'll clear the room if he keeps playing, then we can go back for seconds."

Wink's mouth opened, probably to protest, then her features rearranged into admiration. "That's not a bad strategy."

As the final notes of Joe's next song died a gruesome death, Ella clapped loudly, calling out, "I love your interpretation of *Mary Had a Little Lamb*."

He frowned, his lips hovering over the microphone. "That was *Twinkle, Twinkle, Little Star*."

He cleared his throat, a noise that blasted through the speakers and sent the audience scrambling to cover their ears. "This next song's one I wrote myself. It's called, *Stuck in Dino Land.*"

He began strumming and after listening for several bars, Ella found it indistinguishable from the previous song. Still, she hummed and swung her foot.

When Ukulele Joe was halfway through his set, Jimmy finally showed up. He sat with a harried expression, plunking down a plate of whatever remained at the buffet—mostly vegetables and white meat.

Ella caught Wink's and Flo's attention and gave a not-so-subtle nod in the deputy's direction. During an investigation, Chapman was tightlipped, which was more due to him not being the chatty type than any actual adherence to secrecy during an ongoing investigation. Jimmy, on the other hand, could be a font of information if they played their cards right.

The deputy chewed a dry piece of meat, eyeing the remainder of Ella's smoked ribs.

She folded her hands, leaning forward. "So, what's the skinny?"

"How's that?" The dry chicken seemed to catch in his throat. He pounded his chest and grabbed Rose's punch.

"Oh, I wouldn't—" Rose began but was interrupted by Jimmy spewing out the contents.

"Who let Lou near the drinks?"

After he recovered, he doused his chicken in barbecue sauce before attempting another bite. Ella offered up her water, which he gratefully accepted, and she tried again.

"Did Pauline determine a cause of death yet?"

"Chapman warned me not to tell you anything."

"It's okay. He's not here. You can tell us."

"No, I can't."

Ella gave him an exaggerated wink. "Right. Gotcha."

"No, really. I can't tell you—and stop winking at me."

She lowered her voice and scooted her plate of ribs suggestively. "You can't tell me anything. I get it. Like, you absolutely *can't* tell me that the professor was hit on the head by a blunt object and that he died of some kind of brain hemorrhage." She raised her voice again. "See what I did there?"

He grunted. "I will say Pauline ran tests on the object you're referring to. It's a dinosaur bone, specifically a femur. Most likely from our recent visitors."

Her gaze fell to the rest of the ribs on her plate, remembering the biological matter still rotting on the dinosaur bone, and her stomach protested. She shoved the plate the rest of the way to Jimmy. Before she could blink, he was tearing into them like a velociraptor.

Between bites, he said, "Oh, I almost forgot. The sheriff wants to know if you'll come in tomorrow to help him question our suspect." He looked at Ella.

She floundered for a moment. Her brain filled with a dozen different thoughts related to communicating with the caveman.

"Absolutely, but don't get your hopes up. I think he hails from a time before any writing systems, and I don't know how much spoken language he's capable of."

Stewart dropped his cloth napkin on his plate, indicating he was finished, then draped his arm over the back of Wink's chair. "I wonder how long he's been living in that cave."

"What d'you mean? He wandered in with them dinos," Flo said.

Ella shook her head. "You're a few million years off." Also, judging by the number of paintings that had covered the cavern walls, the man—in the colloquial sense of that term— had been hiding there for quite some time. And, to a lesser extent, so had the professor.

Had they been sharing the space like roommates? She would've paid money to see a spinoff version of *The Odd Couple* featuring those two.

Perhaps Dr. Kaufman had moved into the chamber, unaware that it was already occupied, or perhaps they'd commingled until something had set the caveman off. Either way, why not just move to another section of the cave system? It wasn't like it lacked dark, creepy caverns.

She was pulled from her thoughts when Sal wound around the crowded tables, gliding like an eel, stopping to shake hands. He wore a sports jacket and a smile as greasy as his slicked-back hair above a sharp widow's peak.

Wink craned her head around to see what Ella was staring at. "Has anyone found out why he's got a bee in his bonnet about Chapman all of a sudden?"

"I've been eavesdropping on conversations at the diner," Ella said, shaking her head, "but no one seems to know. Also, I didn't realize how much people gossiped about their neighbors. Spoiler: it's a lot. Like a 'you can't pass gas in your own home without a Keystone Village neighbor knowing' a lot."

"Chapman told me Sal confronted him the other day." Jimmy dabbed at his mouth, dropping the bone of the last rib to his plate with a satisfied grunt. "Came in all hot under the collar, yelling at him about failing to arrest Six for something."

"Did he say what?" Ella asked.

The deputy studied the table, his finger tracing a scratch, and Ella was forced to repeat her question.

He sighed. "I guess I don't see the harm in telling you. Sal claims Six broke his window and destroyed his apartment. And Chapman didn't do a darn thing to punish him."

Oh no. "Are you sure that's what he said?"

Her chest suddenly felt constricted, and she exchanged glances with Wink and Flo, who appeared to be as equally uncomfortable. They were the ones who'd broken Sal's window—well, mostly Flo. Incidentally, the damage had been caused by the plasma cannon and a not-so-well aimed plasma ball.

Subdued, Ella half-listened as the conversation drifted to the high school's upcoming softball season. Since Keystone couldn't play against other towns, the school was relegated to playing against the lodge's retirees and a church team. Stewart and Jimmy spoke in earnest, excited over a new recruit, but all Ella could do was watch Sal slither around the room with his unctuous smile.

The new mayor had a beef with the sheriff, and it was all their fault. He didn't have the authority to kick Chapman out of office, as it was an elected position, but that wouldn't stop him from influencing voters when it came time for the re-election of the sheriff's position in two years.

An hour flew by as they chatted—accompanied by the screeching, off-key serenade of Ukulele Joe—before they rose to head to their respective homes. As they neared the double doors, someone at a nearby table called out Flo's name.

"Oh, hello… Jason," Flo said hesitantly as Ella, Wink, and the others were donning their jackets.

"Norman," the man corrected in a whiny, nasally voice. "We were married, for God's sake."

Ella stopped. She looked at Wink.

Together, they retraced their steps a couple of yards.

"Pardon me," she said to the man, "I couldn't help but overhear. Norman, was it? You and Flo were married?"

"We were never married." Flo shook her head.

"Yes, we were."

"But you have a beard. I don't marry men with beards."

Ella murmured, "So you *do* draw the line somewhere."

Norman rolled his eyes behind wire-rim glasses. "I didn't have a beard then, Florence."

Besides the beard and glasses, he sported thinning, curly gray hair streaked with wisps of blond, and his button-down shirt pulled taut around his mid-section. If Ella were to paint someone with a broad brush—and if they were living in her time period—she would've pegged him as an IT technician.

"I remember you." The confusion in Wink's expression suddenly cleared, and she turned to Flo. "You two were definitely married. The ceremony was at the Half Penny."

"Don't you mean the reception?" Ella asked.

"No, the ceremony."

Of course, Flo had gotten married in a bar.

Wink's eyes were half-closed in concentration. "I think it was annulled not too long after."

Ella addressed the man excitedly. "Norm—can I call you Norm? I have so many questions. For starters, what number are you?"

"… Number?"

"Yeah, which husband? Husband number one? Number twenty?"

"Twenty?" His mouth dropped. "My, my, you've been busy, Florence."

Flo waved away the comment. "I haven't been married twenty times." She paused, glancing at Wink as if to confirm this statement. "Right?"

Wink shrugged. "It's in the double digits, I know that."

Ella draped her arm around Norman. "So, these questions I have. I'm thinking it'll be easiest if I just write them all down and get back to you. What's your phone number?"

Wink made a noise, her eyes wide with a warning. "Remember when we discussed you being too forward for this era? This is one of those times."

This must be because she was a woman asking a man she'd just met for his phone number. Ah, the antiquated social conventions of the mid-twentieth century.

"Fair enough." She dropped her arm. "I'm sure we'll be in touch, Norm."

After an awkward chorus of farewells, they left Flo's ex-husband to his dessert. Stepping out into the cool night air, Ella had a thought and stopped.

"Wink, do you mind waiting a moment and giving me a ride to your place?"

Her boss gave her a coy, knowing smile. "Sure, dear."

After bidding the others goodnight, saying she'd be home late, Ella waltzed back inside the church to the potluck tables. She came out a few minutes later, ladened with two plates covered with cloth napkins. The food was cold and not the most desirable of choices, but it was better than nothing. After rejoining Wink at the double doors, they stepped out into the night.

CHAPTER SEVEN

THE NIGHT AIR was broken by the sounds of Ella's and Wink's car doors closing. The diner owner waved a farewell before hiking up her porch steps.

Turning, Ella aimed for the house next door, pausing to admire the expansive view of the jewels of lights scattered far below. They glittered off the lake like stars. From above, Keystone Village looked like a Norman Rockwell painting. Actually, not only from this elevation; up close the buildings, yards, and people below were idyllic—rash of murders, notwithstanding.

Weedy light from Dr. Kaufman's living room spilled out onto dead grass and dirt—the extent of the man's landscaping prowess. She bypassed the porch and rounded the side of the house, stopping beneath the kitchen window at a set of storm cellar doors inlaid in the ground.

The dishes in her hands balanced awkwardly. A year of waitressing in the diner, and she still balanced food like a drunken clown with an inner ear disorder. She tapped on the door with the bottom of her shoe and waited patiently. At first. When a chilly breeze cut through her jacket, she stomped and called out the inventor's name.

Finally, a sliver of light broke out between the double doors, widening as Will's head emerged like a groundhog checking for an early spring—if that groundhog was handsome, with disheveled hair and bags under his eyes.

"El?"

"Holy Unabomber. When was the last time you slept?" She slipped past him, descending into the basement, catching the scent of his ripe clothes as she did. She probably should have reheated the food in the kitchen first, but it felt too late now.

Her feet shuffled over the concrete floor of the cellar turned mad scientist workshop. Rows and rows of shelves with electrical paneling and wires and tools filled the space, save for a section at the west end. It was devoted to an alcove of consoles and machines, full of lights, wires, and buttons. In the center, on a large workbench, was the heart of the machine, the source of all their problems.

"No offense, but it smells like a men's locker room in here."

There wasn't an available surface on which to set the food, none except for the boxy time device capable of inter-dimensional travel. But he'd probably object to it being used as a dinner table.

Will had followed closely, sniffing the air in her wake. "Is that Betty's green bean casserole?"

"It's not—aaand you don't care."

Without waiting for her response, he'd ripped the topmost plate from her hands, grabbed the fork she'd included, and attacked a cold blob of mashed potatoes with gusto.

"Good God, man. When was the last time you ate—or shaved? Christmas?"

He paused long enough to run a hand down the thick stubble along his jaw before tearing into a roll.

She watched him in admiration a moment before turning a slow circle, taking in the mess. What had been a confusing array of control panels around the perimeter was now a confusing array of control panels on the floor with wires poking out.

A kerosene lantern flickered on a nearby shelf, illuminating the guts of the machines. The lantern was a safe distance away, which boded well for the safety of the equipment but made for poor lighting. She set the remaining plate of food beside the lantern.

"What's with the mood lighting?"

He glanced up. "I turned off power to the basement so I wouldn't electrocute myself pulling those panels off."

"Clever."

On the center workbench, near the humming time device, was a complicated-looking gadget that hadn't been there the last time she'd visited.

He followed her gaze and motioned at the complicated apparatus. "I found that in the professor's inventory." His head jerked towards the dark rows of overflowing shelves behind him. "Took me a while to figure out what it was. It measures gravity waves if you can believe it. It's jake. Amazing. The professor's work is so beyond what we know—at least in my time."

"My time, too."

"Anyway, I've been taking readings around town, measuring fluctuations in the gravity field, recording them, and poring over the professor's math."

"I see. Any progress?"

"Not really. The town's in an inter-dimensional bubble, but that much we already knew."

"Sure, sure."

"The device goes haywire when I near the border, giving me all sorts of wild readings that don't follow what I get in other locations, meaning the field fluctuates. And I can't make sense of the Doc's math in his notebooks."

His jaw clenched and unclenched as he exchanged his empty plate for the next one. "It's like he said: the bubble became independent of the device, somehow. Even if I were able to connect the machine to the field again, the bubble's stable right now, and I'm worried reestablishing a connection would disrupt that. Who knows what could happen?"

"What could happen is that the bubble could transfer to a flux capacitor in a DeLorean, and we could use the car to travel back to the future."

He blinked at her. "The bubble can't transfer to a car."

Shrugging, she moved through the dim light, poring over the open notebooks strewn out on the center workbench. It may as well have been in a different language for all she could understand. Actually, she would've had a better chance of understanding a different language. Then again, wasn't that all math was? The language of the universe? She wished she'd paid more attention to Mrs. Summers during math class rather than pass notes with her friends.

"His work is based on Einstein's posit of gravity waves, right?"

Will nodded, breaking off a hunk of apple pie with his fork.

"And didn't you once say the gravity field was behaving like an inter-dimensional fluid?"

"So, you *were* listening." One of the corners of his mouth turned up, briefly showing off dimples.

"Sometimes it happens, despite my best efforts." She tapped her chin with a finger. "I remember reading once in a science magazine—" she caught his expression and explained, "I was waiting for my chiropractic appointment, and it was the only thing there. Anyway, I remember reading that bubbles followed the physics of a fluid."

"Yes, that's correct."

She rested a finger on the sheets of paper and notebooks full of complicated calculations. "Now I know the inter-dimensional bubble is just a metaphor we're using, but what if it behaves similarly to an actual bubble? Out of curiosity, how much of the professor's math uses fluid dynamics?"

The fork paused partway to his mouth. "Quite a bit..." He let the plate fall to the shelf with a clatter that sent bits of crust flying. "But you just gave me an idea."

"I did? Was that science? Am I doing science?"

He didn't respond.

"Now that you can look at the math from the perspective of fluid dynamics—"

"No," he interrupted, shaking his head, "That is to say, yes, it incorporates fluid dynamics, but that's not the inspiration." He shoved aside papers until he could find a blank sheet. Unable to find one, he flipped a paper over and began scribbling on the back. "Cavitation."

"Bless you."

A small snort was all she got in response.

She sighed, muttering, "Tough crowd," and let him work. She ambled over to the plates of food, and her hand stretched for a cookie.

"If you eat so much as a bite of my food, I'll provide Flo with that atomizer gun she's been begging me to make."

She rolled her eyes and stepped away.

After some time lapsed, with only the hum of the time device and the popping of her lips to keep her company, he said, "Chapman came and saw me today. He told me about the professor."

Ella closed her eyes and drew in a breath. She'd been dreading this conversation.

"I'm sorry, Will." When she turned, she caught the tension in his muscles, the strain in his eyes. "I know he was your friend."

"He stopped being my friend when he ran off, leaving this mess for me to figure out on my own." Beneath the bitterness in his tone, she heard an undercurrent of pain and regret. "His loss is a blow to all of us."

She grabbed a nearby stool and dragged it over to the workbench. With her elbow planted on the notebooks, she leaned forward until he was forced to look at her. "He was still a friend and your mentor."

The inventor blinked, and he whispered in a tight voice, "Yes, he was." He dragged another stool over, a rickety one that teetered on three legs, and sank with a heavy sigh. "But it's hard to mourn when I'm so angry at him. Look at what he did to us. And now it's all on me to fix."

Reaching over, she rested her hand on his. His skin was warm and calloused. "You'll figure it out."

"And if I don't?"

She shrugged. "Then we're no worse off, are we? We'll grow old, you'll take on a protege, someone you can teach all of this to—" she gestured vaguely at their surroundings "—and he or she will continue the work."

"The professor couldn't fix it, and he had ten years. How can I possibly hope to do it?"

She squeezed his hand. "Because you're not doing this alone. Sure, you're doing the calculations and mechanical stuff by yourself, the physics and... where was I going? Oh, yeah. But *you* are not alone. The professor was trying to solve this by himself. You have a whole town behind you. More importantly, I have faith in you.

"My advice? Take a breath and get some sleep. You can't solve this in one night." She straightened her back. "And for goodness' sake, take a bath."

He smiled, a full genuine one this time. After pecking her on the cheek, he stood and retrieved his food. She watched his shadow flicker along the machine wires, recalling the professor's dying words.

He found me.... Don't fix it. He'll use it and change everything.

Don't fix it. The "it" being the time device. A cold dread settled in her stomach, weighing her down. She had to tell Will.

But what if he chose to heed the professor's words? She'd be stranded forever. She would never see her family again. Her friends. Her home.

"El? You okay?"

She forced a smile. "Fine. Did I tell you I met one of Flo's ex-husband's tonight?"

His eyes widened. "You don't say? Which one?" Bringing his plate over, he settled onto the stool again, captivated. "Spare no detail."

Ella's dreams were a mix of dinosaurs and dead bodies. Somewhere in the mix, a caveman emerged in a loincloth and prominent brow ridge, trying to sell her car insurance. She was just teaching him how to high-five, making it the oldest high-five in all of history, when the caveman began shaking her by the shoulders. Through a sleepy fog, she realized that it wasn't just a dream. Someone was shaking her in her bed.

Her eyes shot open. A dark figure loomed over her. Ella opened her mouth to belt out a scream before a wrinkled hand covered her lips.

"Don't scream, Poodle Head. It's just me."

Her heart hammered furiously against her chest. After what seemed an interminable amount of time, Flo pulled her hand away, and Ella gasped for air.

"Cheddar sticks, Flo. Are you trying to suffocate me? My nose is stuffy, and I can't breathe through it." She gulped down lungfuls of sweet air that tasted of freedom and, oddly, chicken. She licked her lips. "Is that—please tell me you just ate. Holy salmonella, you haven't washed your hands since the potluck, have you?"

"Don't be ridiculous. I rinsed them off. I just had a late-night snack."

Ella glanced at the numbers glowing on her phone. "Two-thirty in the morning isn't—wait, did you say 'rinsed'? You only *rinsed* your hands? No soap?"

Flo clambered off the bed or at least attempted to, but it ended up looking like she was both wrestling with the comforter and fighting a seizure.

"Here's a question," Ella said, sitting up and rubbing the sleep from her eyes. "What are you doing in my room at 2:30 in the morning?"

"I need your help."

CHAPTER EIGHT

ELLA YAWNED AND pulled a muffin from her pocket—her emergency snack. "This has to be the worst thing you've done to me yet."

"Well, you didn't have to agree to come," Flo bit back. She held the lantern up, creating sharp shadows on her face like she was preparing to tell a ghost story.

"Yes, I did. What are friends for if not to do favors they can hold over their friends' heads for years?" Her mouth stretched into another wide yawn before she took a bite of muffin.

Ella, Flo, and Wink stood at the entrance to the extensive cave system. Clouds covered a waning moon, and their three lanterns weren't enough to illuminate the dark forest beyond. Wink had picked up Ella and Flo in her car and parked at the base of the eastern Twin Hills, making it less of a hike compared to the day before—or was it technically still the same day? Whenever Sunday morning had been.

"Here it is." Wink had been searching through her backpack. She popped to her feet in much too perky of a mood for the middle of the night.

Ella glared until she realized what her boss held out: a thermos. Unscrewing the lid, she pledged eternal, undying love for Wink, then sipped at the steaming coffee like it was nectar for the gods.

Beside them, Flo hopped from one foot to the other. "Can we get a move on now, please? We're burning oil."

"Crazy old ladies first." Ella swept her hand out, indicating for Flo to enter the dark, creepy cave.

As Flo passed, she gave Ella the finger. Shadows fled their lanterns, their movements putting Ella on edge, especially when she remembered the bear trap and that Spot was still missing.

"Did either of you ever read—I mean, Wink, did you ever read *Journey to the Center of the Earth*?"

"I did."

"Cool, so I'm not alone in knowing what we're in for. You are armed, right, Flo?"

Ahead, the woman let out a snort for a reply.

Three turns later, as the caffeine kicked in, Ella softly hummed *Heigh-Ho* from *Snow White and the Seven Dwarfs* before the echoes grew too loud, and Wink asked her to "stop, please, oh please, just stop."

In the beginning, they followed Ella's markings until the third turn where Flo went left instead of right. The trio descended, and the passage narrowed so much their shoulders brushed limestone on both sides. Ella wasn't usually claustrophobic, but at that point, her skin began to crawl. Just when she was about to suggest turning back, the passage widened into a chamber.

It was smaller than the one the professor and the caveman had been found in, but still on the larger side, about the size of the inn's parlor. She breathed in damp, stale air while, ahead, Flo's light bobbed deeper into the cavern, revealing the rest of the space.

Ella's mouth fell open. "You said it was a small weapons cache."

"It is. This is just one of 'em."

She wasn't a stranger to one of Flo's bunkers. The kooky woman had kept one in a secret speakeasy in the basement of the inn for years. However, at that moment, all Ella could think about was how much time it was going to take to relocate the boxes of ammunition, guns, exotic inter-dimensional weapons, grenades, and—was that a box of dynamite?

Not for the first time did she curse the arms dealers who Flo had stolen the weapons from. Technically, she hadn't stolen them so much as taken ownership after the truck transporting the weapons had been stranded when the town jumped. She'd clearly added to her collection since then, judging by the ancient mace straight from the Middle Ages.

Wink rolled up her sleeves. "Where are we moving them to? I'm telling you right now, I'm not letting you keep all of this at my place."

"Well, it's nice to know how loyal you are," Flo said.

"My loyalty ends at storing dynamite under the same roof where I sleep."

Flo sniffed at this. "It just needs to be moved further into the cave. It's too close to the crime scene right now, and I can't risk that lawman confiscatin' any more."

"Do you have a particular place in mind?" Ella stuffed the remainder of her muffin in her mouth before chasing it with coffee from Wink's thermos. This was going to require a lot of energy.

"Back when I first set up this place, I scouted other potential spots. There's another one deeper in. I chose this one 'cause it was closer." Bending, her back crackling, Flo liberated a shotgun and several rifles from beds of hay—presumably to keep the moisture away. She lay them in a rusty red Radio Flyer wagon.

"Please tell me you bought that wagon and there's not some kid out there wondering where his wagon went."

Flo coughed. "I'm just borrowin' it."

"Borrowing. Right." Grunting, Ella hefted a rocket launcher from its resting place. She may as well help the crazy loon relocate her bunker. Not only was she already down the rabbit hole of crazy, but she was in so deep she owned property.

It didn't take long to burden the wagon to its max carrying capacity. Dragging the red wagon, she followed Wink and Flo into the main passageway, their arms ladened with guns, machetes, and knives. The wheels on the wagon squeaked and protested under the weight. Several times, they had to stop so Flo could recall how to get to the other chamber.

"I don't think it matters if we find the same one," Ella said after the fourth time they had to turn around. Her forehead glistened with sweat despite the cool temperature. "We just need to move this stuff further from the crime scene, right?"

"I think it's this way." Flo marched down the tunnel to the left. A moment later, she reemerged and disappeared down the right.

Wink looked at Ella. "You ever hear of the blind leading the blind?"

Shaking her head, the diner owner followed Flo while Ella trailed behind, mumbling about how she should still be in bed. By the time Flo's voice echoed ahead with "This is it," Ella's biceps ached. And there were still several more trips to make.

She followed their voices into another chamber, then peeled the wagon handle from her cramped hand. It clattered to the rock, echoing around the small space. Her lantern had made the trip nestled between guns and ammo. She held it aloft, wanting to see where to dump the weapons.

"What the..." her voice trailed off. "Do you see what I see?"

The other two stood a few feet away, their loads still cradled in their arms, staring.

"Looks like someone already beat you to this spot," Wink said at last.

Glass containers upon glass containers—ranging from Bradford Farms milk bottles to beer growlers to stoneware jugs—lined the entire chamber, some in crates stacked as tall as Ella. All had been emptied of their original contents, replaced by a clear liquid.

"Did we stumble onto another distillery?" Ella picked up one of the recycled milk bottles and popped off the lid, sniffing.

Flo had already broken into one and was guzzling the liquid. A moment later, she sprayed it out.

"Water," she sputtered, disgusted. "What a waste."

Ella sniffed her bottle and took a sip. "Why hoard so much water?"

At the other end of the small chamber, Wink used her lantern to peer at a moonshine jug, tapping a finger on the brown stoneware. "Maybe the council stashed it here for emergency purposes."

That made sense. She'd heard of small towns doing that.

Ella replaced the cap and returned the bottle to the crate. "I think this is where the professor was getting his water. He had a couple of Bradford Farms glasses in his bolt-hole."

"Hmm, he couldn't have been the one to squirrel all this away," Wink said. "Not without someone spotting him."

The man had been Keystone's most wanted since he'd gone into hiding. Everyone had been searching for him.

"Unless he stocked up on supplies before he ran. He could have anticipated needing to go underground at some point." Ella shook her head. "But why only water and not food?"

It didn't make sense.

"I think you're right," she said after a moment. "I think this is the council's emergency supply and that he discovered it and was stealing from it."

Wink turned to Flo, whose nose was still wrinkled with disgust over the bottles not being filled with booze. "Well, what do you want to do? Search for another cavern?"

She decided to try another chamber. The woman's bouffant was half-deflated as if tired by the hour. It sagged as they trundled deeper down the tunnel. A few minutes later, they stumbled upon another promising alcove, one that was empty.

Ella let out a not-so-quiet sigh of relief when Flo announced it would be good enough.

"It's just temporary, anyway," the boarder added. "When the law dogs aren't wandering these caves anymore, we'll move everything back."

Ella wiped her forehead with her sleeve. "I'm pretty sure I'll be sick in bed that day."

"And I've got a hair appointment," Wink chimed in.

Not wanting to waste more time, Ella unloaded the wagon by gripping one side and tipping it so the contents clattered to the cave floor.

"Careful with those!" Flo rushed forward and gently lifted a rifle, caressing it. "We'll need to bring over the beds of hay, too."

Muttering under her breath about the woman needing a brain scan, Ella returned the lantern to the rickety wagon and wheeled it out for another trip. How had this become her life?

CHAPTER NINE

THERE WASN'T ENOUGH coffee in all of Keystone to stave off Ella's exhaustion. Despite this, she cradled a cup in her hands, fighting the pull of her eyelids as she stared out the diner window.

"Miss?" a voice called out.

She blinked and looked over at a patron, some guy named Rodney or Robert.

"Can I get some more coffee?"

Turning, she lifted the carafe from the warmer, noting the dark liquid sloshing around inside was barely enough to fill a single cup. She dumped it into his mug, sparing a couple drops for her own, nearly whimpering at the puny amount.

Mercifully, the breakfast crowd had fared lighter this morning, and Rodney-Robert was all who remained. After starting another pot brewing, she swung into the kitchen. Wink slumped on a stool at the island, her elbow on the countertop, her chin resting in her hand. She dozed softly, a sliver of drool leaking from the corner of her mouth.

Behind her, Horatio clattered at the griddle, flipping pancakes. As there was currently only one customer in the diner and he'd already eaten, Ella didn't know who the pancakes were for.

She swiped one from the top of the steaming stack and untied her apron before draping it on a hook. "Chapman asked me to pop in today, and now seems to be a good time. We've got a customer at the lunch counter, but he's got his grub and mud." She straightened the pink gingham print of her 1950s waitress uniform, then donned a light coat. "Tell Wink when she wakes up?"

He nodded, then brandished the spatula at her as she stole another pancake.

Outside, the air felt crisp but had a certain warmth fighting through. The sun climbed, trying to dispel the morning chill. It felt like spring and new life. The stupor of exhaustion caused by only three hours of sleep began to retreat.

Just south of the sheriff's office, she passed the library. A pale blue sky reflected in its window, and her steps slowed as she decided on a last-minute detour. Inside the library, the rich scent of old books greeted her as did a hushed, peaceful calm known of all libraries the world over. But there wasn't time enough to linger in the ambiance or browse today.

Instead, she made a beeline for the section she needed and hunted down a book on early European humans. There was only one, which was one more than the inn's library had had. This book—and encyclopedia entries—were all the knowledge the town had to offer on early humans.

After that, she scoured the linguistics section, but was already familiar with all the titles and knew they contained little pertaining to pre-written systems. Wow, did she miss the Internet.

She took the single book to the check-out desk, planning to supplement her reading with the encyclopedias at the inn. No use toting around bricks of books when she had them at home. She'd gotten enough of a workout during the night while relocating Flo's arsenal.

Gabby's surly aunt ran the desk today—which was really just a scratched-up table. While the woman cataloged the return date for the single item, Ella drummed her fingers on the table.

"Lovely weather we're having, hmm?"

She glowered at Ella and handed over the book.

"Welp, good talk as always." Ella waved and hustled out the door. The cool air was a reprieve from the librarian's frigid disposition.

Outside the sheriff's office, Horse stood in the street, reined to a hitching post, munching on grass that grew between cracks in the sidewalk. She petted him a moment before ducking into the squat building, entering a drab world of gray concrete and bars. Dust motes rode on shafts of light from the window facing the street, illuminating Chapman's shoulders like a shroud.

He looked up as she closed the door. His derby hat lay on his desk alongside his boots.

"Where's Jimmy?"

"Sent him to deal with the Murphy brothers."

"What'd they do this time?"

"Dunno. But one of their neighbors called up, said they heard an explosion, said it sounded like it came from their place."

"Maybe they got ahold of some of Flo's dynamite."

"Pardon?"

She cleared her throat. "Her dynamite *lasagna*, that is. That stuff's great, am I right?"

His expression could've been etched from granite.

Squirming under his scrutiny, she turned to the jail cells. It was easy to know which one held the caveman—the third one on the end—due to the odor and the overturned bed, but largely because the two exterior building walls that made up half the cell were covered in paintings.

A creaking protest rose from Chapman's chair as he stood and joined her. When they reached the cell, she pinched her nose.

The sheriff tapped on the bars, and a mound of fur half-buried under an overturned cot stirred at the sound. The caveman's head appeared, and he let out a growl.

"Looks like he's been busy," she noted as her eyes roved from the paintings to the floor. Remnants of chicken bones and other food lay scattered about.

"He didn't like the pie tin we served his food on, took to throwing it. I was afraid he'd hurt himself."

Ella nodded, half-listening, as she studied the person on the other side.

The caveman's nose worked back and forth, sniffing the air. Deftly, he crawled out of the hole of blankets he'd created and stood, and she got a better look at him.

He was roughly her height but powerfully built, robust and solid. A broad, straight forehead rose above prominent brow ridges, his face short and wide. Some features were lost in facial hair that rivaled Grizzly Adams, but she glimpsed a pointy chin.

Her gaze traveled from him to the paintings of animals and stick figures, hoping to God the dark medium he'd used was food of some sort, but the smell suggested otherwise.

Where to begin?

The caveman squatted and picked up a drumstick, nibbling on it and eyeing her warily. She knelt to his level, only a few feet and bars separating them.

Placing her hand on her chest, she said, "Ella." She repeated this a few times, then she pointed at the partially decimated chicken bone in his hands, saying, "Food."

This was met with a blank stare.

Did he even have a language yet? Based on his features, she guessed him to be a Cro-Magnon of the species *Homo sapien* and not the extinct *Homo erectus*, but she was out of her depth. Hence the book from the library.

Sighing, she pointed at the paintings, trying a few more words such as "human" and "animal." The man continued to stare blankly. After a few frustrating minutes of this, she sat on the ground and consulted the book.

Chapman withdrew to his desk. One of his strengths, a trait she secretly admired, was his patience. He lounged back in his chair as if he had all day. The space to work was greatly appreciated.

She ran her finger down a page and skimmed, latching onto anything that would help her. Cro-Magnon had lived 40,000 to 10,000 years ago in Europe and was a member of *Homo sapien.* The features required to produce vocal languages were all present in Cro-Magnon: vocal tract, the structure of the brain, and the size of the spinal cord, leaving little doubt in researchers that they'd had their own language.

If Cro-Magnons did have a *written* language, they'd left no evidence of it. But they had produced art, traded long-distance, and held burial ceremonies.

The book went on to describe the migration and trade patterns of Europe at the time. Included was an artist's rendition of Cro-Magnon. She glanced from it to the fur-clothed man in the jail cell and found more resemblance than not.

This shifted her paradigm about the man. He wasn't some animalistic brute, and she felt ashamed to have let those thoughts creep in.

Closing the book, she searched her memory, recalling anything she could from linguistic studies and academic articles regarding early language pre-writing. A study done in 2012, if she recalled correctly, surmised that the emergence of human language was based on phonemic diversity. Coupling that information with a paper published a year earlier that hypothesized ancestral language would have a subject, object, verb (SOV) order, and that led her to… well, she had no clue. But it was something, the *beginning* of something, really.

The depth of cataloging and deciphering a language, its morphemes, coding, syntax, grammar, it overwhelmed her as much as excited her. This could take a lifetime.

To begin, what she needed were words—his words. She needed him to speak in context, and visuals were the best way to accomplish that. Unfortunately, it seemed the caveman wasn't cooperating, most likely because he was scared. For him, this experience would be the equivalent of her being abducted by an advanced species of aliens and taken to a new planet.

Getting up on cold, stiff limbs, she asked Chapman for a pen and paper. She returned to the cell and drew a stick figure similar to the ones now decorating his cell. It wouldn't win any Pictionary games, but then, neither would his art.

The caveman grunted.

Ella pointed, saying, "Human."

The man stared, nibbling on the chicken bone.

Tilting her head, she tried mimicking the grunt he'd made, but that only drew a perplexed expression.

"Come on," she said. "Just a word. It's so easy, a caveman can do it." She smiled. "No? That's okay. It wasn't that funny."

She sucked in a slow breath, studying him. It felt odd, distant, thinking of him only as The Caveman, so she gave him the name Craig. When she announced this to Chapman, he grunted from his desk.

"Maybe you should be the one trying to communicate with him. You two speak the same language."

Letting out a frustrated sigh, she dropped the pen and paper on his desk, heading for the door.

"You're leaving?"

"I have an idea. I'll be back."

She crossed the street after waiting for a horse and buggy to pass. A bell rang overhead as she stepped into the brick building for the General Store. Seven-foot high shelves overflowing with the town's discarded objects greeted her. It had been a few weeks since she'd stepped foot inside, not since the owner had been killed by her son, along with the help of a neighbor.

She scampered past the register, sparing a wave in the young employee's direction. "Morning, Henry."

"Morning, darlin'."

She stopped in her tracks and spun. Her eyebrows climbed when she saw who was behind the register. "You're not Henry."

In place of a bored-looking young man with a splash of freckles and acne was a cocky outlaw.

Six smirked and tipped his hat in her direction.

"Wh-what in the flying pigs, hell freezing over, is happening? Are you robbing the store? You are, aren't you? This is a holdup." She searched the area for Henry, expecting to find the young man bound and gagged.

Six leaned on the glass counter. Today, he wore a hockey jersey under his usual vest, a walking anachronism.

"I got a job."

"You what?"

"Got a job."

"A job?"

He gave a begrudging nod. "Yep."

"No."

"Yep."

"You? *You* got a job?"

"Me. *I* got a job."

She stared until her eyes began to water. "Huh."

"I'm tryin' to—what's it called?" He pondered a moment. "Go straight."

She rested her elbows on the counter opposite him, saying again, "Huh." Her tongue clicked against her teeth with skepticism. "Well… good for you."

They stood in awkward silence a moment before he pulled a pocket knife from a trouser pocket, then proceeded to drag the point of the blade across the glass, getting as far as half an inch before she ripped it from his hand.

"Part of going straight means no vandalism."

"That don't sound right."

Flipping the blade home, she handed it back. "I don't suppose you know where the art supplies are?"

"Thinking of takin' up a hobby?"

"Something like that."

He tipped his head lazily in a direction. As she turned down the aisle, she heard his blade flip back open. Shaking her head, she surveyed her options and ended up grabbing a sheaf of handmade paper made from old, recycled paper and leaf fibers. It would cost a pretty penny, but that was her only option.

After that, she gathered brushes with bent tips and congealed paint. The latter was acrylic, which would mean adding water to see if she could coax life back into it.

At the register, she dumped the contents on the counter. The jewelry beneath the glass caught her eye—more specifically, the charms. "Add in that silver charm, the star, too."

After he unlocked the case by picking it with his knife, he unceremoniously dumped the charm in her outstretched palm, then rang her up. This involved a lot of punching of buttons and cursing. Finally, the ancient till popped open with a harassed *ding*.

She dug crinkled bills from her billfold, noting her dwindling funds. Payday couldn't come soon enough. It wouldn't be long before she'd have to barter like many of the locals.

When Six pulled her change from the drawer, he grabbed a couple of extra dollar bills and stuffed them into his pockets.

"There it is." She was both disappointed and relieved at the consistency in his illicit activity.

She remained at the counter, staring.

"What?" After an extended silence, he huffed and withdrew the pilfered cash, returning it to the register. "Saw your timber, will ya? This goin' straight business is dry as bones."

She waved cheerily, gathered her items, and bid him a good day to which he replied that she was "off her chump."

"I can't hear you," she called out in a sing-song voice as the door closed behind her, drawing satisfaction at having said the last word. Crossing to the sheriff's office, she gave a wide berth to Horse's freshly made pile of excrement on the pavement and stepped back into the dim building. Time to see what Craig had to say.

CHAPTER TEN

ELLA BEGAN MAKING progress in her communications with Craig the caveman once she implemented the paint and paper she'd bought. With his interest now piqued, he produced sounds she could record on her phone while panning the lens across his art. He'd taken a shine to the medium and had been reluctant to give the brush and paper back, his hands now covered in ominous red paint.

Later, when rewatching the recordings, she'd write out his utterances phonetically. After establishing nothing more than a few guttural articulations of complex consonants she *hoped* were words, she booked it back to the diner in time to cover the late afternoon rush. If she could just establish a baseline with the Cro-Magnon, she might be able to question him about the murder.

Her hopes weren't high. Random articulations were a far cry from, "Why did you kill the professor?" but it was a decent starting point.

A few hours later, Ella sipped a blended concoction she'd made, reveling in her accomplishment. An apple seed crunched between her teeth, which she promptly spit into a napkin.

The kitchen door swung in, and Wink stopped short. "Wh-what's this? What have you done to my kitchen?"

Remnants of fruit and puddles of juice decorated the island countertop like the gruesome aftermath in a horror movie.

"Don't worry. I'll clean it up. I made a smoothie." Ella preened and handed over the cup for Wink to try.

The diner owner took one whiff and recoiled. "Did you add peppermint extract to this?"

"Yeah, it's not very good. But the point is, I made a smoothie. We drink them all the time in my era. I call this one…" Her mind searched and latched onto the first name that sprang to mind. "Jamba Juice. Yep, Jamba Juice."

"That's an odd name."

"Is it? Well, it's a name I made up. Just now, right off the top of my head. It's in no way the name of a franchise in the twenty-first century." Wink continued to gape at her. "Oh, a smoothie is this delicious drink, similar to a sorbet, but with more liquid. And sometimes there's dairy or a milk substitute. Actually, maybe it's more like a milkshake—"

"I know what a smoothie is. And I don't care about the mess. I'm glad you took the initiative to make something, even if it tastes as if it came from a compost pile."

"That might be the grass I added."

It took Wink a moment to recover. "What I don't understand is why you used my food processor to make it instead of the blender."

"Because we don't have a blender, silly."

Wink pointed at a contraption on the counter.

"That's a blender? I thought that was Horatio's pancake mixer." She squinted at the appliance. "Ah, so it is a blender. I see that now. When did we get that?"

"We've always had it."

"No, I don't think so."

She didn't want to admit that she'd just assumed blenders hadn't been mass-produced in the 1950s. Sometimes, Wink got tetchy when Ella implied they were less advanced.

"Well, I learned something today." Ella took a long sip from her minty, earthy fruit drink, winced, and let it dribble from her mouth back into the cup. "Mm, delicious. It really hits the spot."

After walking to the sink, she poured the contents down the drain, a strained smile fixed in place. "Yep, nothing like a refreshing smoothie on a nice sunny day."

The back door burst in with enough force for the knob to create a crater in the sheetrock. Flo stood on the threshold, sucking wind like it was going out of style. Behind her, Horatio shot them a perplexed look from his perch on a stack of pallets. He preferred to take his breaks outside, which Ella tried not to take personally.

"It's open," Flo breathed out.

"What is?" Wink wiped a rag on the island, mopping up some smoothie ingredients. "And close the door. You're letting flies in."

"Preferably," Ella said, "close it with you on the *other* side."

Flo shook her head. "We gotta go. Dot's house just opened."

The effect of this last statement was immediate. Wink dropped the rag and spun. "What? Are you sure?"

Ella dumped a banana peel from her failed experiment in the garbage. "Wait, are you that winded just from running over from the inn? Goodnight, woman, that's only a few yards."

"Never mind that." Wink was at the back door, throwing her apron on a hook. "Come on! We have to move!" She turned to shout something to Horatio, but he was already stepping inside.

"I heard. I can cover here. You'd better hurry."

Ella stood in the middle of the kitchen, trying to catch up on what was happening. Grabbing Ella by the elbow, Wink dragged her out of the kitchen and through the diner.

"My apron," Ella protested, tugging feebly with her free hand at the ties.

"Take it off in the car," Wink said.

Behind them, Horatio called out through the pass-through, "Bring me back some kitchen utensils!"

Ella's behind barely touched the backseat of Wink's Oldsmobile before the vehicle peeled out. Sliding across the seat, she scrambled for a buckle. The car lurched, picking up speed. As soon as they left the town proper, Wink pressed the pedal to the metal.

"Will someone tell me what's happening?" Ella's grip tightened on the buckle as Wink slammed on the brakes to make a hairpin turn up the eastern Twin Hill.

The diner owner glanced back in the rearview mirror. "Dot's house was in foreclosure. It just got bought, and the new owner opened it to auction off the items inside. Kind of like an estate sale."

Now she understood. In a town with limited resources, certain items were in high demand.

In the passenger seat, Flo dug through her purse, murmuring under her breath. Ella caught disconcerting phrases, such as, "can't use the pepper spray in close quarters" and "brass knuckles might work against Gladys."

The car climbed the steep hill, winding around the corkscrew road at a breakneck speed. Ella had been to Dot's property before, with Six, and the familiar street and gravel driveway brought back fond and not-so-fond memories—mostly of being shot at. The cabin sat tucked among towering pines at the end of a winding driveway where a slew of cars was already congesting the gravel lot in front of the residence.

Flo was already unbuckled or, perhaps, never had been. Her door swung out, and she leaped to the gravel with the car still moving.

"Flo!" Ella yelled after her. Surprisingly, the older woman landed on her feet. "Nut job."

Gravel spat out as Wink brought the car to a sliding stop. The moment the Wink turned off the engine, she was out the door, hot on Flo's heels. It was all Ella could do to unbuckle and throw herself onto the gravel drive to keep up.

"Looks like the word got out," Wink said when they'd caught up to Flo.

"We can thank Miss Johnson from the Community Services Office for that," Flo spat. "That ol' Nosey Nellie's got a big mouth."

If Ella thought the potlucks were chaotic, it paled to the bedlam inside the cabin. She lingered in the doorway, surveying the vultures picking over Dot's abandoned belongings, terrified to step inside. A very harassed man stood nearby, a clipboard clutched to his chest like a shield, as others shouted at him, asking how much such-and-such items cost.

"Ladies, please," he hollered at a group of women gathered in the dinette area. "Check the tape first before asking. Many items are already labeled."

Ella enjoyed the breathing space the porch provided. Taking another step back, she nearly tripped over Dot's collection of garden gnomes. She fought a smile as she picked one up, remembering her first encounter with these particular lawn ornaments. Six had given her one as a present her first Christmas in Keystone, a symbolic gesture of their budding but tenuous friendship at the time.

Her gnome had been looking rather lonely on her dresser recently. Once she located the tape with the price written out in marker, she decided her gnome needed a buddy.

If the cheap cost of the little statue—the name Tubsy seemed to fit—was any indication of the bargains inside, it was worth braving the maelstrom. Taking a deep breath, girding herself, she told Tubsy to wish her luck and plunged into the cabin.

The flow of bodies, like an ocean undertow, sucked her around the living room. Couch cushions were overturned. Angelica, occasional gardener for the inn when Rose and Jimmy were too busy, toted a lamp made of antlers.

Ella opened her mouth to say a friendly hello to the woman but was already being swept away in the sea of bodies, in the direction of the wood stove. Also, the gardener didn't appear to be in the mood for a friendly chat as she was currently brandishing the lamp—sharp points facing outward—at a man who claimed he'd seen the fixture first.

Voices shouted. The cabin smelled of stale air and sweat. Shoulders bumped shoulders. It didn't take long for her to be sucked into the frenzied spirit, snatching items that caught her eye without looking at prices. A pile of books. A lamp without antlers. A radio.

Ladened with her bounty, she located Wink in the kitchen and deposited her treasures next to the woman's growing mound of bowls, spatulas, and beaters.

Without looking up from the cookbooks she rifled through, Wink nudged a cupboard near the floor with her foot. "This one hasn't been looked through yet."

"Is it because I'm the youngest one here and you all can't bend that low?"

Wink shot her a nasty look before jabbing a finger at a blond-haired gal. "Jenny's here. I could ask her. She'd get first dibs—"

"I'm on it." Ella sat cross-legged and rooted around inside, pulling out her phone for a light. As she pulled out a cast-iron skillet, she tuned into the conversation buzzing around the kitchen.

"Norm bought this place a few weeks back but only recently decided to open it up," a woman with dark skin, sporting a curly bob and poodle clips, was saying.

"Norm?" Wink asked.

"That's right. Norman Baxter."

Ella looked up, mouthing, *Flo's ex?*

The diner owner nodded.

Another woman, wearing a white sweater and pearls, asked, "Why buy this dump? Doesn't he have that lovely, large craftsman down on Lake Drive?"

The first nodded. "It seems like a step down, doesn't it?"

Wink's chest swelled. "Maybe he wanted a smaller house to keep up, one with more property. He is a bachelor, after all."

"Oh sure, dear. We weren't implying those who live on the hills don't have desirable homes. Your place is lovely. It's just some of them—" Her face pinched as she looked around Dot's kitchen "—haven't been maintained well."

"I didn't think you were implying my place was undesirable." Wink's words had a bite to them.

Ella stayed out of the conversation, not wanting to get involved. She didn't know which house Norm was moving from, but most of the residences surrounding the lake were on the posh side—certainly larger and newer than this cabin made of rough-hewn logs and creaking floorboards.

It did seem a rather odd move. Then again, for the expansive lot and trees, she would have been tempted, as well.

"Did you hear Norm bought this place?" Wink asked softly as Flo, who dropped her items with a loud *clunk* on the counter, joined them. A familiar shotgun lay amongst the treasures, the very same weapon Dot had used to chase off Ella and Six. Ah, memories.

"He did?" Flo scratched her beehive hairdo. "Hmm, bit of a step down, don't you think?"

Wink shrugged.

"D'you know he was in the pokey?"

Ella looked up from stacking pans. "You remember *that*, but you don't remember getting hitched to him?"

"Or his name," Wink added.

"It's been coming back to me." The woman tapped the side of her head.

"What was he in prison for?" Ella asked. "Drugs?"

"No."

"Money laundering?"

"No."

"Murder?"

"Uh-uh."

"You don't remember, do you?"

Flo's eyes closed partially in concentration. Ella could almost hear the hamster wheel spinning beneath her bouffant.

"I wanna say it was... embezzlement?" After another moment of deep concentration, she shrugged and gave up.

Still on the floor, Ella aimed her phone into the cabinet and plunged in up to her shoulders to be sure she'd emptied it of everything. The contents she'd pulled were stacked on the counter, and Wink was sorting through the items, arguing with Mrs. Sweater—whom she'd addressed as Shirley— about who should get the cast-iron skillet.

As Ella twisted around, her light hit on a rectangular object above. Frowning, she inspected it before probing it with her finger. It appeared to be foil wrapped around a thin object, taped to the underside of the counter.

She pried it from the tape, and her breath caught in her chest. It couldn't be. Was it...? Gingerly, she peeled back a corner of the brightly colored foil.

Chocolate.

The smell of the bar was intoxicating. She screeched and jumped, hitting her head on the underside of the cupboard.

"El? Are you okay?" Wink asked.

Flo's face appeared. "If it's a rat, I got you covered." Her eyes widened to the size of dinner plates when she spotted the precious foil treasure, and she whispered reverently, "Chocolate."

"Not so loud." Ella shimmied out of the cupboard, folding the foil back over the bar.

Sweater Pearls's head whipped around so fast she probably got whiplash. "Did you say chocolate?"

All around the small space, other heads snapped up like prairie dogs, eyes on Ella and Flo.

Ella forced out an awkward laugh. "What? Nobody said chocolate. Get your hearing checked, Shirley."

The gal with the curled bob pointed at the chocolate bar. "Then what's that?"

"What's what?" Ella bent her head forward as if she was hard of hearing.

"That thing in your hands. Right there. It looks like a candy bar."

"Hmm? I don't see anything. Flo, do you see anything?"

Flo shook her head.

"Now you're putting it in your pocket." Curly Hair stalked closer for a better look.

Ella had slipped the candy inside the pocket of her waitress uniform. But it was too late. The rest of the 1950s Stepford Wives began converging on her.

Wink stepped in front of her, a barricade of dark fuchsia hair, hands out in a placating gesture, using her voice-of-reason tone. "Ladies, ladies. This is Ella's score. She found it."

"That's right." Ella's chin jutted out. "Finder's keepers or whatever."

Wink glanced back at Ella pointedly. "It's her choice what she wants to do with the chocolate, say if she wanted to share it with her two best friends who've kept her out of trouble."

"I think you mean *in* trouble. You two are the source of many of my problems."

One of the women protested, saying, "She's got to do it right. She's got to buy it."

Ella's hand fell to her pocket protectively. "Of course, I will. It's not like I was planning on stealing it. But one way or another, I'm walking out of here with this candy, even if it means fighting every last one of you. If I can punch a little girl without batting an eye—" even if hitting Sally that one time had been an accident "—then I have no qualms beating up senior citizens."

To prove her commitment, she raised her fists and adopted a boxer's stance.

Was the candy probably a holdover from the town's first jump, making it ten years old? Sure. But in that moment, she didn't care.

"Hey, back up, Shirley."

Shirley, in all her sweater and pearl necklace glory, had been trying to flank her. The woman's eyes flitted behind Ella, and she gave a subtle nod. Ella realized too late Shirley had been a decoy.

Someone attacked from behind, and her body flew forward, ramming into the counter. Pain shot up her hip as she brought her elbow around, connecting with a cheek.

Wink dove at Ella's attacker, and they crashed to the floor. It took a moment for Ella to register who Wink was grappling with: Jenny. More than a small part of her was thrilled at seeing Wink getting the better of the blond, a nice red mark blooming on the gal's face. She only had a moment to revel in Wink's victory, however, before Shirley swooped in.

Ella held up a hand. "Take another step, woman, and I'll drop you faster than my fifth-grade boyfriend after I found out we were distantly related."

Shirley stared.

Ella cleared her throat. "Forget I said that."

Then she bobbed sideways as Shirley lunged. The older woman fell forward, missing Ella by afoot.

"Eesh, your aim's as bad as Flo's—" She cried out as Shirley performed a perfect foot sweep, and she toppled over. Her other hip took the brunt of the impact, and she lay on the floor, groaning and questioning her life choices.

Rolling to her stomach, she coughed out, "You wouldn't happen to be related to a little girl named Sally, would you?"

"She's my granddaughter."

"Figures. I thought I smelled the same stench of fire and brimstone." Just as Shirley grabbed for the chocolate in Ella's pocket, Ella rolled and brought her knee up into the woman's stomach.

New threats emerged as more joined the fight. Soon, bodies of all ages wrestled on the floor in a tangle of sensible sweaters, pearls, and elaborate hairdos. Ella felt her pocket being tugged on, dragging her with it.

Like a toddler throwing a tantrum, she thrashed about, indiscriminate of who she hit. More than one nose crunched beneath her fists. In the process, she caught an elbow to the lip.

An ear-shattering boom split the air, causing her to freeze and others to scream. The smell of gunpowder wafted over them, and the frenzy stilled.

Flo stood over the tangle of limbs, Dot's shotgun in her hands, looking like Granny from *The Beverly Hillbillies*. Overhead, the ceiling was dimpled with buckshot and pinholes of light, which made Ella question the state of the roof if a few pellets were able to punch through it.

Flo shook her head, clicking her tongue as if scolding children. A piece of ceiling calved off and hit the ground inches from the senior citizen's feet.

"Ella leaves here with the chocolate. Any of you have a problem with that, you can talk to Betty here."

"You already named your gun?" Wink's voice garbled out from beneath Jenny. "You haven't even bought it yet."

Ella, who was currently held in a choke hold, gasped, "You hear that, Shirley?"

With a chorus of reluctant harrumphs, the women slowly disentangled from the dogpile. Shirley let up her pressure on Ella's windpipe, albeit reluctantly.

As Ella climbed to her feet, the room filled with the percussion of joints cracking, a drumline of aged bones. She didn't waste any time before scooping up her items and darting for the man with the clipboard.

Several minutes and an empty billfold later, she sat in Wink's car, dabbing her bloody lip with her apron and grinning.

"Well, I think that went rather well."

Flo used her sleeve to polish her new gun, cradling it like a child. "I agree."

Wink, who was shoving tissues up her bloody nose, looked back at Ella. "Does that mean you'll share?"

CHAPTER ELEVEN

ELLA LICKED HER fingers and savored the flavor, letting the chocolate linger on her tongue. Despite its questionable expiration date, it tasted heavenly. Divine. It brought back memories of s'mores, hot chocolate, Halloween, and gorging herself on Valentine's Day candy she'd bought on sale after the holiday.

It had taken every ounce of willpower she possessed to wait until after work before eating the treat—willpower in the form of a woman in pinkish-purple hair who'd threatened to tie her to a stool if she abandoned the diner while in the throes of an early dinner rush.

Ella had divvied up the chocolate bar amongst the three of them. Now, her portion held teeth marks where she had nibbled it. Folding the wrapper over the remainder, she stuffed it deep into her underwear drawer. By God, she would savor every molecule of it.

Collecting the library book on prehistoric humans from her nightstand, she headed downstairs to the conservatory, but not before popping into the kitchen to see if Rose wanted help with dinner. As she'd expected, the woman shooed her away, threatening her not to come near the stove.

In the conservatory, she settled at the bistro table, the taste of chocolate still on her tongue. Star jasmine vines climbed the lattice nearby, stretching towards the sun-drenched glass overhead. As she cracked open the book, Fluffy curled around her feet. She spent a good few minutes scratching the Maine Coon's chin before he ambled away and rolled in the dirt of a nearby planter.

Now that she had more time to read, she didn't skim, and instead delved into the topic of early modern humans. The book speculated that Cro-Magnon's linguistic competence and "cultural sophistication" were probably why their counterparts, neanderthals, had gone extinct. Judging by the state of Craig's jail cell, she would argue the point of cultural sophistication, but whatever.

The next paragraph detailed Cro-Magnon's skill at crafting stone and bone tools, shell and ivory jewelry, and paintings—producing the first examples of art. Said tools consisted of retouched blades, end scrapers, and something called "nosed" scrapers, along with a chisel and other tools used for smoothing and scraping leather.

Cro-Magnon's dwellings were most often found in deep caves…

No surprise there. But they had also lived amid rocky overhangs and even primitive huts or lean-tos. Cro-Magnon was thought to have been a settled people, only moving when necessary due to hunting or environmental changes.

What followed were images of carved statuettes of humans and animals, as well as engravings and reliefs. Next were photos depicting cave paintings of proficiency beyond Craig's kindergarten style. Perhaps he was a poor representation of his kind.

Her gaze drifted from the book to the snoozing feline in the plant bed. These paragraphs supported her decision to decipher Craig's language using art. Like language, art required a shared system of meanings in order to communicate its message. It was symbolic.

Needing a break, she headed back to the kitchen for a pre-dinner snack. As she passed the neglected check-in desk in the entrance hall, the phone rang.

"Keystone Inn and future home to an alien invasion, this is Ella speaking."

Chapman's voice shouted back. *"Ms. Barton? Is that you?"*

"Sheriff, you don't have to shout."

"I can't hear you."

"Turn the phone around."

"Is Jimmy in?" His voice continued to blare out at a deafening decibel level.

"Yeah, hold please." Setting the phone on the mahogany surface, she continued to hear Chapman's tinny voice as she searched out the deputy.

He was in the study, reading a book. Why he wasn't doing so in the library was a question for another time. She told him Chapman was on the phone and she hoped he wasn't too attached to his hearing.

Jimmy picked up the receiver as she turned the corner in the hallway, resuming her snack mission. She paused. Ordinarily, she wasn't one to eavesdrop, but she was curious as to why the sheriff rang, hoping it wasn't serious.

"What can I do for you, Sheriff?" Jimmy asked. A pause followed. "Sal's? I'm guessing you want me to talk to him for a reason and not just for a haircut... The professor? Did Sal say why Dr. Kaufman sneaked into town to talk—oh, that's odd. He say what sort of questions the man asked?"

There was a soft creaking of floorboards as Jimmy shifted his weight around. "Charlotte? What's his late wife got to do with Sal?"

Ella's breath caught in her throat. The professor's wife had died in a hit-and-run years back, just after he'd moved here from Germany.

"Ah, yes. I don't imagine he would tell you that, given his opinion of you at the moment. I'll see if I can't get more from him."

Ella was churning over this information when she realized the deputy had hung up and his footfalls were getting louder, heading her way. There wasn't time to make it to the kitchen. If he found her in the hallway, he'd know she'd been listening, so she darted to the nearest door and hid in the room beyond.

The last time she'd been in here had also been for concealment, and the time before that had been for her first tour of the manor. She'd never quite figured out the drawing room's purpose, and the owners didn't seem to know either because they never used it. But it did provide an excellent hiding spot.

The moment she could no longer hear Jimmy, she ducked into the hallway and retreated to the north wing upstairs, her snack forgotten. Pausing in the hallway in front of her bedroom, she eyed a radioactive green glow oozing beneath Flo's door, wondering how concerned she should be before shrugging it off. At this point, she only got involved if there were explosions or the smell of something burning.

Around seven o'clock that evening, they gathered in the kitchen for a late family dinner. Wink provided creamed corn and rosemary garlic mashed potatoes, along with a dessert from the diner, while Rose cooked the main course. Breath held, Ella surveyed the dishes and let out an audible sigh of relief when she didn't spot a single gelatin mold. Maybe the innkeeper was finally picking up on their not-so-subtle hints.

The clanking of silverware preceded everyone gathered at the table. Ella sat beside Will, the picture window that overlooked the lake at their backs. Wink and Flo sat across from them, arguing over whether Flo could rest her elbow on the table. At one end, Rose settled demurely into her chair, the end opposite her conspicuously empty.

"Where's Jimmy?" Wink asked, unfolding her napkin, then shoving Flo's elbow away. Her nose still appeared puffy, and her words came out nasally after the whole chocolate ordeal.

"Out. Said he had to run down the street for a chat with someone. Police business is all he told me. He said he'd be back soon."

Ella bit her bottom lip and caught Wink's eye, hoping she could convey that she had information on Jimmy's whereabouts.

"Something wrong, Poodle Head?" Flo asked loudly.

"Nope, nothing."

"Really? Cause you look constipated. I bet it was the 'you know what' from Dot's house."

"Very subtle." Ella cleared her throat. "Are we waiting for someone more? Can I dig in?" Her fork shot out before she reeled it back in under Rose's glare.

After the innkeeper said grace, they passed a single dish around at a time. It was nothing like the free-for-all potlucks, or even what Ella had grown up with, everyone reaching across the table, fending for themselves.

A hefty chunk of lemon and dill trout dropped to her plate with a splat, then she passed the dish to Will. He'd been unusually quiet since sitting down, seemingly preoccupied. But then again, so was she.

Why had Dr. Kaufman talked to Sal, of all people, about the night Charlotte died? And just before his death, too. Why look into it after all this time?

Perhaps going into hiding had made him reminisce about the past. They'd never found the driver who'd hit her.

Beside her, Will stirred, and Ella realized it was because Wink had addressed him—both of them.

"What's with you two tonight? You didn't have a row, did you?"

"No. At least I don't think so." Ella turned to Will. "Did we have a fight I don't know about?"

He patted her hand, saying to Wink, "We didn't fight. I just have a lot on my mind at the moment."

Ella's attention returned to her food, her appetite waning. There was something deeper bothering her that she, so far, had been able to avoid thinking about. But Will's presence tonight forced that thought to the forefront again, like an ugly, stubborn rash.

"Don't fix it. He'll use it and change everything."

She knew she should tell him the professor's final words, tell Chapman too, but she risked losing the chance to ever return home if she did.

"He found me."

If "he" was the professor's killer, then "he" was currently behind bars decorating his walls with toothpaste and poop like a caveman version of Martha Stewart. But if the professor had been referring to another sinister "he," then that man was still at large, which was disturbing on another level.

To draw herself out of her reverie, she brought up Six's recent change of employment status.

"At the General Store, you say?" Wink asked when Ella had finished. Around the table, their expressions ranged from suspicious to incredulous.

"I know. Can you believe it? We should start a pool now, taking bets, to see how long he lasts—what are you doing?"

Flo had pulled out something that looked like tinfoil origami. It opened at one end, similar to a paper hat, and she stuffed it on her head. It only covered a section at the very top of her hair, nowhere near her scalp.

"It's for the aliens. Six got a job, huh? That's the equivalent of hell freezing over."

At the end of the table, Rose's lips pressed into a line at the mention of "hell" at the dinner table, but even she seemed to agree that the outlaw's employment was a sign of the end times.

Beside Ella, Will's face had darkened, and he muttered several unsavory words about the frontiersman, ending with calling him a scoundrel.

"Scoundrel, hmm?" she teased. "Do you kiss your mother with that mouth?"

There was no love lost between Will and Six, and she suspected part of it stemmed from Ella and Six's friendship.

"Teeth," Flo blurted out abruptly.

Ella blinked.

An extended, awkward pause followed before Ella broke it. She nodded and smiled wide in an intentionally conde-scending way, pointing at her own teeth. "Yes, Flo. These are teeth. We use them to eat and masticate—" Flo opened her mouth "—it means to chew."

The boarder leaned over her plate, her eyes earnest behind her thick glasses. "His teeth. How does Spot eat?"

Using her fork and knife, she held them in front of her mouth at a downward angle, imitating the saber-toothed tiger's ginormous incisors.

Ella began to respond but found she had nothing—not even a pithy quip. So, she settled for a profound "Huh" instead.

Will's brow furrowed. "Doesn't he eat how dogs normally eat?"

"You didn't tell him?" Wink said in Ella's direction.

Ella dabbed her napkin at her mouth. "Hey, Will. Spot's a saber-toothed tiger." Without pausing, she said to Wink, "Of course, I told him. Who do you take me for?"

Rose's fork dropped. "A saber-toothed tiger? Are you certain?"

"He's either that or a mutated lion bred with a bear who needs an appointment with a dentist."

"Is anyone gonna answer my question?" Flo looked around. "How's he get food past those choppers?" To further demonstrate her point—as if she wasn't already being clear —she kept the utensils held to her mouth, shoved her face over her plate, and attempted to eat her trout. As expected, the silverware fangs got in the way, sending fish bits scattering.

Ella slipped her phone out and began to record. "Can you turn your head a little more to the light? That's it."

"Florence Henderson, you get your face out of your food this instant." Rose took a slow breath, adding, "I can't believe I had to tell a woman nearly twice my age that."

"Crazy knows no age," Ella said.

Across from her, Wink nodded sagely.

When the meal evolved to a dessert of apple pie with cheese followed by food comas, Chester made his grand appearance. His furry gray head poked out of Wink's purse on the hook at the back door. He blinked bleary eyes as if waking from a long snooze. His whiskers twitched as he sniffed the air, then lured, no doubt, by the smell of pie, he climbed down.

"Pearl Winkel, how many times have I asked you not to bring that varmint into my kitchen?"

Chester, in all his velour tracksuit glory, chose that moment to leap to the table. Jumping, Wink scooped him up before he took a swim in the pie.

Rose's cheeks colored, and her hand had an iron grip on her pearl necklace. As Wink coaxed Chester back into her purse, the back door opened, and Jimmy strode in. He made it one step before some invisible signal from his wife sent him backtracking and brushing his feet on the mat.

"This looks delicious," he said, taking his place at the end. After slopping a generous helping of now cold mashed potatoes onto his plate, he caught the tension in the room. "What'd I miss?"

"Nothing out of the ordinary," Ella answered. "Oh, except Flo smashing her face into her food, but don't worry, I got it on video." She considered her present company, adding, "And by that, I mean, I recorded a movie of it on my phone."

"Sounds like our standard meal, then."

Ella eyed Will's uneaten crust—a look he caught, probably because she wasn't being covert about it. He nudged his plate in her direction, and she ate a bite of the flaky leftovers.

Chewing, she turned her gaze on Jimmy. "How's the investigation going?"

His expression turned suspicious instantly, and his tone came out guarded. "It's going just fine. Why do you ask?"

"I'm just making small talk. Can't a lady ask how a death investigation is going without being suspected of ulterior motives?"

"Not if it's you," Will and Jimmy replied at the same time.

She feigned offense, then shrugged. "Yeah, that's a fair point."

Reaching up to her beehive of hair, Flo pulled out a toothpick and began working it over her teeth, pausing to aim it at Jimmy. "What's the point of having you be a law dog if you ain't going to tell us anything? I thought that was the whole point of you going to work for the man."

"As always, Flo," he replied dryly, "you've got a good grasp of the situation."

The boarder beamed, the slight going over her tower of hair.

"I will say this: our initial guess as to how Dr. Kaufman died is wrong."

The table fell silent.

Ella abandoned the crust on her plate, and even Chester poked his head back out of Wink's bag, most likely disturbed by the prolonged silence.

"What's that?" Ella finally said. "He had a wound on the back of his head. There was a freaking dinosaur bone nearby with a bit of blood on it. Are you saying that's not what killed him?" Her mind raced with other possibilities. "Ah, I see. Is this tricky coroner wording? Like the blow to the head wasn't what killed him, but internal hemorrhaging caused by the blow did?"

Jimmy shook his head. "You're overcomplicating it. The blow to his head, Pauline says, wasn't fatal."

With a "Huh," Ella reclined in her chair, more perplexed than the time she'd tried to follow a makeup tutorial on YouTube. She glanced sideways to see how Will was taking the news.

His posture was rounded, his face somber.

"I can't say more than that." Jimmy looked over at Ella. "I heard you stopped by to try to communicate with our person of interest."

It wasn't lost on her that Craig was a person of interest and not a suspect.

For the next several minutes, she regaled them with details of her interview with the caveman and her attempts at communication using paint and paper. Encouraged by Flo's bored expression, she painstakingly and methodically expounded on her analysis of each painting and the possible interpretations for each articulation the caveman had made.

Even Will looked bored to tears by the time she finished. But she felt immense satisfaction at the snores now emanating from Flo.

"So," Will said, "to summarize, you didn't get anywhere?"

"Nope."

After that, the conversation turned to the inventor's progress—or lack thereof—on the time device. While he updated Rose and Jimmy, who hadn't heard the latest, Ella joined Wink on her side of the table, and they played their new favorite game of seeing how many objects they could hide in Flo's hair without waking her. They managed two green beans, three sugar cubes, and her grimy toothpick before the woman stirred.

Once Jimmy had finished eating, they cleared the table and put leftovers in the refrigerator.

"Will, I loved your interview in *Keystone Corner*," Wink said, placing a stack of dirty plates on the counter beside the sink.

Ella, arms elbow-deep in suds, looked up in time to see the inventor's ears turn red as he murmured a "thank you."

She prodded him with a soapy finger. "You were in the newspaper? Why didn't you tell me?" Not that the local rag was anything to brag about, but since the village existed in its own bubble outside the scope of the rest of the world, being in the weekly town newspaper was as close to five minutes of fame as a person could achieve.

"It's not a big deal." He rubbed the back of his neck and took the dish of trout from the table to the counter for Rose to put away.

He wasn't getting away that easily. "What's it about?"

"The time device." His eyes traveled everywhere but to her. "It's really not a big deal."

"What aren't you telling me? Did you say too much? Wink, he didn't blame us for breaking it, did he?"

"But you did break it," Wink said, wiping the table with a rag. "I was there."

"Let's not split hairs."

"It's not broken," Will cut in.

"Then why don't you want to talk about your interview? Do you not like the attention? I'm sure Flo could give you pointers on how to bask in the limelight." At the table, the old boarder paused amid culling the green bean from her hair to snarl in Ella's direction.

"No, I just…" His hand went from his neck to his freshly shaven jaw. He'd cleaned up since last she saw him. "I think I made things worse."

"We're stuck in a time-traveling town, and the inventor of the device responsible for our problem now lays in Pauline's cold storage. Also, there's a saber-toothed tiger on the loose, and we were recently overrun by giant dinosaurs. How could you have possibly made things worse?"

Wink nudged her. "You're really bad at pep talks."

"I'm sorry," Will said. "I'm just not in the mood to talk about it."

"Fair enough."

After that, he drifted away, gravitating towards the swinging door with Rose and Jimmy as they talked about getting a card game going in the parlor.

"You in for some Bridge?" Wink asked Flo, who'd just discovered the sugar cube.

The woman grunted and bit down on the cube. "Got some work to do in the lab."

She was still combing through her cotton candy hair when she loped into the hallway and disappeared. A short time later, as Ella and Wink were finishing up the last of the dishes, the floor vibrated with faint booms from the basement.

"Her room was glowing earlier. I was too scared to find out why."

This didn't seem to surprise Wink. "Was it green? Once, I made the mistake of rushing in when I saw that, thinking it was some sort of gas leak…" Her eyes unfocused, staring into the distance.

"What was it?"

Wink shook away the memory. "To be honest, I'm not sure. I don't remember anything after opening the door. I blacked out, and when I came to, I was in one of the guest rooms down the hall, my clothes soaked with sweat, and had hearing loss for a week."

Drying her hands on a towel, Ella made a mental note to never, ever go into the crazy woman's room if it was glowing.

On her way to the parlor, she noticed the door to the study open, the warm light of a lamp emanating out. Will stood at the desk, rooting through the drawers.

"I'll meet you in the parlor," she said to Wink, earning a knowing smile from her boss.

"Take your time, dear."

"That's creepy, just so you know," Ella called after her. When she stepped into the study, Will glanced up. "If you're looking for my stash of chocolate, it's not in there."

"No, I was—you have chocolate?"

"Hmm? No, of course not. Don't be ridiculous."

His blue-green eyes narrowed, clearly not believing her. "I see. Rose asked me to find another deck of cards, but I don't see any in here."

Striding over, Ella reached up to the mantle and pulled out a cigar box. Inside were several well-used decks. He joined her, closing the distance between them, bringing with him the heady scent of sandalwood and machine grease. Right on cue, her stomach plunged to her feet as it did any time he was in close proximity.

"Can I ask you something?" she asked, her voice cracking.

"If it's whether I like chocolate, the answer is yes." The crinkles around his eyes melted away as he studied her very serious expression.

"It's about the professor."

He stepped back, and she took a breath.

"What is it?"

It ate at her, this horrible secret of the professor's final words, his final warning. She'd always prided herself on being honest and straightforward. Secrets only hindered relationships.

She took a breath. No, not yet. The possible consequence of telling him was too great, and she wasn't ready to risk it. But soon. She just needed more time.

Instead, she found herself asking the other question that had been weighing on her. "What do you know about Dr. Kaufman's wife Charlotte?"

The corners of his mouth turned down. "Know about her? I never met her."

"Right, but what do you know about the night she died? That first time we sat for tea in his living room, he mentioned she'd been killed while out for a walk, and they'd never caught the guy."

He stuffed his hands into his trouser pockets. "Yes, the sheriff at the time suspected the driver fled town. It happened at night, before Keystone began jumping."

"What year, do you know?"

His lips moved silently as he calculated. "It was shortly after they moved here, which would've put the accident around 1945 or 1946."

After swiveling her head around to be sure no one was eavesdropping, she closed the nearest door with a soft click.

The other one opened into the north hallway, but was far enough away she didn't worry about being overheard.

In a soft voice, she told him about the telephone conversation she'd heard between Jimmy and Chapman. When she finished, she said, "Why would the professor risk coming into town, asking about that night?"

Will's brow furrowed. He began pacing before the empty fireplace, pinching his chin with his fingers, looking very much like Sherlock Holmes minus the cap and pipe.

"I don't know. That doesn't make sense."

"Perhaps," she said hesitantly, "he wasn't in the right frame of mind."

"It's possible, I suppose. But if not, why ask questions now? After all this time? What changed?"

All the same questions she'd been wondering herself. Pausing, he draped his arm on the mantle and rested his forehead against it, staring vacantly at the hearth as if posing for his portrait to be painted.

"You realize there aren't flames in there, right?" She rested her hand on his back, leaning into him. Despite the freshly shaven face, his features sagged. Shadows crept under his eyes, his hair slightly disheveled. He looked exhausted.

"Look, the time device can't be solved overnight or even in a week. Why don't you go home and get some rest?"

"I will." He straightened slowly, his eyes locking with hers, a heat burning behind them. He grabbed a deck of cards. "After I beat Wink."

CHAPTER TWELVE

THE KITCHEN FOR the diner looked like a tornado of flour had blown through it. But Ella hardly noticed as she cut a warm slice of gingerbread pulled straight from the oven.

She leaned on the island counter, her elbow smashing an eggshell, and savored the flavor.

"Well?" Wink looked expectantly at her.

"It's close. Really close."

The woman's face fell. "But it's still not right?"

Ella shook her head, hiding her disappointment for Wink's benefit. "Sorry."

Wink took the mixing bowl to the sink. "Perhaps it tastes off because I made it and not your mother. I grew up eating my Nana's lemon bars. When I began baking, I begged for the recipe, but no matter how closely I followed it, they never tasted the same."

"Maybe." She broke off another hunk of gingerbread before grabbing a dishrag to wipe the counter. "Or maybe it still needs more molasses. I appreciate you trying, though. It means a lot to me."

After cleaning, she swept into the railcar to refill her coffee, her well-worn sneakers squeaking over the black-

and-white checkered floor. Grandma's Kitchen was experiencing a lull at the moment, so she was alone.

The last customer who'd sat at the counter and paid his tab with screws, nuts, and bolts had left his edition of *Keystone Corner* behind. She'd had a heck of a time trying to hunt down a copy so she could read Will's interview, and here one was, delivered by a man in a beard and overgrown eyebrows.

Sitting on a stool, she sipped her mud and read. Shelly, Horatio's wife, had written the piece, asking Will questions regarding the time device. The topic, understandably, had dominated the last town hall meeting, every conversation in the diner, and every segment on the radio—whether related to music or not. Introducing a Benny Goodman song? Why not speculate how the time device functioned?

In the article, Shelly asked Will how he first discovered the machine. Ella read intently, wondering how he'd respond since it was the Keystone Gators who'd discovered it.

Shelly noted that the inventor stammered before giving his response. He hadn't been the one to discover it, another had, but he was on the scene soon after. He'd omitted the trio's names, and she suspected he'd done it to protect them. Most of the citizens were up in arms about not being informed about the device immediately after its discovery.

The journalist gave the inventor room to explain his side, expound on why he and Chapman had kept the device a secret for a short time. The professor had fled, and they'd wanted to have control of the situation before too many people became involved. They'd also been hoping the professor would return so they could have answers before going public. As it stood now, they had many questions and few answers.

But you do you have some understanding of how the device works?

Will answered this in the affirmative but wanted to stress to folks how complex the machine was. It wasn't as simple as flipping a switch. If he wasn't careful, he could make things worse.

Ella read on and didn't see why Will had insinuated the interview had gone poorly—until she reached the end. He revealed the professor's motivation for quickly finishing his life's work: to go back in time and change his wife's fate, stop her from dying.

After that, he told Shelly there was a problem with the device, keeping it vague, but he believed the professor had been close to solving the issue.

Do you think you can fix the machine?

"I'm fairly confident I can. I'll sure try."

Breathing deeply, Ella laid down the newspaper and stared out the window as a family walked past. Will's certainty contradicted his earlier sentiments in the professor's basement when she'd talked to him. Understandably, he didn't want the town to panic, but in appearing assured that he could fix the machine, and implying that it was close to being fixed, he'd put himself in a tight spot. People will be expecting it to work. And soon.

Oh, boy, Will, she thought before taking a long draught of her coffee. *You've put yourself in a pickle.*

The bell over the door jingled merrily.

"Afternoon, Mr. Harper. The usual today or will you finally listen to Mrs. Harper and mind your cholesterol?"

An elderly gentleman lowered himself to a stool at the lunch counter. "The usual."

"One heart attack coming up."

He grunted at the joke, took off his hat, and grabbed the abandoned newspaper.

Poking her head into the pass-through window, she hollered into the kitchen. "Burn one, take it through the garden and pin a rose on it."

There was no sense in wasting an order sheet for a hamburger with lettuce, tomato, and onion on a lone customer.

Mr. Harper peered at her from over the newspaper. "Add some fries, will you, doll?"

Through gritted teeth, she hollered to Horatio, "With frog sticks."

Once she set his food in front of him, a few more customers trickled in, and Wink placed them in booths. Ella wiped the lunch counter, then took a soda float over to one of the tables. When Mr. Harper finished, she cleared away his empty plate, the man too engrossed in the newspaper to notice.

She was just about to deposit the dish in the kitchen when her eyes snagged for the first time on the other article sharing the front page, below the fold.

The plate dropped to the counter with a clatter, and she snapped the paper away.

"Hey—"

"Your meal will be $1.05," she said absently.

"You can forget a tip."

"Cool beans. Since you think patting me on the butt and calling me 'doll' equivalent to a tip, I consider that a win."

With a harrumph, he smashed his hat on his head and threw money on the counter before storming out. She hardly noticed, her eyes glued to the newspaper.

In addition to Will's interview, they'd also printed an article that was a "Looking Back at Today in History" that delved into Charlotte Kaufman's death. It was the seventeenth anniversary of the car accident that had killed her. Old black-and-white photos of the accident scene took up the right side of the page, including the car that had hit her.

Several yards from the front bumper lay a tarpaulin, a pair of women's feet sticking out.

It seemed in poor taste to include the photos, the kind of grotesque, sensational journalism she expected from a tabloid magazine and not a small town press.

Questionable integrity of the newspaper aside, two other thoughts struck her. First, she'd been under the impression the accident had been a hit-and-run in that the driver had fled the scene *in* the offending vehicle, but it appeared that hadn't been the case.

Reading the article, she found her assessment of the photos correct and that the driver had fled on foot. There was scant more information beyond mentioning that Mrs. Gilbert Kaufman had been on an evening walk when hit by the black Buick. Two Good Samaritans had heard the crash and had run to her aid, but she was already deceased upon their arrival. Even the journalist (not Shelly) admitted details of that night were lacking and called into question the sheriff's investigation.

Ella whipped out her phone and flicked through photos so quickly they were a blur, past the ones of Craig's cell and past an obscene amount—including video—of Flo with her utensil fangs before she eventually found what she was searching for.

In the professor's hideout, she zoomed in on his copy of *Keystone Corner*, the one that had been on his bed beside the half-eaten slice of bread with jam. It was the same issue as the one she held in her hands. The bottom was folded out, displaying the article on Charlotte's death, the paper wrinkled as if read a dozen times.

She leaned on her elbows, tapping her finger on her chin. Had this article spurred the professor's renewed interest in his wife's death? Why? Was it simply a reminder that the person responsible had never been caught, or did it reveal something—a clue—that the sheriff at the time had missed?

A cloth napkin hit her square in the face, jolting her from her thoughts.

"Finally," Wink said when Ella looked at her. "I've been calling your name. We need a vanilla milkshake for the corner booth."

Later, after Ella delivered the shake, she found Wink in the kitchen. The diner owner was pulling fresh sugar cookies from the oven. Their sweet, heavenly aroma filled the space.

Ella drummed her fingers on the island countertop, listening to Horatio hum a sea shanty. Wink set the tray of cookies on the counter to cool, then slid the next batch in the oven. She turned back in time to swat Ella's hand away from the freshly baked treats, most likely saving her from burnt fingers.

"What's with the thousand-yard stare?"

Hesitating, Ella bit her lip and retrieved the newspaper from the diner.

"I think," she said after Wink read the article, "this is what renewed the professor's interest in Charlotte's death." Earlier that morning, she'd told Wink about the professor seeing Sal only days prior to his death, asking about the evening Charlotte had passed. "What do you remember about that night?"

Wink tucked a stray strand of pink hair behind her ear, thinking. "Not much. I remember hearing about it the next day from my regular customers. They said she'd been out for a walk the night before and got hit by a car."

Ella pointed to the article. "Says here there weren't any witnesses."

"That's right."

"So the driver hits her, then flees on foot?"

Wink glanced at the paper, nodding.

"Why did the sheriff think the driver had fled town?" The accident had happened about five years before the town began jumping, meaning Keystone was located in rural Colorado at the time, within relative distance to other towns. "Could the driver have gotten far? The next town over, maybe?"

"If they'd caught another ride out, perhaps. Back then, the nearest town was about twenty miles north."

Ella reached for a cookie, and this time, Wink let her. "Something's not making sense."

"The sheriff at the time wasn't what you'd call motivated when it came to doing his job. I think the position wasn't what he expected, and he became burnt out by the responsibility."

"What happened to him?" Ella asked before taking a bite.

"He got left behind. He was out of town, visiting his wife's family."

Ella's face scrunched as she did the math. "Wait, his term was up before the jump, right?"

"That's right. He wasn't sheriff at the time of our first hop."

Licking her lips, Ella chewed on this information. With him out of the picture, she couldn't ask him about Charlotte's death investigation.

Wink cocked her head, studying her. "You want to look into this?"

"Was O.J. Simpson guilty?"

Her boss stared.

"That means, yes." Ella edged towards the door to check on their customers. "It's just, it's been a few weeks since we've sleuthed around, and with the professor's probable killer behind bars, it might be fun to solve a cold case."

Wink's manicured eyebrows rose. "I don't see how we could. With no witnesses…"

"Won't be a problem for us. Keystone Gators—"

"… and the driver having most likely skipped town…."

"—unite!"

"Uh-uh. We never agreed on that name."

"You sure? I remember meeting about it and voting."

"No, we voted Flo had to be fully clothed for all of our meetings."

Ella grimaced, recalling a particularly horrifying meeting involving loose skin and sagging underwear.

Her back brushed the door. "Look, with the professor gone, no one else is going to look into it." No one else would care enough to dig deeper. "Also, I'd just like to point out that it'll keep Flo occupied, and if she's preoccupied…" She waited for Wink to finish the thought.

"She won't be getting into trouble."

"More specifically, she won't be making weapons."

CHAPTER THIRTEEN

DURING A LATE lunch break, Ella stopped by the sheriff's office for another chat—or rather, doodle session—with Craig the caveman, poop painter extraordinaire. And she was now armed with something better than one of Flo's weapons: knowledge. Knowledge that Craig, indeed, had a language and could provide information.

Paint, paper, and brushes in hand, she stepped into the drab building. Chapman paused amid hanging a long, buckskin jacket on a hook when he noticed her.

"Ms. Barton," he greeted. His hat dropped unceremoniously to his desk, revealing gray hair swooping back like a wave. "Gonna try again today?"

She nodded, drifting towards the back jail cell. She was pretty sure she'd deciphered the word for human in the Cro-Magnon's language but wanted to confirm it.

At the bars, she let out a soft whistle. Craig had added more artwork to the walls. The medium this time—thankfully—appeared to be toothpaste. On the floor lay a half-empty jar of the homemade stuff from Stewart's Market.

"He's been painting nonstop." One of Chapman's desk drawers squealed as he retrieved an object before he strode over. Reaching through the bars, he offered Craig a lemon square. "Turns out, he's got a sweet tooth."

The moment Craig's eye caught on the dessert, a feral look came over him. His overturned cot, a mound of blankets, and neglected toiletries were an obstacle course as he leaped over it all and snatched away the lemony treat.

He swallowed.

"Good Lord, did he even chew that?" She marveled at the caveman who was now hopping and gesticulating for more, speaking rapidly in that foreign tongue. "You seem to be treating him nicer than the usual occupants. You even gave him an extra blanket, I see."

Chapman grunted, sauntering back to his desk. "He'll be leaving as soon as I can find him a proper home."

"Wait, what? He's not still a suspect?"

Dropping into his chair, the sheriff lounged back and propped his boots on his desk. "No."

"What did you learn?"

"Nothing I'm gonna tell you, Ms. Barton. I believe you'd say, 'None of your wax.'"

"It's 'beeswax', but go on." She stared expectantly, waiting for him to say more.

He tugged the end of his mustache.

She blinked.

Finally, she let out a sigh. "You're really not going to tell me whatever it is you know?"

Still leaning back, his eyes slid closed in response. If he couldn't communicate with the Cro-Magnon, then whatever he'd learned had come from an outside source. New evidence? An eyewitness?

"It could help me establish communication with Craig if you tell me what you learned."

It was a long time before he responded, drawing the words out. "All I'll say is the professor's cause of death rules the caveman out as a suspect."

"But wasn't his cause of death brain hemorrhaging caused by a blow to the head?" Jimmy had said it wasn't, but she couldn't let on that she knew differently.

"I'm not saying anything more."

Perhaps the older physicist had died of a heart attack.

"Was it natural?"

Chapman's eyes opened, and he sat up. "Ms. Barton, if you're not going to be interviewing the prehistoric man, then I suggest you get back to Grandma's Kitchen."

Properly dismissed, she sat cross-legged on the floor in front of Craig's cell, laying out brushes and paint, asking casually, "Where's Jimmy?"

"Out" came the abrupt reply. "And don't think you can try to weasel information from him."

"I don't know what you're implying."

"You already pestered him, didn't you?"

"He clammed up like a vise."

Bristles dragged through a blood-red paint as she thought. If Craig was off the hook for the professor's death, then Chapman had no need for her to further communicate with him, especially if he'd died of natural causes. The blow to the head could've been caused by a fall, and the dinosaur bone coincidence.

But the very fact that Chapman wanted her to continue to attempt conversation with Craig implied he was still looking for answers. Why else try to establish communication with an eyewitness?

There was only one way to confirm her suspicion.

She wiped the brush off on a rag she'd brought, standing and making a show of packing up her supplies.

"You leaving?"

"Yeah, I was just thinking there's no point in questioning him, right? And I should get back to the diner. I'm sure Wink needs me." She watched his reaction out of the corner of her eye.

His chair creaked as he leaned forward. "I'll call over and see how she's faring. I'd still like you to see if the caveman —"

"Craig."

"—saw anything."

"Saw anything? You mean like the professor fighting with another assailant?"

Chapman ignored her question and lifted the phone from its cradle. He held it at arm's length like it was a dirty diaper, while a stained finger turned the rotary dial.

His eyes flicked to her as a tinny voice answered the telephone.

"Hello?" Chapman shouted into the receiver. "Wink, is that you?"

The man really needed to know how to use a phone properly.

"Try talking louder," Ella suggested. "It helped me." Wink was going to kill her.

After much back and forth and lots of screaming, he finally hung up, saying Wink could spare Ella a while longer.

"Also, she mentioned not coming back without a proper apology and a hearing device for her. I'm not sure what she meant."

Turning her attention back to Craig, she found him smearing toothpaste on the concrete wall, creating either a deer or a cat with antlers.

On the paper, she painted a stick figure and mimicked the sound he'd made in her video. Her mouth felt like it was full of consonants and marbles.

Craig's hand hovered over the concrete. He jerked his head around and looked at her stick figure, repeating the word.

She smiled. Now they were getting somewhere.

Excited, she pointed at Craig and uttered the same word, then she pointed to herself and repeated it. Did the word mean "man" or "human" or was it Craig's real name?

He repeated the word, which didn't clarify anything. What she needed was more context.

Indicating herself, she uttered the word again but followed it with her name. Then, she pointed at Craig, repeating the first part, hoping he'd fill in with his name.

He spat out a word that sounded like "Ikngerrant-kenhe."

After several attempts at contorting her tongue to produce the same syllables, it still didn't sound right. She tapped the end of the brush against the paper in thought. "How about Craig for short?" She pointed at him, said the word for what she now comfortably felt was "human" followed by "Craig."

After that, she painted a rough representation of the mouth of the cave, adding shading and perspective. If she mimicked the two-dimensional, caveman style he used, all lines and no perspective, she feared the cave entrance would look no different from a round rock. So she did her best to make it appear three-dimensional, but it ended up looking like a squashed donut.

Finishing with a flourish, she turned the paper around, but he'd already grown bored and returned to his artwork.

"Craig." Nothing. "Yoo-hoo, caveboy. Batman."

He turned sharply when she whistled, a slightly annoyed expression on his face at the interruption. She pointed at her painting, her eyebrows raised. Gestures were culturally defined. For all she knew, the simple act of tapping her brush could be highly insulting.

His head of long, matted hair tilted. This was followed by him uttering a couple of syllables. When he repeated them, she wrote them down phonetically, unsure if it was all one word or multiple words.

How to ask him something as complicated as "Was anyone else in the cave with you?"

She chewed the wooden end of the paintbrush, thinking. Dropping it abruptly, she whipped out her phone and flitted through her gallery until she found the video she'd taken at the crime scene. After glancing at the sheriff to be sure he was preoccupied, she paused the video when the camera had accidentally panned to the professor's body while she'd fumbled for the button to stop recording. It was a blurry glimpse, and Chapman and Pauline partially obstructed the view, but it showed part of Dr. Kaufman's deceased form, none the less.

When she showed the stilled frame to Craig, his eyes doubled in size, and he stumbled back. After a moment of cowering, he scuttled forward and poked the screen, muttering under his breath, awed by the technology.

Ella said the word for human again and pointed at the body on the display, saying, "Professor."

Craig leaped in the air, limbs flailing wildly, as he yelled. He slapped the concrete wall, shrieking words at the top of his lungs, words that meant nothing to her.

Quick as lightning, Chapman was behind her, pulling her back, his hand on his pistol.

"I think I scared him with my phone," she said, still shaken by the outburst.

Craig settled in the corner, no longer screaming like a banshee. He eyed her warily.

"Must be stressed by his new surroundings." Chapman's hand fell away from his holster.

Through the bars, she took pictures on her phone of the new toothpaste artwork, then the sheriff escorted her to the front door after she'd gathered her belongings.

"Just when I thought we were getting somewhere." She let out a frustrated noise.

When they reached the front door, she paused with her hand on the knob, considering what she was about to say. He still didn't know about Sal's broken window, that the Keystone Gators were the reason the new mayor was gunning for him.

Her mouth opened and hung there. Through the window, she watched a bicyclist pedal down the street.

"Hey, I read that recent article in *Keystone Corner* about Charlotte Kauffman's death," she said. His eyes narrowed a fraction. "The car's in more photos than a Kardashian in a gossip column. When the professor first mentioned his wife had been killed by a hit-and-run driver, I'd assumed they'd fled in the vehicle. Wouldn't it have been easy for the sheriff at the time to track down the owner of the car?"

"I reckon he searched."

"And he couldn't figure out who it was registered to?" Then she remembered who she was talking to. "You see, all cars are registered to an owner…" His face didn't so much as flicker with understanding. "Oh, a car is sort of like a horse and buggy, only the horse is actually an engine. Its power is measured, oddly enough, in units called horsepower—"

"I know what a car is, Ms. Barton. We've ridden in one together."

Yes, she remembered his white-knuckled grip on the seat while he complained about Will's blistering speed of twenty MPH.

While they'd been talking, Chapman had drifted to the row of filing cabinets and was rifling through them. A moment later, he brought out an aged, stained folder.

"Here it is. The report from that accident." His mouth turned down.

"Are you confused about what that paper is? It's called a case file."

"Not that." He flipped to another sheet, letting out a small grunt. "Sheriff Johnson determined the car came from Lou's lot."

The word "lot" was generous for that sea of rusting metal, but she didn't say so.

"Interesting. Meaning it was stolen?"

"Yes, but Lou didn't report it until after the accident."

That was odd.

After thanking him, she ambled back to the diner, her steps languid to give herself time to process this new information. The whole thing felt off.

If some kid had stolen the car from the lot for a joyride, accidentally hit Mrs. Kaufman, and bolted on foot, then that implied the driver was local. There was another possibility, a more sinister one. Someone could've stolen the car with the sole intention of doing harm, so the vehicle couldn't be traced back to him or her. And if that were the case, that meant they'd targeted Charlotte.

This theory felt like a leap in supposition, so she kept it in the back of her mind. Still, as she tied her apron back on, she couldn't help the fear in her gut that a killer lived in Keystone, one that had gone undetected for years.

CHAPTER FOURTEEN

AFTER DINNER, ELLA stood in the murder room, wearing her home uniform of yoga pants and a faded sweatshirt, waiting. Flo's clunking footsteps announced her presence as she barreled into the room like a storm.

"I grabbed that greased pig in under a minute," Flo was saying to Wink, who trailed in behind her, a harassed expression on her face. "You just don't remember."

Under thick swaths of blue eyeshadow, Wink rolled her eyes. "For crying out loud. That was twenty years ago. Let it go. I beat your time, fair and square."

"You're supposed to do the secret knock," Ella interjected, folding her arms in an attempt to appear intimidating. If she didn't intercede now, their argument could last hours. Once, they'd carried on for an entire day, only stopping when Ella locked them in the basement to work it out.

"Why?" Wink asked. "The door's unlocked."

"Yeah, but secret knocks are for clandestine meetings."

"Are we having a clandestine meeting?" Wink asked.

Ella smoothed out an invisible wrinkle in her sweatshirt. "Sure, let's pretend we are." It seemed far cooler than calling it a gathering of three spinster women with overactive imaginations.

Flo plopped onto the fourposter bed, her expression already arranged in boredom. "You can't just make words up, Poodle Head. Makes you seem not smart."

"And by 'not smart', do you mean unintelligent? Which word did you not understand? Clandestine?" Ella looked at Wink. "I'm buying her a dictionary for her birthday." Flo's hair stood especially tall like it was trying to gain altitude, so Ella added, "Or a comb."

"I think being heavy-handed with a comb *is* the problem," Wink said. The mattress sunk as she joined Flo.

They looked expectantly at Ella.

"Right. Let's start this meeting off right." She yanked a napkin from the nightstand with a grandiose flourish, revealing a plate of snickerdoodle cookies.

Wink's eyes bugged out, aghast. "We *just* ate, El."

"Yeah, but not dessert."

"I watched you eat two slices of rhubarb pie."

Flo's nose wrinkled in disgust. "Ugh, that wasn't dessert. A vegetable's got no business being in a pie."

"Yes, thank you." Finally, she and Flo could agree on something.

After nabbing a cookie, Ella approached the large, antique oval mirror that sat near the window. She took a bite, then exchanged the cookie for a dry erase marker, and soon the stench of ink was all she could smell.

On the left side of the mirror, she wrote Charlotte's name and on the right, the professor's, signifying their two victims. Next to each name, she began a suspect list.

"Suspects?" Wink said. "Isn't the professor's murderer behind bars?"

"Actually…" She told them how Chapman had demoted Craig from a suspect for Dr. Kaufman's murder to a person of interest with intel.

"And Charlotte? 'Suspect' makes it seem like you think she was killed intentionally."

"It just means the person responsible for hitting her and fleeing. It's shorter than writing 'douche canoe who left a poor woman to die'." Biting her lip, she clicked the cap on the marker on and off. "But also, I have a theory—well, not a theory so much as a hunch. And by hunch, I mean an inkling —"

"Spit it out already." Flo chewed on a fingernail.

Bolstered by such encouragement, Ella told them what Chapman had found in the inordinately thin file on Charlotte's death, that the car had come from Lou's lot and that the mechanic hadn't immediately reported it as stolen. She faced the mirror again, leaving Wink to ponder this information and Flo to stare at the ceiling. In each suspect column, she wrote Patience's name.

"Patience arrived after the town began jumping," Wink pointed out. "Charlotte died before that."

"Yeah, but sooner or later, the woman's bound to snap and kill someone. And I want it on record that I was right."

"What record?"

Ella waved her hand dismissively. "You know, just, the record. Whoever's listening."

Flo perked up, nodding. "I know who you mean." She tapped the side of her head, dropping her voice to a loud whisper. "She means aliens."

Ella stared. Then, reaching over to the nightstand, she grabbed a snickerdoodle and shoved in the woman's gaping mouth.

Back at the murder board, she taped the edition of *Keystone Corner* she'd brought over from the diner. She studied it, brushing cookie crumbs from her pants.

"Something in this article triggered the professor to look into Charlotte's death. But what?"

Wink squinted at it from her perch on the bed. "Hmm, nothing immediately jumps out, except the same thing you noticed: the car being on the scene still. Maybe the professor didn't know it had been left at the scene until this article came out."

It was a possibility. Perhaps that was information Sheriff Johnson hadn't divulged to the victim's spouse for whatever reason.

Flo, finished with her force-fed cookie, had scooted to the head of the bed and was picking at the floral wallpaper. "Maybe he clandestined it from Lou's lot."

Ella coughed. "What?"

"You know, the doc might've recognized it as coming from that scrap heap."

"That's a surprisingly good thought, misuse of the word 'clandestine' aside," Ella said. "It wasn't public knowledge that the car came from Lou's lot. Chapman didn't even know until he looked at the file." Her eyes shifted back to the newspaper, ink printed on pulpy recycled paper. "Why Sal?"

"You mean, why did the professor talk to Sal about the accident?" Wink said.

"Yeah, why him of all people? What's he know besides how to give a decent haircut? Don't get me wrong. He also throws a mean baseball and is a doppelgänger for Dracula —" Ella gasped. "Hold on a second. His skin's as pale as snow, his hair's got a widow's peak, and he's also got some sharp incisors... You see where I'm going with this, right?"

Wink shook her head. More paper peeled off in Flo's fingers.

"Have we ever seen him eat garlic or go outside in day-light?" Ella stared at the ceiling a long while, deep in thought, before she shrugged it off. "We'll have to look into the possibility of him being a vampire later. We have a murder and a hit-and-run to solve."

Wink's brow furrowed. "What are you blathering on about?"

"Vampires—and not the sparkly, swoon-worthy kind."

Flo's head twisted sharply. "Vampires sparkle in your time?"

"Some."

She harrumphed. "Well, don't worry. I've got an atomizer that'll disassemble 'em."

"Of course you do—"

"See, the trick is to shoot 'em with garlic pellets mixed with silver. Most folks don't know that."

"Yes, but—wait, silver? That can't be right. That's for werewolves. Right?" She looked at Wink. "Right?"

Wink released a long-suffering breath. "I'd rather be hung by my toes than continue this conversation."

"Right." Ella cleared her throat, collecting her thoughts. "My point was, what does Sal know about the accident?"

"Maybe the professor thought our new mayor could sneak into the sheriff's office and look at the case file for him."

"Were they even friends?"

Flo had returned to the wall and glanced up from a thin strip of overly floral wallpaper she'd successfully peeled away. "I don't think I ever saw the two exchange a single word. How very clandestine of them—" A pillow launched at Flo's face, courtesy of Wink.

"Stop picking at the wall. Rose'll kill you."

"After she makes you fix it," Ella said in an appeal to Flo's lazy side.

Outside the window, the sky was darkening. The room sat on the second story in the south wing and gave an expansive view of tree branches and the roof for Grandma's Kitchen.

"Now the question is, are the Kaufmans' deaths related? Had the professor found the driver, confronted him, and gotten killed for it?"

Wink leaned against the mountain of pillows at the headboard. "Were there signs of a struggle in the cave?"

"Besides the blow to the back of the professor's noggin?" Ella began to shake her head, then stopped. "Actually, I found what I thought were bullet marks on the wall. There was a revolver nearby, but I don't think it'd been fired recently."

"So, whoever killed him caught him by surprise," Wink murmured.

"Or it was someone he trusted enough to turn his back." A breath hissed out between Ella's teeth as she leaned against the dresser. "What is it about his death that rules Craig out as a suspect?"

"What, indeed?"

Flo straightened, suddenly interested. "Only one way to find out."

Ella held up her hands. "Let's not get ahead of ourselves. It's too soon to talk about br—"

"We're breakin' in!" The boarder rubbed her hands together, a Cheshire grin on her face. "I've got this new doohickey I've been dying to try out. Should work swell."

Ella swore. "Can you at least pretend not to be a sociopath sometimes?"

"What's a sociopath?" Wink and Flo asked at the same time.

"Oh, um...." Apparently, the term had come about after their time. "Let's just say Flo is dangerously close to being labeled that." Rocking on her heels, she nodded, satisfied by this vague explanation and left it at that. "Back to the professor. I think to know what happened, it would help if we retraced his steps."

Flo scratched her head, a rather involved process that required her to stick her entire hand into her cotton candy hairdo. "You mean camp in the cave and live off cans and stolen food?"

"Ew, no—"

"Count me in."

"I literally just said we weren't doing that."

"Sounds fun."

"Nope, not happening." Ella had a sneaking suspicion the reason the possible sociopath was so eager to go full-on Bear Grylls was so she could be nearer her precious weapons. "What I meant was, in addition to having a chat with Lou about the car, we should also talk to Sal."

Wink snorted. "You really think he'll tell us anything?"

"No, I think he'd sooner give us bowl haircuts, but it's worth a shot." Staring at Flo, she tried to envision the woman with a bowl haircut.

"Can't we just do the cave thing?" Flo asked. "That sounds more appealing. And what are you smilin' at, Poodle Head?"

"Hmm? Nothing. Tell you what, you do the whole cave thing, and radio us if Spot finds you and makes you kitten chow."

The dry erase marker squeaked as she wrote out Lou's and Sal's names, indicating the Keystone Gators needed to question them, a sort of to-do list. After Sal's, she added a note to bring garlic and a wooden cross as a precaution. If there was one thing television had taught her, it was you could never be overly prepared when dealing with a possible vampire.

Next, she wrote "COD."

"Cod?" Flo asked. "I don't like fish. Can't we eat chicken? It tastes clandestine."

"You know," Ella said, "I don't think you know what that word means."

Wink rolled her eyes. "COD stands for 'cause of death', dummy."

Ella's hands absently capped and uncapped the marker lid again as she tried to devise a means of getting the latter information without resorting to another break-in.

"We could probably pry the information from Jimmy," Wink said before slapping the backside of Flo's head to stop her from peeling off more wallpaper.

"I tried that at dinner earlier."

"*That's* what that was? You asked if he still had bowel issues after eating dairy."

"I was just warming him up, showing him I cared. He didn't need to go into detail about it. That's on him." It was going to be a while before those images were scrubbed from her brain.

Like a growing vine, Flo's hand slowly crept to the peeling wallpaper again. "We could threaten him and see if he spills the beans."

"Let's call that Plan B," Ella said. The moment Flo looked away, she mouthed to Wink, *Sociopath*.

They spent the next half-hour spitballing ideas on how best to get the information they needed. Ella had to admit, begrudgingly, that short of drugging Jimmy, the next best option—really, their only one since Wink put a stop to Flo torturing him—was to break into Pauline's office.

Once they'd decided on that course of action, planning became a breeze, largely because this wasn't their first break-in and mostly because the entirety of their plan consisted of picking the lock on the front door and wearing dark clothes.

Later, Ella descended the staircase with the other two, feeling like she needed a stiff drink. Flo abandoned them near the kitchen where she disappeared into the basement of horrors.

In the kitchen, Rose stood over the largest soup pot Ella had ever seen, and Jimmy stood nearby, helping.

"What are you cooking?" Ella leaned over the pot, took a big whiff, and gagged. A putrid scent lingered in her nose and on her tongue. The pot held brown water colored by tannins and smelled like the inside of her gym bag a month after forgetting to take her sweaty clothes out. "Yum, is that a broth?"

Jimmy took a large bucket from near the back door, his muscles straining, and he poured it through a cheesecloth strainer set up in the sink. More of the same brown water sloshed over the cloth, dribbling through it into a second bucket.

Rose placed a lid over the pot on the stove and turned up the burner. "Ukulele Joe made an announcement on the radio about an hour ago."

That's when Ella noticed the Zenith Bakelite Tube Radio still on. Amongst the background gurgle of sloshing water was the tin-quality screeching of one of Joe's serenades as he searched for the right key.

"Something broke at the water treatment plant," Jimmy chimed in. The couple's turn-taking in conversation played out like a tennis match. "And they're not sure when they can have it fixed."

"They set up a refill station for folks at the water tower near Twin Springs," Rose continued. "They're saying what's in the tower will last us a few days at most."

Lifting the lid on the giant pot, Wink sniffed. She immediately recoiled, pulling a puckered expression. "Did you get that water from the septic tank?"

That thought hadn't occurred to Ella, but it certainly would explain the smell.

"Don't be silly." Rose hip-checked the diner owner away.

"We pulled it from the lake." Jimmy beamed as if toting liquid from a tepid water source yards from their backdoor was something to be proud of.

"Did you learn nothing from our weeks in the desert five years back?" Wink asked.

Rose's ruby-colored lips turned down. "We had to use up our reserve water in the basement to put out that fire."

Ella's interest piqued. "Fire? Oh, wait. Flo lives here. Never mind. No need to explain."

"I forgot about that one," Wink said, her eyes glistening as if recalling a fond memory. "Flo was testing some sort of flame retardant material for clothing."

At the sink, Jimmy snorted. "I've never heard a dryer make that noise before. Sounded like a dying cow, then *poof*. Flames as tall as the ceiling."

"Yes," Ella said. "She has that effect on things."

Wink swept a hand at the buckets of water. "I can fill those at my house. I'm on a well."

"I wouldn't want to trouble you." Rose mopped her brow using her frilly apron.

"No trouble at all."

This back and forth of social niceties continued for some moments until Wink won out. Rose then turned to Ella, saying pointedly, "This means we'll have to conserve water."

"I don't know why you're looking at me. Do you not want me bathing or something?"

"You can bathe at my place," Wink said. "I *insist*."

Ella made a show of sniffing her armpits. "Come on, ladies. It's not that bad. I turn my underwear inside out as often as the rest of you."

"You do *what*?" Rose gasped.

"I'm kidding."

Wink's eyes narrowed. "I don't think you are."

"I didn't bring up water rationing because of bathing." The innkeeper laid a gentle hand on Ella's shoulder as if preparing her for troubling news. "This means until we get drinkable water from Wink, we can't make coffee."

It felt like the kitchen, with its obnoxiously bright lemon drop yellow walls, closed in on her, and Ella heard herself stammering, "W-what? You shut your mouth."

"I beg your pardon?"

Wink stepped into Ella's closing field of vision. "Don't go getting your knickers in a twist, El. I'll have to transport water to the diner, anyway. Just have your morning cup of joe there—or five cups, or however much you're drinking now." She looked over her shoulder at the innkeepers. "I've seen her go a morning without coffee. She scared away all of my customers."

Ella felt the tension in her body ease. "Don't be dramatic. It wasn't that bad."

"You threatened Horatio with a knife."

"Yes, but it was a *dull* knife."

The floor vibrated with a boom.

At almost the same moment, Ella and Wink blurted out, "Not it," touching their noses for good measure.

"Ha!" Ella pumped her fist in the air in triumph. "I win. You saw that, right?" she asked Jimmy and Rose. "I was first."

Grumbling, Wink shuffled towards the door, dragging her shoes over the checkered linoleum to go see if Flo had caused any new fires.

CHAPTER FIFTEEN

ELLA FOUND SHE couldn't sit still and play cards in the parlor with the impending "mission" in a few hours. When she tried turning in early for a quick nap, sleep eluded her.

So, she hitched a ride with Wink to her house for a quick bath to wash burger and fry grease from her pores, then headed over to the professor's house. As expected, Will was working in the basement, flipping switches and tracing the panels' exposed wire guts with a finger before scribbling notes.

His hair was unkempt, and the stubble had returned. She watched from the darkness for a moment. His ability to entrench so deeply in a task was admirable, but she knew how all-consuming that could be, that hyper-focus. All other needs faded to the background.

"When was the last time you ate?" She strode into the lantern light, the breakers still off.

He glanced up, and his eyes slowly focused on her. "Wink brought me lunch."

"It's past dinnertime. Or supper, or whatever you people call it."

"I'll eat soon." He returned his attention to the panel on the floor, turned a dial, checked the readout, and made a note. When he finished, she helped him tuck the wires back into the metal casing and screw the panel back on. Once he'd tightened the screws on his side, he moved to switch places with her, but she held out her hand for the screwdriver. He watched her intently as she sunk her screws in.

Turning, she noticed the blackboard in the room for the first time—actually, *blackboards* as there were three, all sprawling with complicated equations. "Holy John Nash. Yikes."

Will followed her gaze. "I wanted to try the idea you inspired. It's related to cavitation."

"And?"

He let out a sigh as he strode over and faced the middle board. "And that'll take some time."

Well, at least that wasn't an immediate, *it didn't work, and we're all doomed.* "You'll get it." Not sure what else to do, she patted his back awkwardly.

His dimples surfaced faintly. Turning back to the mess of panels and wires, he seemed eager to tackle the next. So, she stood by, handing tools and offering helpful tidbits, such as, "That looks important" and "Remember that important-looking switch you told me not to touch? I flipped it."

It didn't take long before she was relegated to sitting as far away from the wires, buttons, and toggles as possible, only able to watch. While he worked, they ventured onto the topic of slang and idioms from her era.

"Bee?" he asked while scribing a gauge reading.

"No, *bae.*"

"Bay? As in an ocean bay?"

"That's a homophone of it, yes. But it's spelled b-a-e."

He used his pencil to scratch his chin. "And what's it mean again?"

"I think it's a diminutive term for one's significant other, like babe or honey." She inched closer to a glowing panel that had been reattached, freezing when he gave her a stern shake of his head. "Then, there's 'lit'."

"Lit?" He pointed at one of the glowing doohickeys on the nearest console, then at the lantern.

"No, it means 'cool,' or in your case, 'the cat's pajamas.' At least, I think. That teen I was tutoring could've been pulling my leg."

"Ah! Pulling your leg. Now, that's an idiom I understand."

"See?" She gave him a hearty thumbs up. "You're not that old."

His eyebrows knitted together. "Who says I'm old?"

"Hmm? No one. Certainly not me. I mean, if you want to split hairs, from my perspective you're nearly a century old."

Nearing eleven o'clock at night, when Will showed no signs of going home anytime soon, Ella wandered outside and into the house, bored. She had an hour to kill before walking to Wink's for their late-night, illicit activity.

Tired floorboards creaked beneath her feet as she moved from the living room to the dining room like a ghost. It smelled of dust and neglect. The power was on in this section of the residence, Will having only turned off the breakers for the cellar. The fact that there was power at all still flowing in the abandoned house must've been the sheriff's doing.

The dining room had been taken over by books. A bookcase spanned the southern wall, the contents overflowing to the table. Its wooden surface was reduced to slivers glimpsed between yet more books and journals and loose papers full of complicated equations. Half the books and notes were written in German.

Running her fingers along the spines on the bookcase, she paused periodically to slide a book out, glance at the cover, then slip it back. A particularly well-used one caught her eye, and she pulled it out. The book came from the Keystone library, clearly never returned. Gabby's aunt's face flashed before Ella, and she shivered. The librarian had probably charged Dr. Kaufman with enough late fees to bankrupt a country.

That familiar perfume of old book floated up as she cracked it open. It was written in English and focused on the Duquesne Nazi Germany Spy Ring. Pages were dog-eared and heavily annotated. They whispered in the silence as she leafed through it, stopping every once in a while to decipher the professor's chaotic handwriting written in German, the penmanship worse than a drunk doctor's.

As she moved to set the heavy book on the table, several loose notebook papers fell out. Collecting them, she angled them toward the light, finding crooked hand-drawn lines accompanying more indecipherable notes. They reminded her of either sentence diagrams she'd had to draw in school or timelines for historical events. Squinting and reading, she realized that was exactly what they were: timelines.

Sheet after sheet, nearly all of them began with WWII as a starting point. The name "Duquesne" stood out, and she flipped to the title page of the book to be sure she hadn't conflated the name for the Nazi ring of spies in the United States with something else. She hadn't.

More historical events populated the timeline—only, they weren't events she remembered. Granted, her grasp of history was flimsy, but this paper, for example, had Germany winning the war. Maybe she couldn't remember who fought in the war, but she was pretty sure that hadn't happened. The timeline stopped with a single word: Armageddon.

Goosebumps broke out over her arms, and she swallowed past a dry throat. She flipped to another paper, another timeline. Its major events varied slightly from the first's, closer to the history she knew, but were still off. The moon landing happened in 1972 instead of 1969. The Wall Street Crash of 1929, known as the Great Crash, only lasted a month instead of two.

Two of the three homestead acts between 1862 and 1909 had notes indicating they hadn't happened. She remembered from a college history class that the acts had resulted in an influx of farmers moving to the Great Plains. This, along with other factors, such as ripping up prairie grass, had led to the Dust Bowl.

On the face, these changes seemed positive because it would mean farmers' crops wouldn't be decimated at a time the country sorely needed them, but along the edge of the paper was written the word "Apocalypse."

She rifled through more papers. What were these? The professor playing games of "what if?" A more plausible, more ghastly alternative presented itself. Who knew if these had been created before or after his invention was completed, but what if, along with going back in time to save his wife, he'd planned on going back to alter history? What if that had been the intended purpose for the device all along, to go back and change the outcome of the war?

Dr. Kaufman had never struck her as the genocidal type, but he had been conscripted to work for the Nazis before the United States had brought him over as part of Operation Paperclip (originally called Operation Overcast).

Her legs felt weak, and she sank to a chair as she imagined a world where the Nazis had won. The professor's final words echoed in her mind: *Don't fix the device.*

CHAPTER SIXTEEN

ELLA SWEPT HER gaze north up Main Street. Nothing moved among the abandoned antique cars and dappled light cast by street lamps.

Beside her, Flo hunched over the lock for the front door to the funeral home, cursing. Wink stood a few yards south on the corner, also playing lookout.

A metallic clatter came from the door as Flo dropped one of her lock-picking tools. This was followed by another string of profanities.

"I thought you said you could get us in," Ella said.

"I said I'd try."

"I distinctly remember you saying it'll be a walk in the park."

Usually, they spent more time planning their break-ins. Instead, their meeting had devolved into seeing how many cookies Ella could fit into her mouth.

Something snapped in Flo's hands.

"Uh-oh."

Ella turned sharply. "What uh-oh? Is that like an 'I forgot to turn my oven off' uh-oh or an 'I overestimated my skills and ruined the lock and now Chapman will know someone was trying to break-in' uh-oh?"

Flo's lips pursed, and that was all the response Ella needed. Muttering under her breath, she shone her phone on the lock. Sure enough, the long, skinny tool similar to what dentists used to torture their patients—what Flo had called a tension wrench—had broken off in the lock.

"Well, that's useful." Shaking her head, Ella motioned Wink over, but the woman's back was to them. Cupping her mouth, she made a *caw-caw* noise.

"What is that?" Flo asked.

"A crow."

"What sort of crow's going to be making noise this late at night? Do an owl."

"I don't want to—" But Flo was already hooting. Though it sounded more akin to an owl with laryngitis, it wasn't a million miles off from the real deal.

"Will you two keep it down?" Wink hissed, striding over, her heels clicking softly on the sidewalk.

Ella pointed at the woman's feet. "What'd we say about footwear?"

"These were the only dark pair of shoes I have that are clean."

"Fine, but if things get hairy—which, let's face it, they will—I'm leaving you behind with ol' Harry Houdini here."

"Fine. What's taking so long?"

"Butterfingers broke her wrench thingie in the lock, so we can't get in."

Wink shrugged, glancing up and down the sidewalk. "Alright, Plan B, then."

"Sure—wait, we have a Plan B?" Ella glanced sideways at Flo to see if she knew this, but the boarder was too preoccupied practicing bird calls under her breath.

"When this one's involved—" Wink hooked a thumb in Flo's direction "—I always have a Plan B."

She led them around the side of the building, skittering in the shadows. Ella hummed theme music for them until Wink shushed her. When they reached the back alley, they found a second door in addition to two oblong windows five feet off the ground.

Ella and Wink turned, expectant, towards Flo, who was still several yards back.

"Hey, Poodle Head, how 'bout this one?" Flo's lips puckered, and she whistled a bright melody before Wink slapped a hand over the woman's mouth, cutting her off mid warble.

Wink pointed at the door, glaring.

"It's a warbler, by the way." Flo pulled out her toolkit. "Or maybe it's a chickadee."

"Yeah, I didn't ask," Ella said, sweeping a gaze up and down the alley. The buildings abutted a wooden fence that ran parallel to Main Street, creating the alley. "How about that lock, though?"

After inspecting the door, Flo's knobby hand probed around in her kit, and she grunted. "Uh-oh."

Ella let out an exasperated breath, tipping her head back, summoning patience so as not to strangle the woman.

"I don't have another wrench," Flo said.

Wink pointed up at the windows. "Then it's Plan C."

Since Ella didn't see a ladder or a means by which to open the window, she wasn't sure how Plan C was an option.

"No, that ain't Plan C." Flo gestured for the backpack she'd coerced Ella to tote.

Reluctantly, Ella handed it over. The straps had been digging into her shoulders, so it was a relief to have it off. But at the same time, anything the crazy woman had packed for their "mission" was sure to either explode or maim.

While Flo borrowed Ella's phone for light and rooted through the bag, Ella paced, keeping an eye on both ends of the alley. A pebble skittered from her shoe and across the ground. Turning, she kicked a bigger rock, only it didn't roll like the first. It plopped onto its side after one rotation and stopped, revealing a flat, unnatural bottom and an object hidden beneath.

When she looked up, Flo was placing charges of some kind on the door, and Wink was wrestling her away, explaining how blowing the door was in no way stealthy.

"Behold!" Ella held up the key she'd found, so it glinted in the wan light. After unlocking the door and breathing on her fingernails like an expert, she muttered, "Amateurs," then gestured for them to go through first. No way was she stepping into the creepy, dark funeral home before them.

Returning the key to its hiding spot, she said, "At some point, we should really discuss what passes for security in this town."

Wink stepped through the doorway first, her voice floating out. "Most places don't get broken into."

"Except by us," Ella pointed out.

Wink conceded this point, but added, "It's quite safe here."

"Is it though?" She inclined her head towards Flo, who was taking the charges off the door and stowing them in her backpack again, her lower lip jutting out in a pout.

Ella tiptoed through the doorway last, and her light swept their new surroundings. "Well, this isn't creepy."

They stood in the funeral home's showroom. She'd been in here once before, but it had been during the day, with the lights on, and even then, she hadn't wanted to linger.

Funeral caskets lined the wall and took up a row in the center, all the lids open. Every move of her phone caused the shadows to dart. It wouldn't have surprised her if a dead body rose out of a coffin at any moment, even though they were all empty.

"Nope, nope, nope." Her eyes averted to the floor, and she jogged for the door on the far wall. "Flo, quit pushing m—" Flo's jostling caused their feet to tangle.

They tripped, falling right into a beautiful monarch blue casket. It was far too heavy to budge from the impact, but it did lay open at waist height, the cushions inside perfect for breaking their fall.

Ella's face landed on the pillowy interior which wasn't so bad, all things considered. It was like falling onto a cloud— until she remembered what she'd fallen into.

"Get off me!" she yelled, her words muffled. Flo lay on top of her, both of them partially inside the coffin. "Oh my God, it smells in here."

Wink's voice came from somewhere above. "How can it? It's brand new."

"I can taste it!" Ella continued her futile thrashing beneath Flo, who had several pounds on her. She elbowed the woman's soft ribs, earning a grunt that got the old broad moving.

She popped out of the casket, sucking the open air into her lungs. It smelled of freedom—if freedom smelled strongly of embalming fluids. Flo's hair was a mess, like a cotton ball caught in a gale-force wind.

Shooting her a death glare, Ella spoke through clenched teeth. "You're dead meat, Henderson."

Wink patted her shoulder in sympathy as she passed. "Let's just get a move on, shall we?" The moment the diner owner turned her back, Flo's mouth twisted with a rictus grin.

"Smile all you want, but you just got a glimpse of your future, your very *near* future."

Once in the lobby, they turned left down a hallway near the front door. A different odor took over, one that smelled of cooked meat. Ella breathed through her mouth, not wanting to dwell any further on the scent or the door labeled Cremation Services.

Pauline's autopsy room was part of the funeral parlor, mostly because the building already had all the necessary equipment needed for autopsies once the town had jumped and been cut off from a medical examiner. The room served as both office and exam room, with the door for the cold storage room set in the far, exterior wall. With two autopsy tables, shelves of medical equipment, and a desk, the already cramped space felt, appropriately, like a coffin.

She smiled to herself, about to repeat this observation to the others, but Wink had discovered the autopsy folder for Dr. Kaufman on Pauline's desk.

"Really?" Ella tried to hide her disappointment. "That was surprisingly easy. I mean, usually by now, something goes horribly awry for us. It was just sitting there?"

She and Flo scooted around to join Wink at the desk as she opened the folder. A nearly blank piece of paper lay inside, a single note scribbled on it.

To Ms. Barton and gang, better luck next time.

The sheriff's messy signature was at the bottom.

"Darn, law dog," Flo spat.

"Well, you got to give him props."

"I don't know what that means."

"You have to admire his foresight," Ella said. "Now that I think of it, I'm surprised it took him this long to thwart us." When she noticed Flo's blank expression she said, "Oh, 'thwart' means to—"

"I know what thwart means, Poodle Head. I was just thinking over our next move."

"Really? Because your thinking face looks exactly like your confused face."

Wink dropped the file back on the desk. "It also looks like her constipated face."

"Eesh, I'm not going to ask how you know that." Ella tapped her finger to her chin. "What now? Can I offer my suggestion again about plying the doc with alcohol? After a few drinks, she'll talk your ear off about anything. And I mean *anything*, including her first time on a nude beach—"

"Especially," Flo interrupted, "if we slip something into her drink."

"For the last time, we're not drugging her." Wink shook her head, adamant. "And the fact that you two agree on that is cause for concern."

While they brainstormed ways they could find out the professor's cause of death, they searched the room, trying to disturb as little as possible. At least, Ella and Wink tried. Flo haphazardly shifted items and touched nearly every surface in the room.

"Yes," Ella said, peeking into a box, "touch all the things, Flo. I think that lamp over there doesn't have your finger-prints, yet. Why don't you go touch that?"

She replaced the box and looked in the next one. If she remembered correctly, Pauline kept the belongings of the deceased in a box on this shelf until it could be cataloged.

Over by the cold storage door, Wink stood, hands planted on her hips. "We could..." She inclined her head towards the door. "... check out the body."

"We'd just turn into popsicles. I don't see how Pauline's incisions will tell us anything more. Besides, I already saw his body."

But Wink was already opening the door, letting a blast of cold air whip out.

"Huh, well it's empty."

Ella looked up. "Really?"

"He must already be in the embalming room."

"This isn't also the embalming room? I just assumed."

Flo tilted her head. "Next door."

With no body in the room, that meant Pauline had completed her autopsy. It had been over forty-eight hours, so it wasn't too surprising.

Shaking off the mental images an embalming room conjured, Ella pulled out the next box. "Jackpot." It made a scraping noise as she hefted it off the shelf.

"What good is looking at the professor's stuff, anyway?" Flo asked.

"Maybe we'll find a clue," Wink said.

Hovering over the box, Ella didn't respond. Her motive was different. Yes, she was hunting for hints of the professor's killer, but more importantly, she was searching for any sign as to who the enigmatic "he" was Dr. Kaufman had referred to as he lay dying. Keeping the secret from her friends gnawed at her. They were a team, but she wasn't ready.

"Nothing out of the ordinary," Wink noted.

The contents of the box Ella had pulled had come from the professor's nest in the cave: the newspaper, bottles of water, the revolver, and other odds and ends. She sniffed the water, finding it had no smell.

With a frustrated sigh, she replaced the box.

Wink checked her watch. "We've been here too long."

The trio was weaving around the cramped tables to the door when Ella noticed the counter along the north wall, full of syringes, catheters, scopes, and pathology and forensic equipment. At least, she assumed that was the intended purpose of some of the equipment. Parts of machinery had been Frankensteined together, built in a way that screamed homemade.

Pauline was from the 1990s and lamented the fact to anyone who'd listen that she didn't have proper equipment. Once or twice she'd mentioned offhand to Ella that Will had attempted to recreate a gas chromatograph, a blood gas analyzer, and centrifuge. She'd rattled off the names of other equipment, but Ella had stopped listening at that point.

Tucked in the corner was an avocado green refrigerator. "Did you check the fridge?" she asked Flo, who'd been in charge of searching that section.

One side of the boarder's mouth quirked up. "No. Maybe you should go have a look-see."

Ella didn't move. "You already peeked inside, didn't you? Is it gross? Are there body parts in there?"

"Just her lunch."

Wink stood by the door, checking her watch and tapping her foot.

Ella was still staring at the appliance. "What sort of lunch?"

"El! You can't be serious." Wink gave her a light tap on the arm.

"Ew, no. I'm asking for a different reason." Although now her stomach rumbled with hunger. Striding forward, she steeled herself for what she'd find inside and cracked open the refrigerator.

Blood. There was blood everywhere, but mostly in vials labeled and stoppered, amongst labeled containers full of stuff her eyes refused to linger on. Also, meat-like objects. It was like a butcher shop.

She found the "lunch" Flo had referenced, a very familiar-looking strawberry jam. It was labeled, as well, with "Kaufman" followed by a long number.

She looked from it to the toxicology equipment. "She was testing the professor's food."

"Testing it? As in, for poison?" Wink asked. "Hmm, that's interesting, but it doesn't mean she found anything."

Ella nodded absently, thinking. Why the jam and not the water or other food found at the scene? Recalling the crime scene and the partially eaten slice of bread with jam smeared atop, it was safe to conclude that it had been the professor's last meal.

Too bad she didn't know how to use the equipment, so they could test the contents of the jar themselves. Maybe Will did, but that would mean another break-in and bringing the inventor with them. Unscrewing the lid, she put the jam to her nose.

"El, what are you doing?"

"Even I know that's a bad idea, Poodle Head."

The pungent odor of the room and the sweet scent of the jam were nearly overpowering, but there it was, a faint note riding at the end: the smell of bitter almonds. She'd seen enough murder mystery shows and read enough Agatha Christie to know what that meant.

How had she not smelled it on him before in the caves? Then she remembered her nose had been stuffy.

"Cyanide," she said. "The professor died from cyanide poisoning." No wonder the sheriff had ruled the caveman out as the killer.

She turned to leave, stopping short. "Uh, Flo? Your back-pack's smoking."

CHAPTER SEVENTEEN

"FLO," WINK SAID, panic seizing her voice, "why on earth is your bag smoking?"

Flo spun like a cat chasing its tail, trying to see the smoke. "I don't—" Her eyes widened. "Quicklime!"

It took a moment for the word to register. That's when Ella remembered the small explosives Flo had wanted to use on the backdoor, the same explosives she'd stuffed in the now smoking bag.

Without asking why in the jelly-filled donuts Flo had thought it a good idea to pack Greek fire for this excursion, Ella ripped the bag off the woman's shoulders. She leaped for the cold storage and ripped open the door.

The bag flew through the air and landed on the shelf where a body usually lay. She slammed the thick door closed and took two leaping strides across Pauline's lab towards the hallway. Wink was diving through the doorway, dragging Flo out by her hair.

"But my bag!" Flo's exclamation was punctuated by a *kaboom* behind Ella.

The force of a train slammed into her back, sending her crashing into the other two. They landed in the hallway in a dog pile. No one moved for several seconds in the prolonged stillness that followed.

Ella realized two things. One, she'd just survived a death-defying leap from an explosion that belonged in an action movie starring Bruce Willis. Two, she was pretty sure she was deaf, except for the very loud ringing in her ears. From head to toe, her entire body felt like it had been tossed about in a blender.

"I taste purple," she croaked out. "Is that possible?"

Groaning, she rolled over and surveyed the damage. The door for the cold storage room dangled by its top hinge, scorch marks marring the room beyond.

She coughed. "Maybe Pauline won't notice. A little scrubbing, a new door, and it'll be good as new."

The last sinew of hinge gave, and the door fell with a crash that was felt rather than heard through her stuffed ears.

"What?" Wink shouted. Her mouth opened and closed as she attempted to pop her ears. "How much quicklime did you have in there?"

"What?" Flo hollered back. A spiderweb of cracks covered one lens of her glasses. "I can't hear you."

Ella motioned for them to massage their ears, then climbed to her feet. There was no way half the town hadn't heard that blast. If they were discovered, Chapman would throw them in the slammer for sure this time, and, as much as she liked Craig the caveman, she had no interest in being stuck in a cell that smelled like a truck stop bathroom.

"We have to get out of here." She wobbled, standing.

"What?" The other two said in unison.

Ella pantomimed leaving before tugging them to their feet. Sprinting through the building, they burst out the back door and into the night. As the ringing in her ears abated, she heard the clop of horse hooves coming down Main Street.

"Crap!" She shoved the others down the dark alley, away from the approaching sheriff.

Sprinting down the narrow pathway in the dark, jumping crates and dodging trash bins, Ella experienced a horrible sense of déjà vu. The last time they'd been running from Chapman down this same alley, Flo had used a firecracker to create a diversion.

The boarder kept veering left on account of not being able to see out of that side of her glasses. Like a pinball, she slammed into Wink before bouncing back on track.

Ella's boss wasn't faring much better in the low kitten heels. At one point, she kicked them off and scooped them up, opting to run barefoot. Three blocks later, the alley ended abruptly in a fence. They skidded to a halt.

"What now?" Ella rotated, scanning their surroundings, while Flo bent over her knees making hacking noises. If they backtracked and cut up the side of the bank there, they could get to Main Street, which would get them home. But the road also had street lamps and the sheriff.

She eyed the fence that ran parallel to the buildings, while Wink asked Flo, "Just how much of that powder did you have?"

Flo, her hand clutching her ribs, shrugged. "Whatever spilled from the container. When we got back from campin', the lid had loosened, and some powder coated the bottom of my bag. I guess the consideration from my water canteen—"

"Condensation," Ella corrected.

"That's what I said, Poodle Head. Anyway, it must've interacted with the powder and caused the fire."

"Which ignited your explosives," Wink concluded. "Thank God they were relatively small."

Ella gaped at her.

"Well, the room was still intact, wasn't it? I say we got lucky, all things considered."

Ella didn't share Wink's optimism, but now wasn't the time to belabor the point.

Back up the alley, towards the funeral parlor, nothing moved. Unfortunately, she also no longer heard Horse's hoofbeats, which meant Chapman most likely had discovered the epicenter of the explosion. "At least the storage room was empty, and you didn't blow up the professor."

"Wouldn't have hurt nothing if I had." Flo's breathing was less labored, though still a bit raspy. "Not like he can get more dead."

"Stop."

"It's not like he woulda felt it."

"There's a special place in hell for you."

Wink intervened. "Hell aside, the bigger concern is how long we have until Chapman hunts us down and locks us up."

"I say by morning," Ella said. "Also, I call the cell furthest away from Craig."

"What makes you think he'll know it was us?" Flo asked.

Both Ella and Wink faced the woman, letting their expressions answer her question.

The back door for the funeral parlor burst out and slammed into the building. The trio bolted for the shadows, squatting behind a stack of broken pallets and two metal trash cans.

They froze.

Chapman's silhouette stood out, looking up and down the alley. The moment he ducked back into the building, Ella and Wink popped to their feet before helping Flo to hers, pulling her up by her hair.

The list of people in Keystone who would cause explosions in the middle of the night was a short list, and Flo and

Six occupied the top two spaces. Chapman would be a fool not to gallop straight to the inn on Horse to see if Flo and Ella were home.

"We'll have to risk Main," Wink said. "We can avoid the lights." She began jogging back the way they'd come, her trespassing heels dangling in one hand.

"Wait! Where do you think he'll be heading any minute now?" Ella said.

Wink skidded to a stop. "Drat!"

"Where?" Flo asked, looking from one face to the other.

"The inn, dummy," Wink said.

Ella motioned frantically. "Hurry! We have to beat him there." And they had to avoid Main Street as much as possible to do so.

She grabbed for the fence. Her feet ran up the wooden post, and she pulled herself up, not unlike a clumsy, out-of-shape pole vaulter.

Straddling the fence on her stomach, she glanced down to see Flo gawping. "Ain't no way I'm gonna do that."

"Help me." Wink elbowed the senior citizen out of her stupor as she began stacking pallets beneath the fence.

"Well, that works, too," Ella grunted.

It didn't take long for Wink to get frustrated. "No—that's not a pallet. That's a trash can. No. Still a trash can. There you go. Now move it over here. No—*here*. Follow my voice, dummy."

Ella's stomach scraped on the top of the boards before she slid down the other side and dropped onto soft grass. The sound of stacking pallets came from the other side, followed by Wink and Flo arguing about who climbed up first.

They'd never reach the inn before Chapman at this pace, which left one option. A diversion had worked the first time; maybe it could work again.

She stood in someone's backyard, considering her options as she listened to Tweedledum and Tweedledee behind her struggle to get over the fence. What could she use to draw Chapman away from the inn?

Pressing her nose to the fence, she instructed them to knock over the metal trashcans before they climbed over.

"What'd she say?" Flo asked without the slightest concern for the level of noise she was making.

Wink let out an exasperated sigh. "Never you mind. Just get over the fence."

The damp grass made for treacherous running as Ella crossed it. She checked to be sure the coast was clear, hearing Flo hit the lawn behind her with a *thump* followed by an "Oof."

Ella slid past a doghouse to a stop where the grass met a cracked concrete driveway. Ducking under a window, she ran at a crouch. The clatter of metal trashcans being knocked over rang out from the alley, loud enough to wake the dead.

"Atta girl, Wink," she whispered. That should distract the sheriff.

A growl came from behind.

Her voice quivered. "Flo?"

She spun in time to see fangs bearing down on her. Crying out, she stumbled back, falling onto her haunches. The dog —a Rottweiler with an ear-splitting bark—lunged.

Time slowed as she zeroed in on those sharp teeth, the foam-flecked lips, and the chain trailing away from the dog's collar, unfurling to its limit. The dog yelped as it came to the end of its tether and dropped like a rock.

"Ha!" She scrambled to a sitting position. "That's what you get Cujo."

The dog, still within reach of her leg, lunged. He bit down as she scrabbled further back. His teeth missed skin and bone but managed to skewer her pants. With jaws like a vise, the dog clenched down on the loose fabric.

Each tug of her leg only resulted in him tightening his hold as he shook his head from side to side. She swore under her breath. The one time she wore loose clothing, and it bites her in the leg.

She clawed at the ground in a feeble attempt to crawl away. Glimpsing across the dark yard, she spotted Wink tumbling over the fence, joining Flo. Every precious second Ella wasted on this losing game of tug of war was costing her.

A light flicked on inside the house, the owner probably awoken from all the noise. Before she could chicken out, she kicked off her shoes, unbuttoned her jeans, and slipped out of her pants. The dog took off with her jeans. Moments later, the sounds of fabric being shredded emanated from the doghouse.

After collecting her shoes, she sprinted to join Wink and Flo at the driveway, and the trio tore across the concrete as they heard the back door crashing open.

"Who's there?" a deep voice hollered.

Cold air nipped at Ella's exposed legs. Hopping along, trying to pull her shoes back on, she trailed behind Wink, matching Flo's pace.

"Nice skivvies, Poodle Head."

"Hey, you know what I say: sky's out, thighs out. At least my underwear doesn't reach my belly button." She shot Flo a pointed look.

Ahead, Wink turned sharply down J Street. The patter of feet behind Ella made her glance back.

"Tryin' to break into my house!" A man, with more hair sprouting beneath a white shirt than was on his head, brought a shotgun to his shoulder.

"Duck!" Ella grabbed Flo and yanked her around the corner just in time.

Boom. A stop sign and the corner of the homeowner's own house caught the spray of buckshot.

"What is with you people and guns?!"

If Wink's trashcan serenade hadn't been enough to draw Chapman, the gunshot was certain to do so. Now, speed was a higher priority than being spotted, and Ella didn't bother skirting the light. Her sneakers slapped over the sidewalk, her bare thighs flapping in the wind, as she raced towards the inn.

"You know, I have to say, this is kind of freeing." But Flo was no longer running abreast. Having lagged behind, she trailed in the distance.

Ella crossed Main Street, glancing left and right, and let out a breath when she didn't spot the sheriff. Passing Wink in the front yard, she reached the stoop for the inn first, vaulting the steps. In the foyer, she gasped for air and waited for the others.

Straining, she tried to listen for Horse's hoofbeats, but either Chapman had dismounted and was on foot, or they were too far away to hear over the faint whine in her damaged ears.

Wink vaulted the steps next, breathing heavily as she slipped past Ella into the dark entrance hall.

Looking out into the night, Ella counted, "One Backstreet Boy, Two Backstreet Boys..." She got up to five Backstreet Boys before Flo hobbled up the steps, and Ella could shut the door. The boarder appeared about ready to collapse.

"Nope, not yet." Ella propped her up, veering her towards the grand staircase.

Wink had already made herself scarce, presumably in one of the many guest rooms. Ella and Flo were halfway up the steps when a muffled neigh sounded outside.

Her heart hammered against her chest. Throwing Flo's arm over her shoulders, she half carried her friend to the top, hissing for her to be quiet when she griped about Ella's rough handling.

The muffled tinkle of spurs up the stoop told her Chapman was at the front door. He pounded his fist aggressively, one of those officious, come-open-this-door-right-now knocks.

Ella released Flo at the top with a "good luck" and darted a short distance down the north wing to her room. Once inside, she left her door open a crack and put her ear to it, listening.

Someone shuffled past. Judging by the heavy footfalls and not-so-soft cursing, Flo was making for her bedroom.

She continued to listen as Jimmy, in a sleep-addled voice, opened the door, shocked to find the sheriff there. Chapman's spurs jingled as he stepped inside.

"Sheriff? Something the matter?" Jimmy's tone changed, the deputy waking to his duty.

"Where are they?"

"Who?"

But Chapman wasn't stopping to have a conversation. Steps up the stairs.

Frantic, Ella leaped onto her bed and scrambled under the covers, sending a frightened Fluffy skittering under the bed.

Light flared from the hallway, bleeding through the crack she'd left.

"They've gone too far this time," Chapman was saying outside.

She realized that her black, long sleeve shirt was still exposed, suspicious clothing for pajamas. Quickly, she pulled the silk comforter to her chin and squeezed her eyes closed.

Behind her lids, the light brightened as her door creaked open.

Thud. Thud.

"Ms. Barton, enough with the ruse."

Ella didn't move.

Chapman cleared his throat loudly. Her eyelids fluttered, and she rolled her head. Squinting, she said in as throaty of a voice as she could muster, "Sheriff? That you?"

Keeping her comforter to her chin, she sat up, blinking bleary eyes at him. "Everything okay?"

Instead of answering, he sent Jimmy to Flo's room. The innkeeper turned deputy hesitated. "You sure that's a good idea, sir? The last time I woke her during the night, she blew a hole in my wall."

"Get her" came Chapman's tight reply. The moment Jimmy left, he rounded on her. "Where were you tonight?"

"Here."

"All night?"

"Where else would I be?" She smiled innocently. "What's this about?"

He began pacing. "I let you three get away with many things. Trespassing. Breakin' and enterin'. Arson. Vandalism. Yes, I've been lenient with you." He faced her, his face in shadows. "But blowing up part of Pauline's autopsy room—you've any idea the damage you've caused tonight?" Taking off his hat, he strode forward, his duster billowing out like a wraith. "One of you coulda been seriously hurt."

She swallowed. "I'm sorry, but I don't know what you're talking about. Did you say part of the autopsy room blew up? Yikes." She feigned a gasp. "Was the professor... is he...?"

His mustache bristled. "His body's intact."

"Perhaps the killer had something to do with it?"

Silence stretched between them until, at last, Chapman said, "Perhaps." But his tone indicated he didn't believe it.

His hand rustled with something, clothing she hadn't noticed he'd been holding, and he held it up to the rectangle of light spilling from the hallway.

Her jeans.

"You recognize these dungarees?"

"Nope."

"Really?" He studied them, fingering the shredded material. "Seems they're about your size."

"If you mean small and fashionable, then I agree. Sadly, they're not mine. I mean, how often do you see me in blue jeans?"

He didn't say anything, probably because she had a point.

"Don't get me wrong, I like jeans, but the fabric doesn't really have give. I find after a few donuts, an elastic waistband is better, don't you? Besides, when I sit in jeans, I get what's called a muffin top." She proceeded to give a disturbingly vivid description of what a muffin top was.

Just when she was comparing her muffin top to an actual blueberry muffin, he shoved his hat on his head, marching for the door. "Ms. Barton," he said, interrupting, "if I find out you were involved, I won't be lenient."

"So, what you're saying is 'No more Mr. Nice Guy', right? Go on. Go ahead and say it. Oh, and can you use a tough guy voice when you do? Wait! Let me get my phone first to record it."

He stared at her for the count of at least four Backstreet Boys before slowly turning and parting. Her door shut with a soft *click*, and she threw her head back on her pillow, letting out a long breath.

From the threatening yells and subsequent crashes in the hallway, it sounded as if Flo chased Jimmy from her room by pelting him with random objects. It ended with the sound of glass shattering, probably the vase that had decorated the table at the end of the hall. Rose was not going to be pleased.

Jimmy stopped outside Ella's closed door, saying to Chapman, "Maybe it'll be best if you come by tomorrow to question her."

Chapman grunted. "I don't think I'll get much more from them." With that, their footsteps faded down the stairs.

Soon, the rush of adrenaline ebbed like a receding tide, replaced by guilt. And shame.

Rolling over, she told herself the damage wasn't so bad. Replace the hinges and scrub the storage room, and it'd be as good as new. Maybe they could find some way to help without appearing guilty.

At least tonight hadn't been a total loss. Along with a bit of exercise, she'd learned that Dr. Kaufman had died from cyanide poisoning. And all it had cost her was a pair of jeans.

CHAPTER EIGHTEEN

FAR TOO EARLY the next morning, Ella sat in her waitress uniform on a stool in Grandma's Kitchen before the diner opened, leafing through a familiar book. Before leaving the inn, she'd gone into the library and pulled the book that had helped solve Kayline's murder, titled, *If Plants Could Kill: One Hundred and One Toxic Plants*. So much had happened since last she'd leafed through the dusty pages.

Since the diner had coffee that didn't taste like lake sludge, courtesy of Wink's well, she'd been forced to come in early for her caffeine fix. She brushed croissant crumbs from her fingers before turning another page.

The section on cyanide was rather robust. It turned out it could only be detected up to two days after poisoning. If the poison was introduced through food, it would produce alkali burns in the gastrointestinal tract, most likely what had caused Pauline to first suspect it.

Further down the page were two lists of symptoms for cyanide poisoning, one for chronic, the other for acute. Two under the latter category matched the professor's state when she'd found him in the cave: difficulty breathing and cardiac arrest. Thankfully, he hadn't had a seizure, which was another symptom. She wasn't sure if either she or Judy could have handled that.

A few manifestations from the chronic poisoning list matched, as well, such as dilated pupils; clammy skin; slower, shallower breaths; and—most telling—a bright red flush. Mentally, she added cyanide poisoning to her list of "ways not to die," right up there with being shark chum.

Taking another bite, she stared out the window at the weak morning light. Surely the chemical compound was hard to come by, which was why Chapman no longer suspected Craig as the culprit. But what about the professor's head wound?

It didn't make sense. Why take a dinosaur bone to the doc's noggin and not wait for the poison to do its dirty deed? The whole point of a poison, besides being lethal, was to kill from a distance.

However, if Craig was responsible for the blow, it seemed odd to attack a man he'd cohabited with for an indeterminate amount of time. By the amount of artwork in the cave and the horde of supplies at the professor's campsite, they both had occupied the chamber for weeks. The real question, she supposed, was who had access to cyanide?

She glanced down at the page before pouring a second cup of coffee. According to what she'd read so far, cyanide could occur naturally.

She massaged her temples. It was too early for deep, analytical thinking. So she set to work prepping for a bustling Wednesday, grabbing her apron from the back, her mind pondering a different death seventeen years earlier.

Lou's shop door loomed open, like a giant maw, waiting to devour all her money. The lemons he sold sat in the lot behind the sagging building, enclosed by a chain-link fence and rusting under a spring sun. Taking a breath, she plunged into the dank garage, wading into the stench of grease and sweat.

This place was a sharp reminder of her first foray into Keystone, of getting trapped and stranded in the village—all because that lush of a mechanic hadn't traded her for a car that worked. Not that she was bitter about it.

Putting her fingers to her mouth, she blew loudly on the off chance she'd finally acquired that skill. She hadn't. The noise came out as a sputter, sounding like a referee under water.

"Hey, Lou!"

She followed the sounds of cursing and the stench of alcohol, locating the mechanic under the hood of a beautiful blue Cadillac Convertible Coupe.

He went from scowling at the car's engine to brightening upon seeing her. "Eleanor!"

"Nope. Ella. Just Ella."

"Since when?"

"Since always, Lou." She leaned against the car, admiring it.

It felt strange to be sleuthing alone, but the diner was busy enough to warrant her and Wink to stagger their lunch breaks. As for Flo, she'd mumbled something about needing to test a new inter-dimensional proximity alarm.

"This is quite the vehicle." She brushed her hand along the metal exterior.

"A 1939, about twenty-four years old. Vera sold it to me."

"Who's Vera?"

"My wife, only she don't wanna be called that. We're—what's the word?—estranged. She lives across town."

She realized she was staring. "I had no idea you were married."

He grabbed a Mason jar from a nearby utility cart overflowing with tools and took a swig, the fumes reaching her nose. Definitely not water.

She glanced at her watch. "It's 11:30, Lou."

"And?"

"And nothing." Critiquing his vices was probably not the best way to get him to talk. "The reason I came by—"

"Ya finally decided to trade in your Jeep?"

"No," she said, rather emphatically. "I wanted to ask you about something, something that happened about seventeen years ago."

He snorted. "Doubt I'll remember. I don't even remember what happened yesterday."

"That might have more to do with you drinking booze like a rockstar than faulty memory. Just a thought." She leaned against the car, studying him. "I came to ask about Charlotte Kaufman's death."

He stiffened before tipping more swill into his mouth. "What 'bout it?"

"The sheriff's report from that night states the vehicle used in her death had been taken from your lot."

"Yeah, so?"

"Were you driving it?"

He looked at her sharply, his eyes focusing. "No. It got stolen."

"Then why did you wait until after the accident to report that?"

"Didn't notice it was missing 'till Sheriff Johnson called me to tow it away."

It wasn't surprising it had gone amiss. His lot was filled with vehicles in various states of disrepair, and he wasn't exactly the observant type.

"Did you have many cars in your lot back then?"

Thinking, he used a wrench to scratch his jowls. "'Bout half the number I got now, I'd say. Many cars get abandoned in Keystone if you hadn't noticed. Especially when they run out of fuel." He'd set the jar of alcohol on the roof of the car, and she subtly dragged it away.

"Did the professor happen to come see you last week?"

"You mean before he was offed? That's a funny question. Ain't no one seen him for the past few weeks. Wasn't ol' Chapman looking for him?"

Half the town had been searching high and low for the physicist. "I have reason to believe the professor was sneaking into town just before he died, asking people about the night his wife died."

"And you think he'd come here?"

"Asking about the car, yes."

Lou licked dry lips, his hand instinctively reaching for the jar, but it swiped air instead. "Only time he ever came 'round askin' questions was just after the accident."

"And what did you tell him?"

"The same thing I told Sheriff Johnson. I didn't recognize the car 'til I drove up to tow it away." He squinted rheumy eyes, searching out the jar, and grabbed it. "Piece of junk, if you ask me. Never been able to sell it."

She sucked in a breath. "The car's still here?"

"Sure is. I scrapped it for parts 'cause no one was gonna buy a car that killed a broad."

"You've got such a way with words, Lou."

His chest puffed out at the compliment.

"Can I see it?"

"The car?" His skin glistened with perspiration as he angled his head, pondering. "Yeah, I guess. Don't see what it can hurt."

Cradling his drink, he led her out back. He'd seemed on edge, talking about the accident, but as they stepped deeper into his domain, his usual affable demeanor emerged.

"See, the man *was* the priest," he said, finishing with the punchline to a joke he'd been telling as they stepped onto the south end of the enclosed lot.

She gave a weak laugh. "Ha. That's funny. And not at all racist or sexist." She gave him a hearty slap on the back, then discreetly wiped the same hand on her waitress uniform.

They stood in front of a black Buick that appeared straight from the 1930s. At any moment, old-time gangsters would come pouring out with Tommy guns. The vehicle was well-used and had more nicks and dents than Chevy Chase's ego after a celebrity roast.

Lou slurped his booze, the contents of which were considerably lower than when she'd first arrived. She wondered if his drinking was why Vera lived across town now.

With one hand on the Mason jar, the other one fidgeted with his greasy coveralls. The laugh lines around his eyes had disappeared again.

After much tugging, she managed to pry open the driver-side door. It creaked and groaned as it fell open. The back seat appeared to be missing, but the front bench seat was intact, as was most of the dash.

Leaning in, she was careful not to touch anything as she inspected the steering column. "Was it dusted for prints?" she asked, glancing at the mechanic through the cracked windshield.

"Yeah, but the sheriff never found none."

"I'm assuming he dusted the door handle and the seat adjuster?"

Lou just gave a shrug and tucked into his booze, his eyes roving the lot. Before shutting the door, she took photographs, noting the distance from the bench seat to the steering wheel and gas pedal. "Did you have to move the seat at all before you towed it?"

"Don't remember. Probably not."

She edged around the trunk, noting that grass grew to the height of the wheel wells. Another car was crammed too tightly on the passenger side for her to squeeze through, so she retraced her steps. Ending at the front, she looked at the dent in the grill.

If this were a TV show, forensic techs would have pulled fibers and DNA from the front of the car. Even if she could do the same, the information gathered wouldn't tell her anything new. She already knew who the victim was.

Nothing amiss stood out. Whatever the professor had seen in the newspaper to renew his interest in his wife's death had nothing to do with the car itself.

As they meandered back to his shop, she listened with half an ear as he told another joke. If she knew what sort of questions the professor had been asking, it would help greatly. But since he hadn't come to Lou, that left only one other source.

What she had to do next filled her with dread, and she looked forward to it like she looked forward to the dentist appointment she needed to make in a town with equipment stuck half a century in the past. Gritting her teeth, she waved a farewell to the mechanic and headed back to the diner.

There was no way she was going to talk to the new mayor without reinforcements, even if those reinforcements were senile and as benign as a jar of Quicklime and water.

CHAPTER NINETEEN

THE CRACK OF a bat was a sweet, familiar sound to Ella's ears. Standing at the edge of the high school's baseball field, she breathed in the scent of dirt and freshly mowed grass. Memories resurfaced of being hunched over in the rain, the smell of her leather mitt, and the excitement as another school year wound down. Her high school stint on the softball team had ended her senior year when her face caught a ground ball on a bounce, chipping her front teeth and splitting her chin.

"Aren't you starting practices a couple weeks early?" She turned from the baseball diamond to Sal, the team's coach—because owning his own barbershop, being a hobby meteorologist, and becoming the newly elected mayor wasn't enough.

"There aren't many other sports they can play."

"Sure, there's football, hockey, basketball, volleyball..." She trailed off as it dawned on her. "Ah, I see. Those would require a large team and other teams to play against."

His slicked-back hair shone in the sun. "We have other sports, but we're limited to what the community and church leagues want to play."

That explained why the team was playing with softballs rather than baseballs. The two other teams in town played softball.

She became briefly distracted as a batter lobbed a fly ball high into the air. The third baseman caught it easily and rocketed it to the second baseman, who slapped his glove on the runner from first base. Both batter and runner were out.

A few yards away, Flo lounged on a wooden bench with a couple players who were waiting for their turn at bat, showing them how to spit properly. Below the bench, Chester, wearing a lime green tracksuit today, scrounged for peanuts and sunflower seeds.

Wink called to him, which resulted in little more than the rodent twitching his bushy tail. Sal watched her tensely. She seemed to notice because she said in a tight voice, "How's the new job treating you? I hope it's not too overwhelming."

"It's going swell." He cleared his throat. "Listen, Wink. I hope we can put this behind us. No hard feelings?" He held out a hand.

Wink studied the proffered hand, her expression guarded. Several tense breaths later, she shook it.

"I'm not going to say the best person won." Her hand fell away. "But I will say the second best candidate for the job did."

Ella nodded. "Better you than Lou or—God forbid—Patience." She shivered.

After telling the next batter to aim for the shortstop, he said, "So what brings you ladies out? I suppose you want to accuse me of the professor's murder?"

"Is that a confession?" This earned Ella a satisfying glare. "We wanted to know why the professor came to see you last week."

Sal's gaze remained fixated on his team. "I don't know what you're talking about."

"So, you want to play it like that? Fair enough." Turning, she hollered Flo's name.

The boarder acknowledged Ella with a nod and waltzed onto the outfield. As she did, she began sprinkling granules from her pockets.

"W-what's she doing?"

Wink smiled sweetly. "Tossing out dandelion seeds."

"What? Tell her to stop!" Sal's face turned red, then purple, then he screamed at Flo.

"She'll stop," Ella said, "if you answer our questions."

He waved a distracted hand. "Yes, fine. Just tell her to stop."

Ella hollered at Flo, who'd somehow managed to reach center field at her snail pace, but her shouts fell on deaf ears. "We have got to get her hearing checked."

"I'll get her." Wink jogged across the grass, leaping over a ground ball that rolled down left field.

Now alone with Sal, Ella couldn't help but notice his cold stare. "Heh, how about this weather, am I right?"

One of the veins on his forehead stood out. After whistling a few bars of Horatio's sea shanty, she said, "So... about that conversation with the professor...?"

Sal threw his hands up. "What do you want to know? Hmm? I already talked to Jimmy—pardon, Deputy Murray—about this. Dr. Kaufman came to see me, asking about that night. I told him the same thing I told him years ago, the same thing I told Jimmy on Monday, and the same darn thing I told Sheriff Johnson that night."

"That night? The night Charlotte died?" Then it dawned on her. The newspaper article had mentioned two Good Samaritans arriving on the scene. "You were one of the two who tried to help."

"I didn't see what happened. I was in my apartment above my shop, heard the crash and went running."

"What did you see when you got there?"

His lungs deflated, his face pinching in a way that said he was reliving a painful memory and had told this story too many times.

"The car was sitting there, headlights glaring, the driver seat empty." He blinked, looking away. "Mrs. Kaufman was on the ground. She succumbed to her injuries shortly after."

"Did you ask her if she saw the driver?"

"She wasn't..." He swallowed.

"Cogent?" she offered, and he nodded. "I'm sorry. That must've been hard."

"Not as hard as it was on the professor."

The outfield team flooded in, swarming the bench, switching positions with the batters. Gloves were tossed, exchanged for bats.

"Who was the other person?"

"Pardon?"

"The newspaper mentioned two people had tried to help."

Sal's mouth turned down. "Norman Baxter."

Ella's body went cold. "Flo's ex-husband, Norman Baxter? That Norman Baxter?"

He grunted. "I didn't know they were married."

"Neither did she."

"It's kind of hard to forget that night, Ms. Barton. Especially when I keep getting asked about it." He gave her a pointed look, a skill he seemed to be improving upon.

At that moment, Wink and Flo rejoined them, the latter's bouffant bending precipitously in the breeze.

"Thanks for your time." Ella wiggled her fingers in a half-hearted wave before nudging the other two towards Wink's parked car.

It was a moment of weakness brought on by empathy over the haunting pain in Sal's eyes when reliving that night. Before she could reconsider, she turned back to Sal and blurted out, "We were the ones who broke your window. I just thought you should know. It wasn't Six. So, if you're going to be mad at anyone, be mad at us and leave Chapman alone."

Instead of raging or blowing a gasket as she'd expected, Sal's voice came out low and constrained. "Do you really think I didn't know that? Did you really think I wouldn't suspect you crazy hags, *first*?"

"Hags? Really?" Ella aimed a thumb over her shoulder back at Flo. "Maybe this one fits that description, bu—"

"That outlaw's caused more trouble than the three of you combined."

"Well, I don't know about that..." She glanced back. Flo seemed to have taken personal offense to Sal's claim.

"It's time he goes. And for whatever reason, Chapman's unwilling to do his job and get rid of that scourge on this town. As far as I'm concerned, that makes him just as guilty of Six's deeds. And need I remind you the sheriff kept the time device a secret?"

"He didn't know about it that long before the rest of the town. Besides, he was only keeping it confidential until he had control of the situation."

Sal's nostrils flared. "He should've told the council about it immediately. *That's* why Chapman should be kicked out of office. It's got nothing to do with my stupid window. That man's not fit to wear a badge."

Seething, Ella felt her cheeks heat up. "Listen here, Dracula. There's a lot about him you don't know. Chapman has his reasons for running the town the way he does."

"And there's a lot *you* don't know, Ms. Barton."

"He's a good man. Does he sometimes take a liberal interpretation of the law, playing his own judge, jury, and executioner? Sure. Could he use a mustache trim? Absolutely. Also, he could stand to smile once in a while—"

Wink cleared her throat.

"But the point is, he upholds the law and has done a good job of keeping this town safe. I mean, look what he's up against." She hooked her thumb over her shoulder again.

"Hey," Flo called out.

Wink whispered in Ella's ear that they should leave and tugged on her elbow. Ella shot Sal a parting look she hoped conveyed that their conversation wasn't over before allowing herself to be pulled away.

As the trio traipsed across the field, Flo turned out her pockets, dumping the rest of the dandelion seeds onto the grass. The new mayor wouldn't suffer as much as the groundskeeper would come a few weeks later when the weeds poked through, but that didn't stop Ella from patting Flo on the shoulder in solidarity.

Riding in the back seat, her mind was a tempest of dark thoughts, most of them swirling around Sal.

Wink turned right on Main Street. "Did you learn anything from talking to Sal?"

"Besides the fact that he's a muppet? Yes. He was one of the Good Samaritans who'd tried to save Charlotte."

Wink glanced back in the rearview mirror. "Really? Did he say who the other person was?"

"Norman."

Flo twisted around, the maneuver easy since she wasn't buckled. Noticing this, Wink slammed on the brakes, sending Flo sprawling into the dashboard. After she buckled, she rotated around to face Ella again.

"Did you know?" she asked before Flo could say anything.

"Now that you say it, it sorta rings a bell."

"A very empty bell. I don't suppose you remember him talking about that night?" But the woman's short attention had already flitted to the window where, outside, a dog dragged its owner behind a leash. After Ella called the boarder's name a few times, Flo gave a flippant response that she didn't remember Norm talking about that night.

CHAPTER TWENTY

BEFORE DINNER, ELLA went to the conservatory to read more about cyanide from the book on toxic plants, arranging to meet back up with Wink and Flo in the murder room after dinner. When last she saw them, Wink ran interference in the kitchen to ensure one of Rose's gelatin molds didn't make it to the table, and Flo had descended into the basement to work on a "ghost catcher" after Wink had claimed specters were nothing more than figments of the woman's addled brain.

Fluffy attacked a fly near the bistro table before flopping over and licking himself. Through the partial glass ceiling, a brilliant sunset of gold and pink painted the sky, gilding the plants around Ella in hues of bronze.

She plucked a cherry tomato from a nearby plant before settling in. It only took moments for Fluffy to claim her lap, and he curled up, purring. Chewing, she picked up where she'd left off in her reading, then skimmed, her finger dragging down the page slowly, until she found what she was looking for: naturally occurring sources for the chemical compound. It was, after all, a book on toxic plants.

Amygdalin, a dangerous chemical, could be found in the seeds of stone fruits such as plums, peaches, and nectarines.

If ingested, the body converted amygdalin into cyanide. Cyanide compounds could also be found in lima beans, apples, and bitter almonds. The poison itself was renowned for smelling like almonds but didn't always have a scent.

She glanced down at Fluffy, the Maine Coon's eyes now closed. "Well, looks like I'll be avoiding fruit for the foreseeable future. Not that I ate a lot, to begin with."

Why couldn't amygdalin be more prevalent in vegetables? She'd have no problem avoiding that food group.

As she read on, she found she may have been hasty in her decision. Apparently, the amount of amygdalin in the seeds of stone fruit varied widely, even amongst the same fruit picked from different geographic locations. The amount ranged from negligible to "chew on those seeds and you'll die a horrible death."

Because the amount of amygdalin varied so widely, it was difficult to gauge how many seeds were required for accidental poisoning, but a footnote read that there were reported cases of intentional poisoning using just a few ground-up cherry pits.

It looked like fruit was back on her menu—except for maybe cherries. Those she'd give the hairy eyeball next time they showed up in one of Rose's gelatin molds.

The book went on to describe death by cyanide poisoning in grisly detail. As she was entranced by a particular passage about how it deprived cells in the body of oxygen, a distant bell rang, Rose's way of calling them all to dinner after she'd gotten tired of shouting throughout the large manor. Setting the book aside, Ella gave Fluffy a parting scratch under the chin, then left the conservatory, praying the innkeeper hadn't prepared anything with fruit.

An hour later, Ella stood in front of the murder board. "Alright, let's rehash what we know."

This statement was met by groans, protests she ignored. "Charlotte Kaufman was killed on the night of March 8, 1946, while on a walk. The driver split, leaving the vehicle behind. Sal heard the accident from his place above his shop and came running. Our second knight in shining armor was Norman Baxter, a.k.a. one of Flo's marital victims."

Flo flipped up her middle finger.

Hands clasped behind her back, Ella paused in front of the window, feeling every bit like Sherlock Holmes. And Will claimed she was Watson. What did he know? The man wore suspenders, which automatically undermined his opinion.

"We need to talk to Norm," Wink said. "Get his version of that night."

"Agreed." Ella resumed her summation. "After the three of us expertly discovered the professor's machine, he went into hiding where he survived in a cave on water and canned food, living alongside a caveman. At some point, most likely after reading *this* article covering the anniversary of his wife's death—" Ella tapped the *Keystone Corner* edition still taped to the mirror "—he risked coming into town to talk with one of the Good Samaritans that night. A few days later, he's poisoned and hit on the head."

The big question was, was his death related to either the time device or Charlotte's accident?

The black-and-white image of the car drew her gaze, and she recalled her conversation with Lou. The mechanic had behaved oddly—even for him. What was he hiding?

Turning, she studied their mostly non-existent suspect list, but she found her eyes traveling back to that photo. It itched the back of her brain as if she was overlooking something. Charlotte lay on the ground several feet from the Buick, the front bumper dented in line with the driver-side. It appeared congruent with physics. Yet...

Stepping closer, she leaned in, her nose close enough to smell the ink. There. The cracks in the windshield. She'd noticed them when speaking to Lou. A spider web of lines crawling out from an impact point over the passenger-side. The kind of impact that happens when a person is flipped up over the hood of the car and hits the glass.

Try as she might, she couldn't envision a scenario where Charlotte hit the bumper on the driver-side of the car, tumbled up to the passenger-side of the windshield, impacted it, and then be thrown *forward* in an opposite trajectory and not up over the car.

"El, you okay?" Wink asked.

"Be right back."

She darted down the hall to her bedroom and returned with a couple of items. She set Tubsy, her recently acquired gnome, on the dresser and used a large picture frame to represent the black Buick that had hit Charlotte. Using the props, she reenacted the accident—complete with sound effects—having the gnome hit the frame in the same place that coincided with the damage to the car.

Wink tilted her head, pinning Ella with a perplexed expression. Flo, who'd returned to her wallpaper project, toddled to her feet and insisted on controlling the picture-frame-car.

Reluctantly, Ella complied, and they ran through the scenario again. When she forced Tubsy in a slow motion impact to the bumper, then the windshield, then had him fly forward, Wink let out a gasp.

"It couldn't have happened like that."

Flo's beehive tickled Ella's cheek as she craned her head closer. "What if she didn't hit the glass?"

"You mean, maybe the cracks were there before the accident?"

"Or maybe Charlotte wasn't alone."

Ella's mouth fell open. "You're right." She beamed at the crazy woman. "See? I knew there had to be a brain in there somewhere capable of intelligent thought."

"Don't be so clandestine."

"Aaand there it goes." Ella slipped out of the room, returning a moment later with a second gnome, the one Six had gifted her the Christmas before last.

Wink manned the second gnome as they ran through the accident scenario a third time. Using gnarled hands, Flo slid the picture frame to a stop, making screeching tire sound effects with her mouth.

In Ella's hands, the Charlotte gnome went flying forward after hitting the bumper approximately where the damage was in the photo. At the same time, Wink rolled the second gnome in slow motion over the hood of the car, impacted the windshield, and continued its motion, landing behind and off to the side.

The room fell silent, their hands stilled, as they inspected the scene. The guest room door burst open, and Rose came in, humming. Her kitten heels slid to an abrupt halt when she noticed them.

She looked from their guilty faces to her antique mirror covered in marker to the overturned picture frame and garden gnomes.

Her mouth opened, then closed. Slowly, she backed out of the room, saying, "I'll just put these away another time."

After the door closed, Ella asked, "That can't be the worst thing she's seen in her inn, right?"

Wink had moved to the murder board to inspect the photograph closely. "If we're right, then the second person should've landed here." Her finger thumped a spot off to the side of the road.

"Maybe they didn't get as injured," Flo threw out as she rammed the photo frame into the gnomes, knocking them over like bowling pins.

"Shouldn't there be a second dent in the bumper?" Ella asked.

"I think there is. Look." Wink pointed to faint damage Ella had overlooked. "I'm not a physicist—that's Will's forte— but if someone went over the hood and hit the windshield, that would mean the bumper took less of an impact. Unlike in Charlotte's case." The diner owner's finger swept out, indicating the distance to the body.

Ella digested all of this, nodding slowly, looking back at the picture frame and gnomes. "It fits. From now on, let's assume two people were hit. What are the chances the hospital still has medical records from that night?" If the car was going fast enough to kill Charlotte, then perhaps it had injured the second victim enough to warrant a trip to the ER —or Keystone's backwater version of it.

"They destroy them after ten years," Wink said, her tone disappointed. "I know this because a few months back I had to listen to Shirley gripe during art class about her arthritis acting up on account of her pulling files all day to be destroyed."

It had been a long shot, anyway.

Ella tapped Flo's shoulder. "It's really important we talk to Norm."

"What's that got to do with me?"

Ella exchanged an exasperated expression with Wink before saying, "Could you just call and ask him if we can stop by for a visit? You know, since you wouldn't let me get his phone number."

Her personal questions for Norm regarding his marriage to Flo would have to wait. Top of the list, though, was "Does she look like Kenny G when her hair's down?"

After much coercing and ear-pulling from Wink, Flo caved and said she'd ring Norm up. The Keystone Gators dispersed with a lackluster group cheer led by Ella, the others mumbling under their breath.

Wink, who'd agreed to give Ella a ride up the hill to check on Will, descended the staircase to wait while Ella gathered her toiletries. She may as well get a bath out of the trip.

Downstairs in the parlor, she found her boss chatting with the innkeepers.

"Jimmy?" She dropped her bag of items by the door. "Do you have a minute?"

His smile faltered, and he climbed to his feet. "Sure. This about Pauline's office?"

She coughed. "No, but I heard about that. Terrible business. Is the damage bad?"

"Mostly superficial, but the door for the cold room's no good. Chapman found an old one from a meat locker he thinks'll fit."

Her back to him, she let out a small breath. They'd gotten lucky.

They ducked into the study, and he ran a hand through his thinning hair, watching her. "I can't tell you anything about the investigation if that's what you're after."

"Actually, I wanted to tell you something that might help."

His forehead crinkled, which she took as encouragement to continue.

"I was reading an interesting book earlier." She tried to drape her arm on the mantle, but since she was on the shorter side and it the taller side, the pose was anything but natural. However, she'd already committed, so she went with it.

"It talked about cyanide poisoning and how it can occur naturally in stone fruit. Well, not cyanide itself, but amygdalin, which our bodies turn into cyanide. Anyway, apricot and cherry pits have especially high concentrations. I just thought you might want to look into that. Maybe see if anyone's bought fruit recently in high quantities from Stewart's or the greenhouses." She stopped, finally taking a breath.

He stared. "Where did you hear it was cyanide poisoning? Did you bribe Pauline?"

"No, but it's good to know she can be bribed." She wondered what the doctor could be tempted with. Booze? More pockets for her coat?

"Well, thank you for the information." Striding for the door, he paused. "Ella? Be careful, please. I've got a bad feeling about this one. I think whoever killed the professor is especially dangerous." With that, he marched out of the study, leaving her to brood alone.

While Will devoured the roast beef sandwich Rose had sent with Ella, she updated him on their investigations. His scrawling equations had expanded beyond the chalkboards, spilling over onto the walls.

"I really like what you've done with the place."

He followed her gaze. "Yes, I thought I'd try something new. Those gray walls were getting drab."

"I noticed you turned the electricity back on."

"I'm mostly flipping switches and taking measurements at this point, so there's less fear of electrocution."

"*Less* implies some."

He gave a lazy shrug, shoving bread crust into his mouth.

After he finished, she lingered, helping when she could. However, when she tipped over his tool box, she left the basement and wandered into the house. Now in the dining room, she listened to the muffled pounding and Will's distant cursing coming through the floor. The inventor and Flo really did have much in common.

She considered going over to Wink's to bathe, but instead, settled at the table with the professor's spy book and the timelines he'd drawn up. Her mind kept drifting to the Kaufmans' deaths. Being a visual person, she took inspiration from the timeline sketches and drew out her own for the professor and his wife.

Flipping one of the sheets over, she dragged out a line with a pencil, then marked off branches. Two signified the beginning and ending of WWII, which spanned from September 1, 1939, to September 2, 1945.

On the third offshoot, she noted the Kaufmans' arrival to Keystone as some time in 1945. The next line and date were for March 8, 1946, the date of Charlotte's death. Following that was the town's first jump on August 21, 1951. And finally, she ended with the professor's death the previous Sunday, March 17, 1963.

Leaning back in her chair, she rubbed her eyes and studied the timeline. She didn't glean anything by writing it out other than to sort out the events in her brain. The papers beneath bore the professor's invented timelines, events that had never occurred, and it filled her with dread. The time device had the potential to be a terrible, dangerous machine, capable of altering history and destroying humanity's future.

Don't fix it.

The knot in her stomach tightened, and she struggled to breathe. She caught her reflection in the black window, skin pale, eyes big.

The lights blinked out, plunging her into darkness. What on earth?

She groped for her phone, muttering, "*Now* he turns the electricity off."

He must have thought she'd left. Using her phone as a light, she stepped out into the night. At this elevation, a biting chill cut through her sweatshirt.

Her feet shuffled on the concrete steps into the cellar. Odd noises sounded within, almost like scuffling and grunting.

"Will?"

"El, run!"

CHAPTER TWENTY-ONE

ELLA SKIPPED THE last two steps into the basement. Wielding her cell phone, she shined it around the pitch-black room. Will lay in the main aisle between shelving, clutching his head and groaning.

Kneeling, she rested the phone on the concrete floor and searched him for wounds. "What happened?"

A figure darted out from the darkness, kicking the phone away. It skittered across the floor.

She dove aside just in time as the figure barreled past like a shadowy juggernaut. Then she scrambled to her knees, searching for the assailant. Where had they gone?

The pounding of footsteps.

She spun, glimpsing the intruder fleeing down the main aisle. Her cell phone had landed in the corner, backlighting the figure, revealing the shape of a trench coat and fedora. Then the shadow fled up the steps.

Will had struggled to a sitting position and was clutching his head. "Coward!" he spat at the empty air. "Come back and face me!"

Ella's heart beat rapidly, and she waited for the sound of the attacker to fade before she moved.

"Will, don't." She put a hand on his chest, stopping him from going after the intruder.

Still shaking, she retrieved her phone and inspected his head. A trickle of blood meandered down his forehead, his knuckles cracked and bruising. "Looks like you might have gotten a shot in yourself."

He glanced down at the knuckles, his ears reddening. "It was pitch black."

She considered the odd reply. "So, you hit…?"

"A shelf." His eyes darkened. "What sort of coward jumps a man in the dark? That's not a fair fight. He should come back and face me like a man."

"Alright, Rocky." She shined the light in his eyes to check his pupils, drawing a protest from him. When she tried to help him to his feet, he shook her off. Apparently, the assailant had wounded Will's pride, as well as his head.

Her light swathed the room as she searched for the breaker box. She froze.

"Will," she whispered, pointing a trembling hand.

Sprawled across the concrete wall in chalk were the words, *Fix the machine.*

He spat on the floor for a second time. "A childish prank. Probably the Murphy brothers, angry I haven't fixed it yet. Do they think I'm up here playing cards?"

She didn't think it was the Murphy brothers or a prank or even an upset citizen.

Don't fix it. He'll use it and change everything.

"Will, there's something I need to tell you."

Chapman stared at the chalk letters. His hat lay on a nearby shelf, and his swept-back silver hair nearly glowed under the bulbs in the nutty professor's workshop.

"And you couldn't see 'im?"

"He flipped the breaker when I was over there." Will pointed to the section at the far end that housed the machine.

"Ms. Barton?" The sheriff turned his laser focus on her.

"I couldn't see anything either except—I could be wrong, it was nearly pitch-black, mind you—but I think the intruder was wearing a trench coat and a fedora."

"I'm not sure what a trench coat is. Fedora... that's what you call that Stetson you wear, right, William?"

"Yes, sir. It is."

Chapman's fingers rolled the end of his mustache as he pondered the chalk message a moment more. Turning, he scooped up his derby hat. "I can't spare my deputy right now to come play guard here, much as I want to. You're just gonna have to find a way to lock them double doors from the inside."

He paused to inspect the lump on the back of Will's head and determined it must've been quite the "floorer" for such a good-sized goose egg.

"There's more," Will said as the sheriff started to leave. His gaze flitted to Ella. "Tell him."

She gave a subtle shake of her head. When she'd told Will what the professor had said with his last breath, he'd slumped onto a crate and churned over the words aloud until they sounded foreign to her ears. Anything the professor said carried weight with the inventor, which was why her stomach had clenched upon seeing the conflict on Will's face. He was considering heeding Dr. Kaufman's words, yet, doing so would ensure he never saw his sister again.

"What do you need to tell me, Ms. Barton?"

She swallowed past a dry throat, took a breath, and gave Chapman a rushed, breathy account of the professor's final moments.

When she finished, he stared quietly before, at last, saying, "So, the professor thought that infernal contraption shouldn't be fixed, and this fellow—" he inclined his head at the scrawled message "—demands it should be. That about the sum of it?"

She nodded. The tension she'd been holding in her shoulders eased when he didn't chide her about withholding information.

Will folded his arms. "What do you want to do?"

Chapman, who'd been carrying his hat, mashed it onto his head. "I'll not let some *curly wolf* bulldoze my town, intimidating folks, dictating what we do. The council and the mayor decide that, and fixing the machine's their top priority."

But the council didn't have all the facts, Ella thought. Looking around, she realized all three of them had a bias. All three of them were transplants to the village and had a strong motivation to return home—more than those on the council would. Except for that nut job Patience, the council members were native to Keystone.

"So," she began tentatively, "we don't tell anyone about the professor's warning?"

"For now."

Torn, Ella stared at the message scrawled on the wall, remembering how well it had gone the first time they'd kept a secret related to the time device.

Wink stared at Ella, eyes wide. "How scary! You should've come and gotten me!"

It was the next morning, and the Keystone Gators sat in the diner in their usual corner booth just before it opened.

"I wanted to, but Will refused. I'm not sure his ego could have withstood anymore bruising by admitting he'd been bested in a fight." She gripped the warm brew of coffee in her hands. Her fingers had gone cold while retelling the ordeal the night before.

Wink consoled her by scooting forward another bear claw.

"Is he okay?" Flo asked, a crease forming between her brows in uncharacteristic concern.

"Will? He's fine. Nothing aspirin and a bandaid didn't fix."

"But is his face fine? They didn't ruin that handsome mug, did they?"

"No—"

"'Cause he's got those dimples."

"Stop."

"And those dreamy blue eyes."

"Gross, you're old enough to be his grandmother." It wasn't the first time she'd had to remind Flo of this fact.

"You say that like it's a bad thing."

Ella dropped the donut back onto the plate. "Well, there goes my appetite."

She brushed her fingers on a napkin, eager to change the subject. "Any news on the repairs at the water treatment plant? I'm getting tired of using lake water every time I need to flush the toilet. It does not smell good, let me tell you." She then proceeded to describe the pungent odor until Wink interrupted her.

"What do you think the person who attacked Will wanted?"

Flo blinked spider-leg mascara eyelashes at Wink. "Weren't you listening? They want the time thingie fixed." Looking at Ella, she twirled her finger around her ear, indicating Wink had a few screws loose.

Like she was one to talk.

"That's what the message said. I think it's someone upset about getting stranded." She took a long drink, avoiding their eyes.

Leaning back in the booth, she listened to her two friends argue. They were like a family now. But they were born and raised in this town, unlike her and Will. This was the only home they'd ever known.

Sure, they were all equally cut off from the outside world, but they didn't have the tortuous past of being ripped away from loved ones, from their home, from their own era. They would never know that deep, heart-wrenching pain.

It didn't mean they should be kept in the dark. They were her partners, and she'd tell them—just not today. She didn't have the energy to have the same conversation for a third time in less than twenty-four hours.

At an unspoken signal from Wink, Ella floated into the kitchen and returned with a smoothie. She slid it across the table to Flo.

"What's this?"

"It's called a smoothie."

"What's it for?"

"To drink, dummy," Wink said.

Flo's eyes narrowed. "What d'you put in it, Poodle Head? You trying to poison me?"

"Not today. Someday, probably. But not today."

The woman prodded it with a ponderous finger. "Looks like a milkshake."

"It's not." Ella made a drinking motion with her hand. "Go on."

"Why aren't you drinkin' any?"

"Because I already had one."

Wink cleared her throat.

"Two," Ella corrected. "I had two. And part of a third. Come to think of it, I should probably take a break from them for a few days."

Flo bypassed the straw and dipped her tongue in the liquid, testing it. "You makin' me a drink seems too... nice. I don't like it. What do you want? You obviously want something."

"Just wondering if that cobweb-filled brain of yours has remembered if your ex ever talked about the night of the accident."

"Which one?"

Ella's face scrunched in confusion. "Which one, what? Which accident?"

"Which ex?"

She already regretted not poisoning that smoothie. She looked to Wink for help.

"For Pete's sake. Your ex-husband, Norm. The man who tried to save Charlotte."

Ella sucked in a steadying breath before saying, "You said you couldn't really remember him talking about that night. Is that still true? Did anything come back to you since then?" She could swear she heard a hamster wheel frantically spinning in the woman's head.

"He never talked about it. I met him after Charlotte passed, before he was sent to the slammer."

"Did you remember what he went to prison for?"

"Nope, but he did a nickel."

Wink snorted. "Don't pretend you know how they talk."

"I think," Flo said loudly, shooting a glare at Wink, "he was locked up from… maybe late 1946 to 1951?"

Ella considered the dates. "1951… He was released the same year as the town's first jump."

"Do you think that means something?" Wink asked.

"No, not really. It's just a date that stands out to me is all."

Wink's voice dipped to a whisper, the sound of rustling leaves, as she said, "For all of us."

Ella felt a pang of guilt for her earlier assumption. Perhaps they did share a similar pain to those stranded.

She forced the thought aside. "What'd he say, Flo, when you called him last night?"

"Says we can stop by his work this afternoon," Flo said before finally slurping the smoothie. She spewed it out a moment later. "Is there sage in this?"

CHAPTER TWENTY-TWO

A LINE OF horses, wagons, cars, and people on foot trailed beneath two large water towers. They held empty buckets, animal troughs, and stoneware jugs, waiting their turn to fill them from the town's remaining water supply.

As it turned out, Flo's ex worked at the water treatment plant. It was located near Twin Springs, off the dirt lane that led to Six's homestead.

Wink's Oldsmobile rounded a copse of pine trees, and a handful of small industrial buildings came into view.

"I had no idea this was here." Ella gripped the seat after a particularly teeth-jarring bounce.

Behind the row of structures that made up the facility were tanks and what looked like swimming pools surrounded by walkways and catwalks.

"Lots of folks back there needing water," Flo remarked.

They parked in front of the nearest building, and Wink turned off the engine. "It'll be a lot worse soon. I'm helping all I can, but there's only so much my well can pump. I also got to worry about robbing the water table from my neighbors."

Climbing out of the vehicle, Ella glanced back at the string of townspeople, her heart going out to them. A light breeze whipped at her clothes as she walked to the structure.

"I wonder why the town doesn't dip into its emergency supply in the caves?"

"Probably waiting for the council's approval." Wink's tone edged with a bitterness she reserved for any time she referenced the council.

Inside, the metal and concrete building hummed with machinery and people—which, judging by their attire, not all were workers at the facility. It was probably all hands on deck and then some until they could get the problem fixed.

The trio located Norm near the east end of the building, shouting gauge readings to a coworker.

"Too bad they don't have walkie-talkies," Ella muttered, wincing at all the commotion.

Norm noticed them and waved them off to the side. A minute later, he nabbed a young man to switch places with him. After he led them back the way they'd come, they clustered near the entrance, which was relatively peaceful by comparison.

Norm took off his hard hat and ran a hand through damp hair, an expression of exhaustion on his face.

"Thanks for meeting with us," Ella said.

He forced a harried smile. "I don't have long. We got to get the pumps going again. By our projections, the town's water towers'll be dry by end of day Friday."

"That's tomorrow," Wink said.

His chest deflated, and he let out a small, "Oh."

Ella opened her mouth, about to ask about Charlotte's accident, when Flo interjected with, "Can we see it?"

"Pardon?"

"The rest of this shindig." The boarder swept a hand around the interior of the building, narrowly missing Ella's head. "I wanna know how all this works."

"You do?" he asked.

Ella and Wink echoed this sentiment. "You do?"

"What? I'm curious."

"Y-yeah, sure." He checked his watch, standing taller at her sudden interest in his job. "I can give a real quick tour."

As they filed outside, Ella kept a skeptical eye on Flo, wondering what she was up to. Norm marched ahead, and they had to power walk to keep pace. Their first stop was at the pools. Ella's reflection rippled at her feet as he rattled off the purpose for each basin.

After he prattled on, he concluded by saying, "The water comes from both the lake and underground spring."

The sound of water falling into the nearest pool wasn't unlike a soothing waterfall—except for the smell.

"Aren't you worried about tapping out the underground aquifer?" Ella asked. "I'm sure it's got a finite supply now that it's cut off from whatever was feeding it before the town began... you know." Most of the locals detested the phrase "time travel" and generally liked to pretend Keystone Village was normal.

"Actually, it's replenished often with the run-off from the hills, along with all the rainfall and snow we capture while in certain climes. Remember when we got snowed in a year back?"

How could she forget?

"That's kept us supplied for over a year. Also, folks capture rain for their gardens, which helps."

She nodded. "Explains all the rain barrels in people's yards."

The sun broke from behind a cloud, warming her skin. As they ambled around the glittering pools, steam rose from the surrounding concrete, wet from a recent drizzle. Who knew how long this season would last, but it had the smell of spring and new life.

"The council's pretty stringent about how much can be collected so we don't rob from the aquifer, and they've set strict limitations on water use. Also we, uh, recycle."

"Recycle?" Ella stopped short, considering this. "You know what, I don't want to know more. Some things are better left with a little mystery." The smell emanating from a nearby pool was enough to curb any further curiosity on the matter.

A metal gangway rattled under them, and Norm pointed at the different surrounding buildings, explaining the entire water treatment process. The first step was coagulation and flocculation.

"We add chemicals that have a positive charge, which neutralizes the negative charge of dirt and other particles. This binds them together"—he interlaced his fingers —"which creates larger particles called *floc*. Floc settles to the bottom."

He indicated another structure. "That one's for sedimentation."

"Fascinating." Flo put a hand to her chin in a thoughtful pose. "What happens next?"

Grinning, he crooked an arm out for her, and she linked hers through it. Together, they strolled alongside the pools as if they were in a park, his voice nearly drowned out by the roar of the water pumps.

Ella gave Wink a frightened look and mouthed, *What is happening?*

Norm's voice rose over the din. "Next is filtration, using gravel, sand, and charcoal. Last is disinfection. Once the water's cycled through that, it's pumped to those two tanks you see there." He pointed at the elevated storage tanks with the line of people snaking below. "They hold about 675,000 gallons in total."

With the tour ended, he escorted them back inside the main building where one of his coworkers approached and talked to Norm about one of the pumps.

"So," Ella began once he'd rejoined them, "do you mind if I ask, what happened to the equipment? Did a pipe break?"

"We're still working the problem. At first, that was our assumption. We thought one of the pipes busted on account of pressure loss and reduced flow rate, but now we know it's somewhere in one of the pumps."

The coworker, who'd remained within earshot, called out, "It was sabotaged."

"We don't know that for sure."

"Sure we do. Someone messed up them valves. No way those seals broke that way on their own."

Ella glanced at Flo and Wink before asking who had access to the building.

"Just me and a couple other guys," Norm answered. "That's how I know it wasn't sabotaged. None of them would do that. They know what it'd do to this town."

"Could someone have broken in?" Wink asked. "Picked the lock?"

"Kinda a hard lock to pick," the coworker said. He stood tall and gangly, like a toothpick.

"What about forgetting to lock the door?" Ella asked.

They both shook their heads. Norm took off his hardhat and wiped his forehead. "I locked it myself. Ming here even checked, didn't you, sport?"

Ming's head bobbed up and down. "I forgot my lunch box after Norm locked up. I fiddled the knob, then realized it wasn't worth chasing him down to unlock it. I'd just get it the next day."

If the door had been locked, then how else could the saboteur have entered?

Nearing the door, Ella inspected it. There were no signs of forced entry, and the deadbolt appeared sound. It was the type of lock she had yet to see Flo—the self-proclaimed expert on lock picking—overcome.

Along the same exterior wall was a window about ten feet off the ground. Could someone have used a ladder to gain access through it? Her head craned up, studying it. Getting back out would've been a challenge.

"The door was still locked when you arrived for work the next morning?"

They both said it was.

She pointed up. "What about that window? Does it open?" It appeared to be a single pane that didn't slide or have hinges, but it was hard to tell from ground level.

Norm shrugged. "If it does, we've never opened it. I could get a ladder and check." His watch caught the light as he checked it again. "But it'll have to be later."

"I'll do it," she offered. "If you point me in the direction of a ladder. I'd really like to take a look up there."

Norm's expression was difficult to read as he pondered this. Ming offered to bring a ladder over instead, earning a shrug from Norm. It took less than a minute to drag a step ladder in place from a different part of the facility.

As Ella climbed, she noticed Norm had decided to stick around despite being pressed for time. The window sill was rife with dust and cobwebs—except for a portion in the middle. It had been wiped clean. The window opened in, with hinges at the top. And it was unlocked.

Frowning, she snapped photos with her phone, careful not to touch anything. Maybe Jimmy or Chapman could dust for prints. Putting her phone away, she noticed stiff threads, shavings of some kind, on the sill. Carefully, she pocketed a few fibers, then descended the ladder.

"Thanks," she said to Ming and Norm.

"Find anything?" Wink asked.

"I think the culprit entered that way." Turning to Norm, she said, "I'm sure the sheriff will want to take a look."

He dipped his chin in acknowledgment.

Ming wandered off, leaving Norm to linger pointedly near the exit. "Florence said you had questions for me?"

Wink opened the door. "Do you mind if we talk where it's a bit quieter?"

They stood outside again.

Ella shielded her eyes from the sun. "We wanted to ask about the night of Charlotte's accident."

His eyes widened. "How d'you know I was there? The newspaper didn't print my name."

"Sal," Ella said. "I don't blame you if you don't want to talk about it, but would you mind telling us what you saw?"

"Why's everyone asking me about that night all of a sudden? I'd been able to put it behind me." His chest heaved with a deep, shuddering breath. "It was about nine o'clock at night, dark out. I was stressed about getting a job, renting some hole in the wall room at the edge of town. Of course, if I'd known how small my cell would be, I would've thought it a mansion."

"What d'you go in for?" Flo asked, which earned her an elbow jab from Wink.

"You can't just ask a person that, dummy."

His mouth quirked up in a weak smile. "It's fine. I don't mind. I guess we never caught up once I was released. They charged me with tax evasion. But I can't help that I'm an enterprising man, can I?"

It was a phrase Ella would've expected to come out of Six's mouth. "Tell me, Norm, in your enterprising ways, you didn't also happen to fence certain, hard-to-obtain objects, did you?"

"You mean like drugs?"

"What, no. I'm talking about chocolate. Nature's drug."

"No, sorry."

Wink waved her hand in dismissal. "You were talking about the night of the accident."

"Yeah. Anyway, that night I was stressed and needed some air. I was a few blocks away when I heard tires screeching and someone screaming. I ran towards the noise." He stared past them, eyes glazing over. "When I got there, I saw a figure staggering off into the orchard a few blocks north, and the driver-side door open. And Mrs. Kaufman—" his voice cracked, and he swallowed. "She died right there in my arms."

A hollow feeling came over Ella, one she'd been able to bury the past few days.

"I'm so sorry," she whispered.

Would that moment in the cave with the professor haunt her for years as this did him? Carrying this weight as an adult was difficult enough. How much harder must it be for Judy, a young kid?

"What was the figure wearing," Wink was asking, "the one who ran away? Could you tell who they were?"

He hesitated. "It was dark. And I'd only just moved here, so I wasn't familiar with the locals yet."

"But you did see him, didn't you?" Ella pressed.

He hedged. "I saw a general shape."

"And," Wink said, "after living here for some time, thinking back, do you recognize that person?"

"They were definitely male. I can't say for sure, but—keep in mind, it really was quite dark and I'm sure I'm wrong, which is why I never said anything to Sheriff Johnson later— but a few months after the accident, I took my car to Lou's to get repaired. When I saw the mechanic, I couldn't help but notice he had a similar build."

He released a breath that sounded both relieved and anxious.

Ella's mind raced. "And he—this person—was the only other one you saw at the scene besides Charlotte?"

"That's right. And Sal, of course. Look, I really need to get back to work."

He took a few steps before she called him back.

"Sorry, two more questions. You said we weren't the first to ask recently about that night. Who else has been asking questions?"

"The professor, as a matter of fact. Scared me half to death. He just showed up at my house like he wasn't the town's most wanted man, asking what I saw that night and if Charlotte had still been alive when I found her. Stuff like that."

"Did you tell him the person running from the scene looked like Lou?"

"I told him I saw the general shape of that man, yes."

"Last question," Ella said. "Why doesn't the town use its backup supply of water to give out to people?"

He blinked at the abrupt change of topic before his eyebrows lowered. "What backup supply?"

"You know, all the bottles and stuff in the caves."

His confused expression said he had no clue what she was talking about. He nodded a farewell—mostly aimed at Flo—and headed back into the building.

The car ride down the dirt lane was more subdued than the funeral parlor they'd recently blown up. When Wink pulled up to the curb in front of the inn, she voiced aloud what they'd all been thinking but had been too reluctant to say. "Do we really think Lou ran her over?"

The hum of the engine died, and they sat in silence. Unbuckling, Ella leaned into the front seat, her head between the two women.

"It would explain why he didn't report the car stolen until later and why he didn't mention being at the scene of the accident."

Flo took off her glasses to clean the cracked lens. "Could be why Vera left him. Maybe she knew?"

"It's possible," Wink admitted.

"She didn't leave him because of the drinking?" Ella asked.

"That's also possible. Although, she loves her booze almost as much as he does."

"When did he start hitting the bottle so hard?"

Wink hummed, thinking. "Let's see… the first time I saw him show up drunk to a party was a couple years after the war. I think it was that Christmas Betsy got chased by that goose. You remember that?" She aimed her question at Flo.

The boarder's mouth twisted with glee. "That was a fun party. Let's see… that was when I bought Bobby's Winchester 1894 off him."

"About, what would you say, '45? '46?"

"About then, I reckon," Flo agreed.

Ella leaned back in her seat. "So, he started drinking heavily about seventeen years ago, right around the time Charlotte died."

"Seems like an awfully big coincidence." Wink shook her head. "But how do we prove he was driving the car?"

An idea was taking root, growing and blossoming in Ella's mind. "Ladies, what do you say we go for a drink?"

CHAPTER TWENTY-THREE

"WHERE'S WINK?" ELLA asked, burrowing deeper into her hoodie. As night had fallen, the temperature had dropped.

"Dunno." Flo breathed into her hands. "But if she doesn't show her mug soon, I'm goin' in without her."

The Half Penny stood out like a lighthouse, the windows awash with a dim glow that spilled onto the sidewalk. At this hour, it was the only establishment open on the slumbering Main Street, a beacon that ensnared citizens on their way home with the promise of forgetting their troubles, if only for a short while.

Ella and Flo waited rather impatiently outside. Flo's nose pressed against the hazy glass as she peered into the saloon-like, dingy interior.

"Looks like they've got a special going on Six's moonshine."

"Don't forget why we're here." Headlights appeared in the distance. "Finally."

As soon as Wink pulled up to the curb, Flo bolted into the bar before Ella could stop her, mumbling something about all the good booze being gone.

"Yeah, don't wait for us or anything," Ella hollered at the closing door before shrugging apologetically at Wink, who was exiting her car.

"I'm surprised she waited this long," Wink said.

The diner owner joined Ella on the sidewalk, sporting a teal tracksuit, her hair pulled aside in a barrette that caught the light, glittering like a disco ball.

"That might've been because I gave her a wet willy and told her I'd give her another if she didn't wait."

"What's a wet—"

Ella licked her finger and stuck it in Wink's ear.

"Ella Barton! That's disgusting!"

"Hey, I didn't come up with it."

"Do all the people in your era do that?"

"Sure, why not? It's the new handshake." From the expression on Wink's face, she didn't buy it.

"Sorry, I'm late. My house is being used as a water-filling station right now, and I had a mess of people in my yard fighting over the faucet. I had to step in when Hank Cooper began swinging my rake around."

As they stepped inside, she explained how she'd left Chester at home, snoozing on the couch after a heavy meal of dried cranberries and nuts.

The finish on the wood floor was worn bare in places. Clouds of cigarette smoke mixed with boisterous laughter, like cumulus happiness. The establishment was as eclectic as its patrons, part leftover saloon pre-prohibition days, part holdover speakeasy. A raucous game of poker was happening in the corner, Six conspicuously absent from the table.

Flo hovered at the periphery before elbowing her way into the game, squeezing between sabertooth-loving Harold and a man with mutton chops the size of Texas. A chorus of dissenting groans rose.

Ella scoped out the rest of the place. About half of the patrons appeared to be from Wink and Flo's era, the exceptions including Leif, Mutton Chops at the poker table, and a man who looked like he'd come straight from a performance of *The Crucible*.

"There." Wink indicated a hunched figure teetering on a barstool, nursing an amber-colored liquid.

The duo cut a path to the mechanic which happened to be within spitting distance of the poker game—literally. An old fashioned spittoon sat on the floor at the corner of the L-shaped bar, and a poker player aimed tobacco spittle in its general direction.

Ella sidestepped the slop and settled onto a stool beside Lou. Thick grime covered the bar top, exuding an odor she'd rather not dwell on. Taking a cloth napkin, she wiped down the surface, then used the fabric to rest her elbows on.

She adopted a relaxed posture. "Ah, that's the ticket."

Blinking, Lou aimed bleary eyes at her. "Evelyn?"

"Okay, now you're just doing that on purpose."

Wink made a show of dragging a barstool over to Lou's other side and parked next to him. She began to lean on the counter but stopped short upon seeing the surface. "I don't think this place has seen a cleaning rag in ages."

"Yeah," Ella said, "it's got a real nice *Cheers* vibe with a side of hepatitis."

"Lucky used to keep it in better shape." Lou tipped back his glass, the dim light glinting off a crack, and emptied it. With a *thunk*, he slammed it down and knocked on the counter, demanding another.

It took several attempts and Lou tossing the empty glass at the bartender—where it shattered at his feet—before the man at the far end acknowledged him. Turning, he glowered at the mechanic, his dark eyes flashing with a dangerous, familiar expression.

"Six?" Ella gaped at him.

The sharp angles in the outlaw's face softened. "Hey, darlin'."

"You're working here, too?"

"Nah, I got the boot from the General Store."

"Naturally. But, hey, you lasted a few days there, right? So that's something."

"Two days."

"Oh." She drummed her fingers on the counter, then wiped them on her pants. "Got to start somewhere, though. This seems like a better fit—" He'd taken the lid off a rum bottle, poured out a shot, and downed it. "Yeah, that makes more sense now."

Lou reached a wavering hand for the bottle, but Six slid it away. "Hey, can I get me some of that?"

"No."

"But you've gotta serve me what I ask for." Lou licked dry lips.

"No, I don't. I got this here job for the free booze."

"I don't think that's how bartending's supposed to work," Ella said as Six threw back another shot. "Well, this can only turn out well." She glanced around Lou to Wink for support, but the woman was preoccupied watching the poker game.

Behind them, with her sweater sleeves rolled up, Flo raked in poker chips like Chester hoarded acorns.

"But that's nothing," Harold sputtered, pointing at the boarder's hand of cards sprawled out on the table. "You got nothing. Just a Jack, an eight, a six—and they ain't even in the same suit."

"But they're all red." Flo fluffed her hair and proceeded to stack her winnings.

Ella shook her head, turning back to ask Six for a cup of water, but he was gone. "What the—" She twisted on her stool in time to spot him rounding the counter and sauntering up to the poker table where he demanded they deal him in.

"I hope you weren't planning on ordering a drink," Ella said to Wink.

With the sole bartender occupied, Lou flopped onto the counter, his gut spilling out as he stretched for the bottle of rum. His fingers slipped off the glass, the alcohol just out of reach.

Before Ella could say "Jack Daniels," Wink had hopped from her stool and stood on the other side of the counter. She poured two shot glasses and slid them over to Lou.

As he tucked into them, Ella exchanged a knowing glance with her friend. At least he'd be liquored up for their questioning.

Slipping her phone out, she opened an app and began recording their conversation. She placed it on the grime-covered counter, wincing as she did, wondering how badly dipping it in a bucket of bleach afterward would ruin the tech.

"What's that?" Lou's tongue flicked over his lips again, and he prodded the device.

"Just something to help me remember this conversation."

Lines creased between his brows, and his mouth murmured with silent words, repeating what she'd said, his brain catching up.

"You told me the professor didn't come to see you last week, remember?"

It took a moment for him to track the abrupt shift in topic. "That's right."

"But he did, didn't he?" Lou's eyes widened, and he began to shake his head before she cut him off. "Don't lie, Lou. It makes Jesus cry."

"I don't know what you're talking about."

Wink refilled his shot glass.

"That's why you killed him, wasn't it?" Ella pressed. Lou sputtered, spraying rum into a mist. "Because he was onto you. He knew you were the one driving the car that night Charlotte died. There's a witness who can place you at the scene."

She was stretching the truth more than she stretched her yoga pants after Thanksgiving, but the bluff worked on TV when the cops wanted their suspects to confess.

"Look, lady, I didn't kill him." His words were beginning to slur. "You got it all wrong."

A commotion broke out behind them. Harold's chair had hit the floor with a *crack*, and he stood, glowering at Flo.

"Don't you be talking about Spot like that." He shoved a finger in Flo's face. "And if ya ever shoot at him again, I'll smack that smirk off ya."

Ella grabbed the nearest object—the rum bottle—in case she needed a weapon with which to help defend her friend. She attempted to break it on the edge of the counter, leaving jagged edges, like in the movies. It rebounded as if it were a bouncy ball.

"What the—is this made of rubber?"

Flo, in a surprisingly fluid motion, produced a pair of brass knuckles—probably from her bra—and slid them on.

"Oh, boy." Ella's grip tightened on the frustratingly intact rum bludgeon.

Lounging in his chair, Six glanced up from the cards in his hands. "Either fight or ante up."

The tension in the air dissipated. Although, as Harold righted his chair, he continued to side-eye Flo, and she was slow to stow the brass knuckles.

Behind the bar, Wink cleared her throat and set a glass of water before Ella.

"Thanks." She drank deeply, tasting dirt and a touch of rotten eggs. The water dribbled from her mouth, back into the glass. "You know, I don't think Six got the Half Penny's water from the tower." She wiped her mouth with her sleeve. "Now, where were we?"

"Lou was saying he didn't kill the professor," Wink said.

"That's right. I didn't."

"Maybe not," Ella said, "but you drove that car into his wife."

The mechanic's face turned red, starting at his neck. "I. Wasn't. Driving." Each word came out as a boozy garble, but emphatic nonetheless.

"Then why lie about the professor coming to see you?"

His glassy eyes fell to his drink, but she realized it was his hands he was studying. Calluses and grease permanently marred them. He brushed his naked ring finger. "When the sheriff rang me to come get the car and I saw it, I knew. I knew she'd done it."

They fell silent.

Wink, who'd been scouring the countertop with a rag, paused. "Vera?"

He nodded.

"Had she been drinking?" Ella couldn't imagine the horror of getting behind the wheel after a few drinks and finding out you'd killed someone.

"Dunno."

"You didn't ask?"

"We don't talk about that night. See, even though she hit Mrs. Kaufman, it was my fault."

Ella's mouth turned down. "Why do you say that?"

"'Cause I was the one out walking with another woman."

"You and Charlotte?" A picture began forming, fuzzy but turning clearer by the second. Ella gasped. "You were the second person who was hit."

"Went flying up over the hood, if you can believe it. I ain't ever walked right since then." He motioned for Wink to pour more rum, telling her to keep it neat after she offered up ice. "It's not what you think. We weren't—she was just helpin' me. Vera and I were having problems, and Charlotte —Mrs. Kaufman—well, she was an ear. She came into the shop from time to time to chat. The professor threw himself into his work the moment they moved here, didn't even help unpack. So, we kept each other company. Before I knew it, we were sharing our problems."

His eyes glistened. "She was the first true friend I had. Vera caught her a few times, told her not to come back. Anyway, that night, we'd had a big fight, Vera and I. When I stormed outta the house, I think she suspected where I was headin'. After—after we were hit and I came to, I saw it was the black Buick that'd done it. And I knew."

"Why did you run?" Ella asked.

His head stooped lower, as if carrying an invisible weight. "I stayed and tried to help all I could, but she was bleeding too much." His voice broke. "There was so much blood. It was everywhere. When I saw someone comin', I got scared. I thought about... about what folks around town would say. And what the professor would think. I panicked. I didn't find out 'til later that she didn't make it."

Looking up, he searched their faces in earnest. "Please don't tell Chapman. I haven't said nothing all these years 'cause I don't want Vera getting locked up."

"But someone died, Lou."

"Then tell him I was the one drivin'. I'll swear to it." His voice rose, his knuckles white on the counter's edge. "It's my fault Charlotte died. If I hadn't asked her to meet me, we wouldn't have been out that night. And Vera wouldn't have come after us." With clumsy fingers, he reached for the shot glass, but Ella rested her hand on his.

"Drinking's not going to help."

"Sure it will. It helps me forget—at least for awhile."

She looked at him with new eyes. Before her, in stained coveralls and a sheen of sweat, was a broken man who used booze to blur sharp memories.

But instead of empathy, an uglier emotion broiled up. This misery of his, she reveled in it. The man partially responsible for her being ripped from her era, her home, her family was in pain. And it made her feel better.

She found she couldn't look at him and stole the rum for herself. Here she'd walked Six through forgiveness, of letting the past go, and she'd preached its importance, but when faced with a similar situation, she'd been found wanting. She was a hypocrite.

"El?" Wink nudged her arm.

"I'm fine—"

The poker table erupted with shouts. Harold flipped it over, sending chips and cards flying like shrapnel. Roaring, he lunged for Flo, his hands going for her throat.

"You take that back!"

The senior citizen swung her brass-enhanced fist around, connecting it with the man's cheek. The blow glanced off due to her lack of any upper body strength. Her eyes popped open, magnified by her thick glasses, with an expression that said she very much regretted what she'd just done.

Harold towered over her, yelling, "That's the last time you bad mouth my pet!"

Ella held up a finger. "Um, sorry to interrupt what's clearly a tense moment, but are we sure 'pet' is the right word for a saber-toothed tiger?"

"That's right," Flo said. "Spot's not a pet because he's clearly clandestine."

"Nope," Ella said.

Harold's face was purple. "You take that back!"

He took one lumbering step and shoved hard. Flo tumbled to the ground, her head bouncing on the dusty floor. She didn't move.

It was like an invisible signal flare had gone up, and the room erupted. A chair thrown by a poker player flew through the air, narrowly missing Six. It crashed against Leif's back. The Viking's chest vibrated in a deep growl as he lumbered to his feet, pulling his ax.

Ella registered all this peripherally, her focus still on her fallen friend. She let out a breath when Flo stirred. Her glasses sported new cracks in the other lens. Half-blind, she fumbled to collect her mammoth-sized purse.

"Does no one understand the meaning of the word clandestine?" Ella tried to holler over the bedlam.

Wink rounded the counter, a broken bottle in her hand.

"What—how'd you do that?" Ella scanned the rapidly deteriorating situation. "Looks like Flo's got this."

The boarder had pulled the dismantled pieces of The Hammer from her purse and was rapidly assembling it.

"I thought you confiscated that from her?" Wink ducked in time as a chair whipped past. It slammed into the bar, shattering bottles.

"I'd like to see *you* try taking it when she's got a flamethrower pointed at you." Ella searched the chaos for Six. Any minute now, he'd step in and put a stop to this madness.

There. The outlaw turned bartender was squatting by the overturned poker table, shoving poker chips and money into his pockets.

He paused to deck the guy next to him. Then in a blink, he whipped his weapon from his holster and shot in Harold's vague direction.

Ella hunched down. "Six! This isn't the Wild West!"

As Harold used the poker table for cover, Flo shouldered her plasma cannon and aimed.

"Crap! Take cover!" Ella yelled to no one in particular as she dove over the counter, headfirst.

Her body slid across the layer of scum like a greased pig. It was almost fun until the tumble down the other side where she cushioned her fall using her hands, landing in a heap.

A terrible boom split the air, and a turquoise plasma ball hit the back of the bar. The few surviving bottles exploded. Glass and booze rained down. Three Backstreet Boys later, she pried her hands from where they'd been protecting her head and assessed the damage.

She found Lou a few feet away, out of the blast radius. He was behind the counter with her, rifling through the debris and pocketing any intact bottle he found.

"Are you serious right now?" She popped to her feet. "And dial back your power, Flo, before you kill someone!"

Half the patrons were fleeing through the front door—notably those from the twentieth century on up. The other half overturned tables, creating makeshift covers like Harold had done with the poker table. Guns poked over the tops. Six leveled his revolver around the room while Leif wielded his ax and used a serving tray as a shield.

Ella held her hands up to the Norseman, pleading. "*Nei*, Leif."

"*Man må hyle med de ulve man er i blandt*" was his response, which roughly translated to "One must howl with the pigs (wait, no, *wolves*) when one is among them."

Ella ducked a flying chair and kept her eyes barely above the bar top. Wink had managed to make it to Flo's location, and together they hunkered behind a pile of chairs, which also served to prop up the plasma cannon.

"I've got the superior firepower, boys!" Light glinted off the spiderweb cracks in Flo's glasses.

The Hammer swung around, aiming at nothing in particular. Wink whispered in the boarder's ear, and, a moment later, Flo shifted the weapon so it aimed at a person.

"I don't wanna hurt anyone," Flo yelled. "I just wanna be on my way. So, this is what's gonna happen. Me, Wink, and Poodle Head over there—"

Ella stuck her head up higher and saluted those who looked her way.

"—are gonna walk nice and slow-like towards the door. Anyone who doesn't wanna see what the inside of their own stomach looks like is gonna let us pass."

Wink motioned Ella forward.

She found her muscles slow to respond. As she rounded the counter, taking the longer route as opposed to the Slip 'N Slide counter, she paused beside Lou. "You have to tell Chapman you were with Charlotte that night and that Vera was driving. It's not like she can hate you more, right?"

She'd taken a single step past him when something Flo's ex-husband had said triggered a thought. The accident had happened at night. Norm had even said it'd been too dark to be sure it was Lou he'd seen fleeing the scene.

"Lou, did you actually *see* Vera driving the car?"

"No." He belched. "Who else would it have been, hmm? She took cars off the lot all the time to run errands. Drove me mad." He stared off wistfully into the distance.

Wink hollered for Ella to hurry.

Jogging, she joined the duo at their chairs. They huddled together, moving to the doorway as a mass, the cannon pointing out.

"Flo," Ella intoned when they'd reached the door, "you remember that bear spray you used on me a while back, the one that made me pray for death? Do you have it on you?"

"In my bag."

Ella began the Herculean task of rifling through the contents inside the purse while still walking. She half expected a grenade to go off from all the jostling.

As they exited through the doorway, there was an awkward moment where all three of them tried to squeeze through at the same time, like in a cartoon, before they spilled out single file.

"Got it." Ella held up the obnoxiously large canister as her feet hit the sidewalk.

"Didn't Chapman confiscate that?" Wink asked Flo.

"Yep." Flo still had the cannon aimed through the open doorway. "What're you gonna do with that?"

"We're past the danger, El," Wink pointed out.

"We are, but they aren't." Before she could lose her nerve, she mashed the button on the canister, aiming the stream inside. As with any weapon Flo possessed, its effects were "enhanced," which she knew, having experienced it firsthand.

"You'll thank me later," she hollered into the bar as the stream hissed out, misting into a cloud.

She held her breath. Her eyes, already leaking like faucets, burned like the pits of hell. Then she kicked the door closed. Cries rose from inside, followed by hacking coughs.

She turned to Wink's car and froze. Several yards south, Jimmy sprinted up the sidewalk, jacket billowing behind like a cape. In the distance came the faint echoes of hooves over pavement. Chapman, one of The Four Horsemen of the Apocalypse, was on his way.

"Time to blow this Popsicle stand." She shoved Wink and Flo towards the car.

As Wink opened the driver-side door, she said, "I don't see any Popsicles."

"It's an expression." Ella hip-checked Flo aside, reaching for the front passenger-side door. "Shotgun."

Flo huffed, shoving her ridiculously large weapon in Ella's face. "How many times do I have to tell you? This is a plasma cannon, not a shotgun."

"We don't have time." Wink started the engine. "Let's go."

Flo shoved Ella back and tumbled into the front with a victorious grin. The cannon became an awkward appendage that hit both Wink and the windows. Frustrated, Ella dove into the backseat.

As they peeled out, Jimmy shouted, "I see you three! Don't think I won't be..." Whatever he said next was lost as they put the Half Penny in their rearview mirror.

Flo rolled her window down to accommodate The Hammer, and a cold breeze blew across Ella's face as she thought over the evening's events. So, Lou hadn't been driving the car that hit Charlotte, which put them back at square one, or near it, anyway.

CHAPTER TWENTY-FOUR

ELLA SIPPED A cup of precious water from a jar, staring at the mirror turned murder board as she had for the past half hour, hoping it had somehow become a magic mirror and would reveal the killers. Wink had gone home, and she heard Flo bumping around in the hallway outside, blinded by her cracked glasses, as she got ready for bed.

"It looks like it's just you and me, Fluffy."

The Maine Coon pounced on a knot in the wooden floor. The soft glow of street lamps filtered through the branches of the large oak outside, the budding leaves and darkness a blanket that hid the diner from view.

The murder board taunted her. Absently, she tapped the end of a marker on the glass. She'd added Vera's name to the suspect list for Charlotte's death. While on her lunch break tomorrow, she planned on hunting the woman down for a chat, if an interrogation could be called a chat.

According to Lou, the sheriff at the time, this Johnson fellow, hadn't found the driver's fingerprints in the car, but maybe he had and hadn't realized it. If he'd found Vera's prints, he could've dismissed them, as their presence wouldn't be suspicious.

However, if Lou was wrong and Vera wasn't the driver, then the lack of fingerprints could be explained by the driver wearing gloves.

In the twenty-first century, it was odd to imagine a person driving with gloves on unless they had a sinister motive. However, her involuntary time in Keystone acquainted her with 1950s attire, where gloves were commonplace.

Her eyes drifted to the suspect list for the professor's death, lingering on Patience's name at the top. The woman had been conspicuously quiet in recent weeks, except at the latest town hall meeting where she'd berated the townsfolk for being heathens and had attempted to set fire to the church.

Vera's name had been added to that list, as well. She had a vague recollection, either from a TV show or an article she'd read, that poison was the preferred method of death and murder for females, Hitler and Socrates notwithstanding. If the professor had figured out Vera had driven the car that killed his wife and he'd threatened her, then it stood to reason she'd killed him preemptively.

But how would Vera have known where to find him? Had she followed him back to the cave?

Ella pinched the bridge of her nose. It fit, but only by leaps in supposition as tall as Flo's hair.

She moved onto the next suspect: Lou. He blamed himself for Charlotte's death. He could have feared the professor discovering the truth and wanted to protect Vera. Typically, there was no love lost between ex-spouses, but guilt was a driving force that freed humans of the shackles of morals, enabling them to commit atrocities.

Considering the professor's cause of death could help narrow the pool of suspects. The problem was, if the poison came from stone fruit, then nearly anyone in town would have access to it.

In all of the previous murders she and the dynamic duo had solved, her gut had been a guiding force. Sure, research, evidence, dumb luck, and copious amounts of coffee had led her to the killers, but her gut usually told her whether she was on the right track or not.

Of course, her gut had been wrong in the past, telling her who the killer was, only for her to be surprised later. And it also hadn't warned her about that supermarket sushi a couple years back. So, its track record wasn't the best, all things considered.

But right now, it told her there was more that she wasn't seeing, more she didn't know. These two cases were fraught with coincidences, making them appear connected. An elaborate tapestry, and she was only seeing the fibers up close instead of stepping back and seeing the whole.

Fibers.

She ran to her bedroom and dug out her waitress uniform. The pink gingham print smelled of burgers and grease. Her hand groped inside one of the pockets and came out with the fibers she'd collected at the water treatment facility. Without a microscope or forensic knowledge, she was left to inspecting them under her bedside lamp.

They looked like shavings from twine, or... rope. That must've been how the saboteur entered and exited the facility. But knowing that still didn't tell her who had broken in, nor did it help her catch a killer. Putting the fibers in an old jewelry box, she returned to the murder room.

Staring at the mirror, she thought late into the night but struggled to maintain focus. Each time shadows cast by the branches waved over the window, her thoughts couldn't help but drift to the intruder in the professor's basement, the shadow with the hat who'd attacked Will. Maybe there was more than one killer on the loose.

* * *

The next day, after changing into her waitressing dress, Ella bounded down the steps. She considered bypassing the kitchen and heading straight to the diner for her breakfast. The water shortage meant there was still no coffee at home, and she also wasn't keen to run into Jimmy.

Her feet whispered across the grand entrance hall to the vestibule. She was reaching for the knob when Rose shrieked deep in the manor, bringing Ella to a stop. What now?

Marching across the room, she homed in on the source of the noise. As she swung in the kitchen door, she asked, "What'd Flo do?"

A streak of fur swept past her feet. She glimpsed a strip of bacon dangling from Fluffy's mouth before he was out of sight.

"That cat!" Rose's lips pursed, and she kneaded her pearl necklace like bread dough. "He's more trouble than he's worth, I tell you."

Jimmy looked up from the same worn edition of *Keystone Corner*, his eyes locking on Ella.

"Welp, got to go." She cut a hasty retreat in the form of a moonwalk back through the doorway.

"Ella! Get back here!"

"I'd love to, Jimmy, but I'm late for work."

"Your shift doesn't start for another half hour."

"I'm sorry, I can't hear you, but this has been fun. We should catch up sometime..." She let her voice fade as the door swung in and out, each time revealing the kitchen and his dark expression.

She paused partway down the hallway, realizing she needed to ask him a question and to tell him about the rope fibers found on the window sill at the water treatment plant.

Cursing, she reluctantly sauntered back. The moment she stepped a wary foot back in the room, he hooked a finger in the air, motioning her to the table.

"Just so you're aware, that's really creepy. If you're going to offer me candy and ask me to get into your van, I'm telling you right now, you better have chocolate."

"I've no idea what you're talking about." Confusion flickered in his eyes, replacing anger.

"You do a really good impression of Chapman."

"I'm offended." He dabbed his mouth with a napkin. "I'm much more handsome than him."

"You sure are, dear." Rose pecked him on the cheek before depositing a plate with a mountain of pancakes and a whole pig's worth of bacon in front of him.

"What were you doing at the Half Penny last night?"

"Who, me?"

"Yes."

"Where?"

"The Half Penny."

"Doesn't ring a bell."

Sighing, he leaned back in his chair, folding his arms, leveling her with a gaze.

She held both of her hands up in "L" shapes and framed him in a shot with an invisible camera. "Yep, definitely have the body language down. Would you mind saying, 'Ms. Barton, I think you're the greatest, and I don't know what this town would do without you'? Because that's what he says to me. All the time."

Jimmy scratched his jaw in thought. For a moment, she wondered if he was actually considering her request, but then he said, "I could take you down to the station and ask you questions, but I don't think that's necessary. We're friends, and—despite the questionable company you keep—I think you're reasonable."

"Thanks? Also, my 'questionable company' is the same company you keep. I just want to point that out."

His face flushed slightly. "Let's start over." Picking up a strip of bacon, he dangled it mouthwateringly close to her face. Grease glistened in the morning light, and it was just the right amount of crispy. "What were you doing there last night?"

Her eyes glued on the bacon, she said, "Can't a gal just go out for drinks with her friends without getting harassed by the police?"

"She can if she and her friends aren't the types who repeatedly cause trouble."

"Well, that's just rude—not really untrue, mind you, but uncalled for."

"Am I supposed to believe it's just coincidence that I get reports of gunshots at the bar, show up, and see you, Wink, and Flo leaving?"

"Yep." Her fingers stretched for the bacon, but he pulled it just out of reach.

"And it's also a coincidence that some sort of pepper aerosol had gone off inside, making it nearly uninhabitable?"

"Yes. Coincidence. But in the off chance it's not, you're welcome." She lunged for the crispy strip of meat and swiped it from his hand, grinning triumphantly. It tasted as delicious as it smelled.

"Do you realize it'll take a week to air the place out? Also, several of the patrons ended up in the hospital."

Saying more would be admitting culpability, so she arranged her face in her best sympathetic expression before swiping another strip of bacon from his plate.

They lapsed into silence, the sound of their chewing filling the void, and he cut into his stack of pancakes. He didn't seem mad. If anything, he appeared slightly amused and fought a losing battle with a grin.

Rose sat with her own plate, pouring orange juice from a pitcher into cups before she offered one to Ella.

"Thanks. I really should get going, though." Despite saying this, however, she remained seated, chugging the proffered juice. "I take it they didn't get the water running yet?"

Rose shook her head, a blond pin curl breaking loose. "No. A radio announcement this morning said the damage is more extensive than they'd thought. They're having to fabricate a new part."

"I miss the days when it was easy to ship something into town," Jimmy said.

Rose's eyes dropped to her plate. When she cut into her pancakes, it was with enough force to cause her fork to screech over the dishware.

"Some folks," Jimmy continued, oblivious to his wife's sudden shift in mood, "have taken to selling water from their wells."

"How very... enterprising of them" was the nicest thing Ella could think to say. After dwelling on this another moment, she told him about her visit to the facility the previous day, her chat with Norm, and about the window.

"Thank you for letting me know. I'll take a look."

"I'm also wondering why the town's not dispersing its backup supply of water."

His face held the same expression Norm's had when she'd asked him about it.

"What backup supply?"

They stared at each other.

"You mean the water tower? That's nearly gone, last I heard."

She made a noncommittal noise, her mind churning. If that hoard in the caves wasn't the town's, then who did it belong to? She shook away the barrage of questions this brought up and shifted to the reason she'd risked his wrath to return to the kitchen.

"Hey, I was wondering if you'd looked further into that stone fruit theory I told you about? About how the seeds can lead to cyanide poisoning?"

Syrup from his pancakes clung to the corner of his mouth. "I brought it up with Pauline. She knew about it, of course, and had already done the math. According to her, it would've required massive amounts of seeds to achieve fatal levels, unless it was cherries—like you said. It might've been possible to get enough—what she'd call it?—amygdalin with cherry seeds to kill him."

His tongue swept over his mouth, finding the wayward syrup. "I plan on asking around today, but I don't have high hopes. Nearly everyone here's got access to cherries."

"But they're not in season at the greenhouses, are they?"

Both glanced over at Rose, hoping she knew.

"I don't believe so, no." The innkeeper sipped her juice demurely. "But that doesn't mean much in this town. Every woman I know who's worth her salt in the kitchen does her own canning or freezing."

Meaning nearly anyone had access to cherry pits, even when the fruit wasn't in season. After grabbing more bacon, Ella scooted her chair back, standing.

"Well, thanks for the chat. And the bacon." She stared out the window a moment, choosing her next words carefully. "Also, if you have time, I recommend looking deeper into Vera or Lou."

"What do you know? Did you find out something?"

"I've found out a great many things. Like, don't wear white after Labor Day and mayonnaise goes bad after twelve hours at room temperature—don't ask me how I know that."

Rose cleared her throat. "Eight hours, dear."

Ella blinked. "You sure? Huh. Then if you'll excuse me, there's a potato salad at the diner I have to throw out." Her hand reached for the back door. "Right, so you'll tell me what you learn?"

"Of course not."

"Great. Cool. Just let me know."

"I won't."

She shot him a finger gun and opened the door. "I expect names by the end of the day."

Whatever he muttered was lost by the click of the door shutting behind her. Her steps were slow, trudging across the grass as she savored the view of the lake. Clouds skittered across its glassy surface.

Inside Grandma's Kitchen, Wink huffed behind a rolling pin, spreading dough over the island, while Horatio warmed the griddle.

"Coffee's already brewing," Wink said without looking up.

"You're my hero." After pouring a hot cup in the diner, Ella wiped down tables, then flipped the sign to "Open."

When she turned around, Wink was at the pastry display, restocking it with glazed donuts and muffins. Waltzing up to the case, Ella lent a hand while telling Wink about her conversation with Jimmy. Only a single muffin happened to find its way to her mouth by the time they finished.

Wink wiped her hands down her apron. "Hmm, that seems a bit..."

"What?"

"Premature, I guess? To go telling our new deputy to look into Vera based solely on Lou's assumption."

"When you put it like that, I did jump on that theory rather quickly considering the source is an alcoholic who can't remember my own name. But it's not like he'll go confessing to Chapman about that night. You saw how desperate he was to keep Vera out of this. He'd sooner dry up." At Wink's expression, Ella added, "What?"

"Nothing, you just seem… more harsh than usual."

"Than *usual*?"

"Towards Lou."

"Am I bitter towards him? Yeah, sure, but not to the level of slashing his tires or sneaking laxatives into his food—wait, that's not a bad idea. Random question not at all related to this conversation, but do you have any laxatives on hand?"

Wink put her hands on her hips, raising one eyebrow. "Uh-uh. I helped Flo sneak some into Milton's milkshake once. That's a mess I never want to clean up again."

"Well, I wouldn't give it to him here."

"And don't think I didn't notice you deflect the topic of your issue with Lou. But we'll save that for another time." Grabbing a sopping rag, Wink began to scrub the milkshake mixer. "So, how do we confirm Vera as a suspect or rule her out?"

"I've been thinking about that. Sheriff Johnson dusted the car that hit Charlotte for fingerprints."

"That's surprising."

"Yeah, I never met the man, but I get the impression his gumshoe work left much to be desired."

"Yes, he didn't show a lot of initiative, always using his arm as an excuse."

Ella stared. "What am I missing?"

"You're not missing anything. He was. His arm."

"Huh?"

"The man had one arm."

"Just the one? Well, good for him. Anyway, the prints—wait, how in *The Fugitive* did the man arrest people if he had only one arm?"

Wink shrugged, distracted by a stubborn spot on the machine. "What's your plan?"

Instead of talking to Vera, a new idea had formed, one where she could gather facts and evidence and not rely on a stranger's word.

"Let's just say, it'll make Flo happy."

"Don't say it. We are not breaking—"

"We're breaking in!" Ella said in much too chipper of a tone.

A resigned sigh left Wink's lips. "Where?"

"The sheriff's office."

CHAPTER TWENTY-FIVE

"ANYONE ELSE FEEL like this is old hat by now?" Ella made her way across the entrance hall towards the front door with Wink and Flo.

When they reached the vestibule, both she and Wink stopped short.

"Forgetting something?" Ella asked Flo.

"If you're talking about my deodorant, how many times do I have to tell you? I don't sweat."

"The pit stains on your garments and your perfume of BO suggest otherwise, but that's not what I meant."

The woman hadn't gotten replacement lenses for her glasses yet, and she was forced to eye Ella sideways to see around the fissures, giving her a deranged look.

Wink paced in front of the door. "I told Horatio we'd only be gone an hour."

"Okay, let's hustle." Ella pointed at Flo's bag. "Take out anything that shoots, sprays, incinerates, or causes serious bruising."

Behind the cracked glasses, Flo's eyes bugged out. "Are you pulling my leg?" Turning to Wink, she said, "Can you believe the nerve of this one?"

"Just do it." Wink glanced at the grandfather clock nearby. "And you're also getting a pat-down."

Ella hissed through her teeth. "Yeah, about that… you're the lucky winner on that front."

"You'd rather go through her purse?"

Ella made a face. Neither prospect sounded fun.

"Over my dead body." Flo crossed her arms, staring them down.

"That's precisely what we're trying to avoid: dead bodies," Ella said. "It's either this or you don't come along."

Crossing her own arms, she mimicked the woman's posture, then became distracted by the way her biceps pushed out like Popeye the Sailor.

After much cajoling—mostly by Wink since Ella had taken to flexing in front of the mirror by the coat tree—Flo submitted her purse for inspection. She spat curses like a feral cat while Wink rifled through the handbag of doom, already having pulled out a revolver, the brass knuckles that had made their big debut the evening before, and throwing stars.

Meanwhile, Ella raked her hands down the woman's calves. Within a minute, a small collection of throwing knives and a second revolver lay on the floorboards.

"Hey, Flo, be honest. Do my biceps look bigger? Because I've been doing pushups—well, not pushups per se, more like lifting Fluffy a few times each morning."

"El," Wink cut in, getting her to focus. She handed Flo's purse back to her.

Once slung over the boarder's shoulder, it no longer created a deep divot. Wink had relieved her of most of the weight, the majority of which had been The Hammer, its disassembled parts now strewn on the floor with the rest of the confiscated arsenal.

"You'll regret this." Flo's voice came out low. "The moment we run into trouble, you'll wish I was armed."

Ella exchanged a glance with Wink. "She's right."

Reaching into the pile, she tossed the brass knuckles to Flo. They seemed the least lethal, considering something resembling cymbals on the floor beside it was humming and emitting blue light.

Ella snapped her fingers. "Almost forgot." Her hand plunged into the woman's beehive.

"Hey!"

It was like swimming through straw with slightly more give.

Flo sniffed. "I was hoping you wouldn't think of that."

After adding another throwing knife and a canister of pepper spray to the pile, they were bounding down the sidewalk. Flo trailed behind, grumbling, while her sensible shoes made shuffling noises along the sidewalk. Ella could practically feel the daggers stabbing her back.

The noonday sun had burned off morning clouds. Up and down Main Street, people bustled in and out of establishments—Sal's Barbershop, the General Store, Jenny's Salon, Stewart's Market, and even the Half Penny. A wagon rolled down the road, pulled by two restless horses.

"How do we lure Chapman and Jimmy out of the office? With candy? I'm sure we can borrow a creepy van from Lou." Ella's feet slapped the sidewalk. "That's, of course, assuming they're not out and about, arresting Six or chasing the Murphy brothers." Maybe they'd get lucky and the duo wouldn't be in the station.

"The Murphy brothers won't be up yet for another couple hours," Wink said.

Ella's mouth turned down as she glanced at her watch. It was past noon.

"But to answer your question, we're creating a diversion."

Ella nodded. "Yes, you said that. But you never said *how*."

Flo huffed behind them. When Ella glanced back, the woman's lower lip was still jutting out.

"Are you still moping?"

"Yes. It's not fair that Wink gets to do the fun part, while I'm stuck with you."

"I love you, too."

Glancing over at her boss, Ella noticed a small smile creeping up. Whatever the two were planning couldn't be good.

Just before they reached the building for the sheriff's office, they slipped into the alley.

"See you clowns later," Wink whispered before slinking between the buildings, heading towards the lake.

Ella's stomach knotted as she watched her friend's retreating back, the gingham dress swaying happily. If they set fire to one more boat, Chapman would throw their hides in jail quicker than she could call him Barney Fife and explain why that reference was insulting.

"Looks like it's just you and me, Thelma."

Edging to the sidewalk, Flo craned her head around the alley corner to watch the station's door—well, door adjacent. Her questionable vision put her looking a few degrees off.

Ella had a thought. "Hey, let's watch from across the street. We can see who's inside."

After backtracking south, they cut across Main, then darted north again until they were in the shadow of the General Store. From their new vantage point, they had a perfect view of the sheriff's office, as well as slivers of the lake, sparkling with sunlight, between buildings.

There was movement in the window, but it was difficult to tell if both lawmen were inside or if it was just one.

Several tense minutes followed with nothing more happening but a bug crawling over her waitressing attire. Bored, she'd taken to explaining *Star Wars* to Flo.

"So, she kisses her brother? Good Lord, if that sorta thing's common in your era, then humanity's doomed."

"You just have to see it to understand."

She fell silent, wondering if the drama club would be up for performing the saga if she wrote a script. She'd watched the original trilogy enough times to quote it verbatim. And, given a year or two, Ukulele Joe could learn the theme score.

A distant rumble drew her attention. What had Wink done? She held her breath, waiting for an explosion.

"Look alive, Poodle Head."

Behind the sheriff's office, a figure shot into the air, over rooftops and the lake. A streak of flames and smoke trailed behind.

"Will's jet pack," she whispered, more to herself. She'd nearly forgotten about it. Her eyes narrowed at the erratic behavior of the pilot. "Is that—is that Wink?"

"Sure is." Flo snickered. "That's our cue."

"For what? To call the funeral home and tell Jensen to expect a new customer?" She followed Flo across the street, steering her away from the library and towards the sheriff's office. "Any chance you'll get your glasses fixed soon?"

In the sky, Wink made a figure eight in a way that suggested it wasn't intentional before plunging out of sight behind a building. A moment later, she popped back up, streaking high overhead.

Ella's mouth fell open as she tipped her head back, watching. "This is bad. Very, very bad. I can't believe Will let her borrow that."

At Flo's silence, she added, "He does know, doesn't he? Florence Henderson! What if she kills herself?"

Flo waved a wrinkled hand. "She'll be fine."

"She looks like a drunk insect."

They reached the front door, and Flo busted it open. It whacked against an interior wall, which was, thankfully, made of brick.

"Hurry! Wink needs help!"

Jimmy, alone in the room, leaped from his desk. "What's wrong? Where is she?"

Flo pointed. "Over the lake. Hurry!"

"*Over* the lake?"

"What don't you understand about hurry? She's got Will's rocket on her back—"

"Jet pack," Ella corrected.

"—and she doesn't know how to work it!"

"She *what*?" Without waiting for further explanation, Jimmy tore out of the building.

"Nicely done." Ella skipped over to the filing cabinet. "Maybe you should keep an eye on Wink."

"What for?"

"In case she sprouts feathers—why do you think? In case she crashes, and we have to rush her to the hospital."

"She'll be fine," Flo insisted for a second time. "It's all for show."

"Then she's a *very* good actress."

The boarder approached the wall of filing cabinets. After a few tugs, she let out a frustrated growl. "Darn thing's stuck."

"That's because that's a table."

Her cheeks flushing, Flo gave Ella the finger before shuffling to the right.

"Still no."

Two more tentative steps.

"Getting warmer. Just follow the sound of my voice—that's it. Right there. Now pull."

The older woman pulled a lamp from atop a cabinet. It toppled forward, and she caught it with her face.

"Yep, you got it." Ella returned her attention to the cabinets, pointedly ignoring the glare aimed in her direction. "They're locked."

They'd been expecting this. Reaching into her Marge Simpson hairdo, Flo retrieved her lock pick set and got to work on the first cabinet.

"I thought your tension wrench thingie broke at the funeral home?"

"It did. This is a hair pin."

Soon, the sounds of cabinet drawers squealing open filled the room as they hurriedly sifted through files. They worked quietly and efficiently, with Ella thumbing over the folders' labels and Flo's nose an inch over the contents of one. At some point in the past, the cases had been filed by year, but beginning about a decade ago, that organization seemed to have given way to "if it fits, put it here."

"What do we have here?" Pulling out a folder, she let it fall open on top of the others. It was dated the same year as Charlotte's accident. The pages rustled as she shuffled through them, then said, "Bingo."

Flo sidled up, standing uncomfortably close.

"Holy rotten diapers, what did you eat for lunch, woman? A sulfur deposit the size of an elephant?"

Flo widened her mouth and released a heavy, stench-filled breath right in Ella's face. A bit of the lunch in question was stuck between her teeth. "Never mind that. What d'you find?"

"The death investigation for that night." The file was thin —too thin.

As she rifled through reports and forms, Flo stuck her finger on one. "What about that?"

"That's a copy of the death certificate." She set the folder down and began taking pictures. There wasn't enough time to read through everything. Her phone made a shutter noise, and she moved aside a page, revealing crime scene finger-print cards with dusty fingerprints taped to them. "Jackpot."

The annotations on the cards read that they'd come from an old black Buick.

"I don't see how that'll help."

"It only helps if you found the file you were supposed to be looking for."

The boarder's eyes clicked with an *Oh, yeah. That's right.*

Her part done, Ella helped Flo search. Five minutes and several exchanges of insults later, they'd located the file for the professor's murder investigation—right in the top drawer of Chapman's desk.

Ella made a *tsk-tsk* noise. "He's getting sloppy."

In comparison with Charlotte's file, it was bloated. Flip-ping through the contents rapidly, she located another set of fingerprint cards. These had been collected from the profes-sor's jar of jam, the one Pauline had sitting in her lab.

Ella laid the older fingerprint cards collected from the Buick side-by-side with these and squinted.

"You know what you're looking for?" Flo asked.

"Sure. Check and see if the whorl's match... or something like that." It wouldn't tell them who their killer was, but it would tell them if the same person was responsible for both deaths. They would finally know once and for all if the two incidents were related.

"Well?"

"Well, you're breathing down my neck again, and I'm about to pass out from the smell." Ella's lip caught between her teeth, and she leaned closer until her nose was inches from the cards. It couldn't be... Oh, no.

Her shoulders sank. "They're not a match."

"Huh? You sure?"

Ella nodded, and Flo snatched up both sets of cards, her hip colliding with Ella's, sending her stumbling. "Lemme see."

"You want to *see*? Woman, you couldn't see the sun if you were in its chromosphere and on fire."

Flo let out a litany of curses, and the cards fluttered from her hands to the desk like moths. "You're right. They don't match. See, on the thumbs, there's that bit there—loops around—looks nothing like this bit here."

Quickly they collected the cards, returned them to the files, and the files to their respective places, then left. Dejection threatened to set in.

"Buck up, Poodle Head. We'll figure out who offed them." But even Flo's voice betrayed doubt.

It felt like they were treading in quicksand, trying to keep from sinking further. No leads. Little evidence.

"Is it just me or do folks seem like they're acting nuttier than usual?"

Flo's question brought Ella out of her melancholy, and she looked up. The afternoon foot traffic was flowing one direction, and rapidly. Gabby shot out of the library like a plasma cannon, nearly bowling Ella over.

"Oh, sorry, Ella. I didn't see you."

"Where's everyone going?"

The librarian's words came out in a breathy tumble as she flung her copper-colored braid over her shoulder. "Mrs. Sanders came in saying that someone's stuck up in a tree— and it's on fire."

CHAPTER TWENTY-SIX

ELLA AND FLO flew down an alley and burst out onto a sunshine-bathed knoll. In the distance, halfway around the lake, a crowd had gathered in the park below a dark column of smoke.

Flo wheezed, "Go. I'll catch up."

Ella pulled ahead, leaving the woman behind. Wind whipped at her face, smelling of wet mud and lake water. When she reached the park and the cluster of gawkers, she slid to a stop and clutched her ribs.

The stench of smoke was nearly overpowering. Slowly, her gaze slid up. Wink dangled from the limb of a pine tree, the jet pack's straps somehow managing to ensnare in a branch. Above her, small flames licked the air. Fortunately, the fire was on the smoldering side, the pace of the flames up the tree languid, looking like dozens of birthday candles.

Since Keystone didn't have an official fire department to speak of, volunteers arrived with buckets, and they created a bucket brigade, starting at the lake and ending at the tree.

Stewart manned the end of the line, still wearing his store apron. He shouted encouragement up to his sweetheart as a fisherman in waders thrust a bucket into his arms. Tepid water sloshed over the sides before the market owner tossed the contents high. Not only did it miss the small inferno, but the brunt of the cold water doused Wink squarely in the face.

"Stewart Benson! You did that on purpose!"

Wink's dress had caught on part of the branch, hiking up her skirt, revealing polka dot underwear. And now, thanks to Stewart's poor aim, her mascara ran down her cheeks in dark streaks, a la the Joker.

Since she didn't seem to be in immediate danger, Ella stepped closer, zooming in on her phone to be sure she got the best angle.

"El, you'll put that contraption away if you know what's good for you!"

"Why don't you just unbuckle the harness?"

"I tried." Wink attempted again, demonstrating the problem. Hanging the way she was put tension on the straps, and the buckle couldn't give.

Stewart looked at Ella. "The sheriff and Jimmy went to fetch a ladder."

As he said this, Chapman called out from behind, telling them to make room. He and the deputy came bounding through, carrying an insanely tall ladder.

A familiar scent hit Ella's nose. Turning, she found Will standing beside her, shielding his eyes and staring up at Wink. "Is that my jet pack?"

"Is it? Huh, I hadn't noticed." She crossed her arms. "Hey, be honest. Does it look like I've been working out?"

"What?"

Chapman had climbed up the freakishly tall orchard ladder and stood on one side of Wink with Jimmy just below him. Both lawmen scratched their chins, trying to figure out the best way to get her down.

"Will you at least cover my bloomers?" Wink bit out.

Jimmy, his face flushing, eyes averted, obliged. As Chapman tugged on the straps for the jet pack, Will rushed to the ladder, his hands held high. "Careful with that."

"He means the jet pack," Ella called up to Wink.

"Thanks for the concern, William."

Will shook his head. "It's not that. The fuel's rather unstable. That's why I stopped using it."

High atop the ladder, Chapman tilted his hat back, peering down at the inventor. "Why in tarnation would you loan out something that could explode?"

Will's features twitched, and Ella knew he was struggling between ratting Wink out, saying he hadn't given her permission, and appearing irresponsible with one of his inventions.

He was saved from having to answer, however, as Wink said, "Can someone please get me down now? I'd like to remind you all that the tree's still on fire." Her arms flailed erratically in another attempt to free herself, slapping Jimmy across the cheek.

The fire had crawled up, leaving charred limbs, and seemed to be burning itself out. Ash and embers fell around the crowd like fireflies.

It took several minutes to extricate the woman from the tree, giving the crowd enough time to gawk despite Chapman ordering them to leave. Since the jet pack couldn't be unstrapped, Chapman and Jimmy had to hoist her down, pack and all. Grunting, they lowered her as far as they could, then let go.

The diner owner dropped the remaining feet to the ground, landing upright. Her arms wheeled around to gain balance, and there was a moment where she gave a triumphant grin before the weight from the jet pack won out.

She fell on her back with a *thud*. Arms and legs jutted up in the air as she thrashed wildly like an overturned beetle.

Ella snapped another picture with her phone. "I think I need to take up scrapbooking." Of course, she'd need to find some way of printing digital photos in a town that still printed black-and-white photographs.

Stewart and Will rushed forward to help Wink to her feet and relieved her of the rocket while Ella brushed grass and dirt off her boss as best she could.

The crowd gave a light applause. Wink dipped in an elaborate curtsey, grinning widely.

"Alright, folks," Chapman drawled. "Show's over."

Ella nudged Wink—who was giving another round of curtsies—towards the diner. "Come on. I'm sure Horatio needs us."

"No, I don't," a voice called amongst the dispersing cluster of people.

Ella spun to find Horatio standing there, a wide grin on his face. "How long have you been there?"

"Since Freddy ran into the diner saying Wink was stuck up in a tree that was on fire." Chuckling, he ambled back to Grandma's Kitchen, muttering, "Stuck up in a tree... Bloomers for all the world to see..."

Chapman stood nearby, shooing the stragglers away, while Jimmy and Will broke down the ladder.

Wink's face was still flushed from the excitement. "That was fun."

"Aside from the whole tree business, you mean."

"Hmm, I suppose."

"You suppose?" Ella caught sight of Chapman over Wink's shoulder. "Crap. Hurry, this is our chance to escape before—"

"Pearl Winkel." Chapman's voice halted them in their steps. "You gotta stay and answer questions."

Wink collected herself, probably mustering what little dignity she had left after half the town saw her undergarments. "Fine, but at the diner. I need a cup of joe after that."

Ella trailed behind, mostly to avoid being roped into questions. She hadn't been on the scene, and she didn't want either Jimmy or Chapman to realize that fact and ask her where she'd been.

Will parted, saying he needed to get back to work, and left before she could ask if he was making headway on the machine. It was probably for the best since everyone and their mother was pestering him about its status.

As they drew near the diner, she discovered the crowd hadn't dispersed, so much as relocated to the side street between Grandma's Kitchen and Stewart's Market.

Flo materialized at Ella's elbow, a sheen of sweat glistening on her forehead.

"Where have you been?"

"What d'you mean? I was in the park."

"I didn't see you. Wait, did it take you that long to catch up? Oh my gosh, woman."

"What's he doin'?" Flo asked, ignoring her.

Ella faced the crowd. At the edge of the gathering, Harold and some woman in coveralls parted, revealing an odd scene. A trailer bed pulled by a forlorn-looking donkey was parked at the curb. Flo's ex-husband Norman stood on the rickety platform amongst a slew of bottles filled with liquid that sloshed with each jiggle of the trailer. In case there were any doubts as to the contents of the containers, a scrap of cardboard was secured to the bed, the word "water" written in what appeared to be orange crayon.

The crowd shouted prices at Norm, competing over each other, their voices desperate. Norm's hand went to his ear as he leaned towards Harold, whose words rose loudest.

"Two dollars for a jug of water?" Harold shouted.

"I'm asking at least three for that size. I'm also willing to trade batteries or bulbs." Norm pushed his spectacles up, then exchanged a crate of recycled milk bottles for a five-dollar bill paid by a woman in a faded floral dress.

Harold spat and strode off, done with the spectacle.

Around Ella, more than a few grumbled about the steep prices, which were, for a town stuck in a 1950s economy, as high as Twin Hills.

"That's profiteering," Ella hollered, then frowned, muttering to Wink, "Right? Price gouging like that?" She wasn't an economist, but she'd been through enough disasters and seen enough predatory merchants who exploited situations to recognize the unethical practice.

Norm's eyes swiveled, homing in on her. "It's supply and demand. I have something the people need. Why can't I make some money on the side?"

Flo grunted, saying under her breath, "I think I'm starting to remember why we got a divorce."

Reluctantly, a man in a bowler hat beside Ella handed over three wrinkled ones, asking if the water had come from the treatment plant. Norm answered that it'd come from his well, then hefted over a heavy moonshine jug.

The glazed part of the stoneware caught the light, glowing like amber, and sparking a thought. Frowning, Ella wiggled between elbows and shoulders to get a closer look as Wink's voice rose above the din.

"I've got free water at my place. Anyone who wants to fill up's more than welcome to it."

"We don't have the means," a woman called out and added in a pointed, bitter voice, "Most of us weren't fortunate enough to get our vehicles modified by Mr. Whitehall."

Another female called out, and Ella glanced over to identify the source. Gladys Faraday offered up the use of a horse-drawn cart retrofitted with a water tank. She'd been using it at least twice a day, filling it with lake water, then hauling it to the greenhouses to water the town's indoor crops.

"I could fill up at Wink's, then park it on Main Street."

Murmurs of agreement and appreciation sounded. Norm's face reddened, but he seemed at a loss for a rebuttal, and Ella could practically see the dollar signs in his eyes bursting like balloons.

A heated discussion followed between the enterprising waterman, Gladys, Wink, and Flo—who stooped to calling him dirty names. But it washed over Ella as she focused on the familiar contents of the trailer. Molasses and tan-colored stoneware jugs. Milk bottles from Bradford Farms Dairy.

Sure, the town was limited on containers, but the presence of these specific ones, and only these as opposed to, say, wooden barrels, gave her pause. Looking up, she studied Norm. He stood elevated on the trailer bed, silhouetted against the noon-day sun. His hands waved animatedly, refuting one of Flo's accusations.

Ella's thoughts churned over the stockpile of water they'd discovered in the cave. Norm worked at the water treatment plant, giving him unrestricted access to the machinery. Also, there was his recent, inexplicable purchase of Dot's house— days before the water plant was sabotaged. A house that, despite being a downgrade for him, just so happened to have a well on it.

What had he gone to jail for? Racketeering?

And here he was, a solution ready and waiting for the problem he created, and at a steep price, no less. The professor had had some of Norm's water supply in his hideout. Had the professor figured out what he'd been planning?

CHAPTER TWENTY-SEVEN

"I KNEW HE was a good-for-nothing piece of—"

"You didn't even remember him," Ella said, cutting Flo off from what was sure to be a foul-mouthed diatribe about her ex-husband. She picked at a club sandwich—her dinner— and waited for Wink's voice of reason to steer the conversation.

"He's still better than half the men you've been with." The diner owner sat across from them in their booth, which left Ella next to Flo, whose hair was emanating a questionable odor.

That's when it struck her that she had yet to see Flo practicing any sort of hair hygiene since the water crisis began. Combing in baby powder. Rinsing it in lake water. Going to Wink's to use the bathtub. She'd done none of those things.

Ella pointed this out. The woman's only response was a shrug, saying her hair didn't get greasy. Ella's olfactory senses begged to differ.

The silence of the closed diner felt peaceful after the afternoon they'd had. Upon returning from Wink's *The Rocketeer* reenactment, the thirsty crowd had bustled from Norm's cart to the diner.

Ella massaged a knot in her shoulder while attempting to take another bite of her sandwich single-handedly. Slices of tomato and bacon plopped onto her plate. Slipping them back in, she said, "I think the best way to catch Norm is to get his fingerprints and compare them to those from the jar of jam."

Wink nodded. "How do we get his prints?"

As one, they both turned to Flo. Unsurprisingly, the crazy woman had stopped listening and was in the process of reshaping her dome of hair. The lack of water and visits to the beauty parlor weren't doing the frizzy tower any favors.

"You ever see paintings of Marie Antoinette?" Ella asked suddenly.

It took an uncomfortably long time for Flo to realize Ella had addressed her. "No, why?"

"No reason. So, how about it? Norm's fingerprints?"

"Well, I don't have them."

Wink pulled in a steady breath, an action the diner owner performed whenever she needed patience, usually when dealing with Flo. "Surely you have an object in that pig stye room of yours that he touched? A gift, perhaps, when you were married? We just need something he would've touched."

"I guess that counts Flo out." Ella chuckled at her own joke, which fell on deaf ears, then felt a pang of regret. Perhaps that had been too harsh. "I'm kidding, of course."

"I don't keep no presents from past suitors."

"Really?" Wink asked. "What about that bracelet you wear on special occasions?"

Flo tensed. "What about it?"

"You said someone special gave it to you."

"And you assumed it was a man? Why couldn't it have been my mother or a cousin?"

"All right. Don't get so defensive." Wink's brows scrunched as she studied her friend. "I'm going to grab a slice of bread. Anyone want some?"

Ella nodded. Wink's freshly baked, homemade bread was worth the extra jog around the lake to burn off.

The moment the door swung closed and the noise of Wink bustling in the kitchen floated from the pass-through, she turned on Flo.

"Donald gave you that bracelet, didn't he?"

Wink, Donald, and Flo had been best friends growing up, and the boarder had harbored a hidden torch for the man until he'd married Wink, which became a source of great pain. That pain stormed in the woman's eyes now at Ella's drudging up. She blinked rapidly, turning away, her lips mashing into a thin line.

"When are you going to tell her?"

"I don't see how it'll change anything." Flo's voice lowered at the sound of Wink's approaching footsteps in the kitchen. "And I don't see how that's any of your business. Stay out of this, Poodle Head."

A moment later, Wink waltzed back in and slid a plate of warm bread smeared with strawberry jam across the table. Ella thanked her and tried not to dwell on the coincidental appearance of the jam. The sweet scent hit her nostrils as she opened her mouth. She stopped, her jaw stuck open before she replaced the bread, unbitten, to the plate.

"Hold on a sec. If we're right—and we always are—and Norm's the one who hoarded all that water, then we can get his fingerprints from one of the bottles in the cave."

"When have we been right?" Wink asked.

Ella waved a hand dismissively. "I'm sure it's happened."

Flo's eyes lit up, the pain that had clouded them moments before vanishing. "We should stalk him."

"If by 'stalking' you mean patiently staking out the cavern chamber from a safe distance to see if he returns, thereby connecting him to the water, then yes, I agree."

"Huh?"

"Ella's right," Wink said. "We do this smart and safe this time."

"I'll get video proof on my cell phone." Ella waved the device around before wiping strawberry jam off the screen. "Oh, crap. Does that mean we're camping out in a cave tonight?" Images of bats and bears flitted through her mind.

Flo rubbed her hands together, bouncing gently in the booth. "Like I said, a good old-fashioned stalkin'."

"Stakeout."

"That's what I said. A clandestine stakeout."

Ella beamed. "Look at that. You finally used the word correctly. See? I knew if you just—"

"The word *stakeout*? 'Course I did, 'cause I'm clandestine."

Ella sighed.

They waited until the cover of darkness to sneak into the cave, taking the chance Norm wouldn't go back for more water in broad daylight. Against her better judgment, Ella not only returned Flo's weapons to her, but she even borrowed a couple for herself.

They weighed down her pack during the tense, anxious hike to the cave, but her thoughts were elsewhere. The flicker of her lantern made the shadows of the surrounding forest dance, and more than once, she whipped out the borrowed pistol to point at nothing.

Once in the cave, she lowered her guard somewhat. Danger could only come from two directions now: forward or back. Her fear heightened again when she saw the bear trap had been sprung.

Leading the charge, Flo wielded The Hammer like she was on some geriatric version of *The A-Team*. However, after the Murdock wannabe obliterated a stalagmite, mistaking it for either an animal or Norm, Ella wrested the plasma cannon away and handed her the pistol.

"I think I should take lead."

"You don't know where you're going." Flo checked the pistol's magazine to see if it was loaded, pointing it uncomfortably close to Ella's face.

Ducking out of range, Ella said, "You can tell me where to go."

She knew to follow the marks she'd made Sunday to a certain point, but after that, they'd have to rely on Flo's memory and vision. They'd be lucky to find the water cache by morning.

Marching, The Hammer resting on one shoulder, Ella hummed the theme song for *The A-Team* on a loop. When they ran out of marks, they stopped at each junction so Wink could carve a notch in the rock.

"Left," Flo called out behind Ella.

"You sure?"

"'Course, I'm sure. I know the way to my own bunker."

After the tenth jab in the shoulder from the boarder, Ella let out an exasperated growl. "If you think you can do a better job, then *you* lead again."

"Fine by me." Smirking, Flo strutted past—and smacked right into a limestone wall. Expletives bounced along the passageway, echoing into the distance, as if a dozen, foulmouthed sailors surrounded them.

She rubbed her nose, glaring at some point over Ella's left ear.

"I'm over here."

"I know that," Flo spat. "You've made your point. You lead. Just know we gotta take a left soon."

From the rear, Wink said, "Maybe we should keep our voices down? If Norm's already in the cave or if he enters now, he'll hear us a mile away."

Agreeing, they fell silent until they arrived at Flo's old bunker ten minutes later. The cavern was a few turns away from Norm's water stash—what Ella had begun calling Watergate, which then required several minutes of explanation as to why it was a clever name. Neither Flo nor Wink found it interesting, and she only stopped talking when Flo aimed her gun at her. They figured Norm would have to pass it to reach his chamber (Watergate), so they set up camp in the old, cramped bunker.

"I still say we should be closer." Flo pulled out a crumpled sleeping bag that smelled of mothballs and was peppered with burn marks, most likely from being too near a campfire.

Wink lobbed a small pebble at the woman. "And I still say you should keep your voice down."

The cloth on Wink's pack moved of its own accord, and Ella jumped, choking back a scream. A moment later, Chester's brownish-gray head poked out. He sniffed the air, whiskers twitching, before he disappeared back into the bag. Clearly, musty caves weren't his scene, especially having spent time in one last Sunday.

Shaking her head, Ella unfurled her sleeping pad. It wasn't comfortable so much as it took the edge off the hard, uneven ground, making her long for the camping days of her youth, full of cots and blow-up air mattresses.

They settled into their sleeping bags to stay warm, keeping conversation to a minimum, so they could hear if anyone approached. One lantern remained lit, turned down until the wick was barely visible.

Ella felt the tug of exhaustion, but there was no way she'd turn in before her elderly friends. Staving off sleep, she pulled out the book she'd brought, the one on Cro-Magnons.

But instead of reading, her eyes traveled the cavern walls, watching the shadows jump. The silence was a pressure on her ears, and it was a relief when Wink made noise as she searched inside her pack.

The diner owner passed around a container of jerky. Ella bit into the meat, instantly regretting it. For the first time since arriving in Keystone, she found one of Wink's creations unpalatable.

"What is this?" There was a strong flavor she couldn't readily identify.

"Trout."

Ella immediately pocketed the rest and did her best to swallow what was in her mouth. It felt like a lump sliding down her throat.

"Mmm, yum," she managed, turning down the container as it went around a second time.

Time seemed to stand still beneath the earth, and she was unaware she'd drifted off to sleep until awoken four hours later by Wink for her shift at keeping watch.

As Wink slid back into her sleeping bag, Ella took up her post at the mouth of the chamber. A mineral formation roughly the size and shape of a large suitcase served as her backrest. The dim, flickering lantern was tucked deeper into the cavern, partially obstructed by Flo's snoring form. That way, if Norm did show up, he wouldn't see the light from the passageway.

Her eyelids felt heavy, and she fought to keep them open. She should have brought coffee. This far from the lantern, it was too dark to read. That left her with nothing but the pressing silence and her thoughts, which were what she'd been trying to avoid ever since her and Will's encounter with the shadowy man in the hat.

Just the recollection sent a cold shiver down her spine that had nothing to do with the icy limestone pressed against her back. Maybe she should borrow one of Flo's handguns indefinitely to keep on her person at all times.

What had the professor gotten himself entangled with? Was Norm also Will's attacker?

She rested the cannon in her lap, its cool metal and weight reassuring. Time dragged on, and she wasn't sure how long she'd been sitting there when somewhere deep down the passage came a scuffling noise. Her body froze, her ears straining.

There it was again. It sounded like the steady rhythm of footfalls on stone.

Her breath quickened, and she checked the dial on the weapon before crawling over and nudging Wink awake. The diner owner's eyes shot open.

Ella put her finger to her mouth to warn Wink to keep quiet. As she returned to the mouth of the cavern, Wink shuffled over and woke Flo. Thankfully, she'd had the foresight to cover the boarder's mouth because the first thing Flo did was let out a muffled sound.

The cannon pressed down on Ella's shoulder as she hid just out of sight of the tunnel. She'd wait for Norm to pass, then follow at a distance. Their plan hinged on catching him in the act.

The echoing noise stopped for some time before starting up again. Beating hard, her heart felt like a drum inside her chest.

Slowly, the steps grew louder.

She practically jumped out of her skin when a booming male voice began humming. This deep in the earth, far from the slumbering town, she figured he didn't have to concern himself with stealth.

Her grip tightened on The Hammer.

Just as the humming was reaching a crescendo, a furry shape larger than a lion slipped past her cover, entering their small hideout. Soft paws padded across the rock almost imperceptibly.

Spot paused feet from where she crouched, close enough for her to hear the predator breathe, close enough to see his fangs. Those large, massive fangs.

CHAPTER TWENTY-EIGHT

ELLA'S FINGER REACTED, squeezing the trigger for The Hammer before her brain had a chance to catch up. A cerulean blue plasma ball shot out and went wide, missing Spot by a good three feet. It exploded against the wall. Rock and dust rained down all around her.

His amber eyes glowed in the lantern light as he growled, then released a spine-tingling scream reminiscent of a cougar only a thousand times louder.

Pop, pop. Flo shot at the beast with her handgun, forcing Ella to dive for the cavern floor.

"You nut job! You're shooting at me."

"Stop!" Wink shouted at Flo.

Bullets stopped flying, and the dust began settling. Scrambling to her feet, Ella coughed and aimed the cannon again at Spot. It appeared the plasma ball and gunshots were momentarily giving the sabertooth second thoughts about proceeding forward.

"Here, kitty, kitty." Wink extended her hand so the "kitty" could sniff it.

"Are you insane?" Ella asked.

Ignoring the question, Wink continued to coo at the feline. "Who's a good kitty? You are. Yes, you're a good kitty. "

Spot's obnoxiously large maw yawned open and snapped towards Wink's fingers. She jerked her hand back in time to save it from becoming prehistoric kitten chow.

"What do you know?" Flo said. "He is a good kitty."

The beast crouched, his hindquarters rising in the air, swishing back and forth in that telltale, feline gesture of an incoming pounce.

"Go!" Ella yelled. "I'll cover you."

Wink grabbed her pack, which held Chester, and sprinted past, into the dark passage. Flo was hot on her heels, the lantern swinging wildly in her hand, her pistol aimed vaguely behind her.

Her back to the tunnel, Ella fired the cannon again. Spot chose that moment to spring into the air, and the shot missed. A sphere of crackling lightning hit a stalactite, dropping it with a rumbling crash to the ground.

He growled and hissed at the debris, buying her the diversion she needed. The last vestiges of Flo's light left, plunging her into deep darkness. Her hands trembled as she groped her way into the passageway.

Spotting Flo's bobbing lantern in the distance like a beacon, she ran. She only tripped twice and stopped counting how many times she pinballed into a limestone wall after ten. The darkness behind her was absolute, and she had no idea if the overly zealous furball was in pursuit.

She hurriedly caught up to her friends, then had to push Flo in the back with the barrel of the cannon to encourage her to pour on the heat. Just after a turn, the trio darted past a tall figure in dirty overalls, holding a lantern, a bewildered expression on his face.

"Hey, Harold," Ella yelled over her shoulder. "Mind calling off your hellhound?"

Whatever he said in response was lost to the heavy slapping of their shoes and Flo's labored breathing. Another feral scream rushed up the passage behind them, sounding alarmingly close.

She heard Harold yell, "Spot, heel!" but didn't want to stop to see if the command had worked.

The tunnel widened into an alcove that branched off three separate ways. She was all sorts of turned around and hoped Wink, who was leading their flight, was faring better. There wasn't time enough to check their markers to be sure they were headed in the right direction.

Ella's legs were starting to cramp, and she wondered how much longer Flo could hold up in an all-out sprint. She spared a glance back.

Spot's dark form bounded towards them.

"Wink! Throw him your jerky!"

Ahead, Wink fumbled with her backpack. A moment later, chunks of dry, shriveled trout flew into alcoves and down side passages.

Ella looked back. The sabertooth paused briefly to sniff a piece, turned up his nose, and continued to give chase. Even a carnivorous prehistoric cat deemed the jerky inedible.

Without bothering to aim, she spun and squeezed off a wild shot. The blinding plasma lit the interior of the cave, revealing just how close Spot was, before part of the wall exploded. A breath later, the stubborn, toothy animal burst through the cloud of debris like a deadly version of the Kool-Aid Man, undeterred.

She let out a frustrated yell. She wouldn't mind making a rug out of the fur-demon.

Harold could be heard far behind, hollering at his pet. Turning to fire at Spot had cost her precious time. Now, she could hardly see, the light from the lantern spilling meekly from around a corner.

"Wink? Flo?"

Their voices echoed somewhere ahead. She groped along the wall, hearing the soft *thump, thump* of Spot's paws behind her.

"Welp, this is my worst nightmare." Her throat began tightening, panic rising. "Marco?"

"Over here, Poodle Head," Flo called out.

"Yeah, that doesn't help me."

Harold's distant lantern came into view, providing just enough weedy light to make out the wide mouth of a cavern entrance. Ella plunged inside and spotted her friends.

She let out a breath, sprinting to join them. Their faces were pale, and sweat glistened on Flo's face. Ella shoved them behind a rock formation, then directed The Hammer at the entrance, fiddling with the settings. Next to her, Flo wheezed and aimed her handgun roughly in the same direction—but slightly up and to the left.

Several things happened simultaneously: Ella realized that the cavern they'd taken refuge in had been the professor's and Craig's hideout, Spot burst into the cavern—followed immediately by Harold—and Ella and Flo fired their weapons.

"No! Stop!" Harold screamed.

Flo's bullets ricocheted. Ella's shot zipped high. The plasma ball was twice the size of the previous one after her finagling of the settings. It hit the top of the entrance, sending rock flying every which way.

A rumble followed, a vibration Ella felt deep in her chest rather than heard. Without warning, the top of the mouth calved off and crashed to the chamber floor in a violent tumult of noise and boulders and rubble.

Silence fell.

The dust cloud reached their position, and she covered her mouth, coughing until she was sure a lung would come up.

Using her shirt as a respirator, she blinked away dust motes in her eyes.

As the cloud of limestone settled, the meager light of two lanterns revealed their situation. And it wasn't good.

"Are you going to help?" Ella straightened her exhausted back, taking a breather.

Flo held up a rock the size of a baseball. "I am." She tossed it onto the growing pile a few yards away.

Harold stood closest to the caved-in entrance and hefted a heavy chunk to Wink, who in turn handed it off to Ella, who then tossed it over to the pile with a grunt after Flo refused to take it.

She shot a wary glance to the side where Spot lay, watching them like they were his next meal. Harold had managed to keep him at bay, commanding him to "stay" near a stalagmite. So far, the beast hadn't discovered Chester in Wink's bag, the squirrel having wisely chosen to remain hidden.

"El, what time is it?" Wink asked, pausing to dab her sleeve over her forehead.

Ella consulted her watch, angling it towards the nearest lantern. They'd extended the wick, illuminating the cavern enough to see, but still keeping it low to conserve fuel.

"4:30 a.m."

How long before they were discovered missing? Surely, Rose or Jimmy would notice their absence.

The cavern was large enough that she wasn't worried about oxygen—yet—but the death glares between Harold and Flo warranted concern. The one thing they lacked was water. Ella and Flo had fled their campsite before grabbing their packs. Wink shared her canteen amongst them, but its contents were dwindling fast due to their physical labor.

She glanced over at Harold. The farmer's biceps pumped like pistons as he hefted another rock from the detritus. "What were you doing in the cave, anyhow?"

"Me? Goin' after Spot. He's taken a shine to these tunnels."

"Yes, dank dark rock, bats, and bears. I see the appeal."

An hour later, during a break, he sauntered over to what remained of the professor's camp, and she watched him from the corner of her eye. Not much of the site was left beyond moldy bread and empty jars, most of the belongings having been carted off during the investigation. He sniffed at a jar of peaches, testing the juice with his tongue before guzzling it.

At the pile of rocks, she aimed her cell phone light at the top of the mound.

"See anything? Are we through yet?" Wink asked.

Ella shook her head, hiding her disappointment as she clambered down the precarious barricade. She gave Spot a wide berth and joined Harold, who'd wandered over to Craig's paintings, peach juice in hand.

"What's it mean?" He inclined his head at the artwork.

"Hmm, that's a question historians and linguists have wondered for years. They theorize that the Cro-Magnons' art held some sort of magical or ritual significance to them. Me, personally? I think they just liked being creative." She nodded at the paintings. "There's a story in there somewhere." This was more of a gut feeling than an observation.

After awhile, she added, "We were only defending ourselves against your demon pet. I'm sorry I got us all stuck in here."

"Spot can't help what he is."

"That's probably true. Hey, here's a thought—and I'm just spitballing off the top of my head—but it's probably a terrible idea to have a prehistoric predator the size of a Volkswagen as a house pet." She lightened her tone. "If it makes you feel better, that soft spot you have for a wild animal capable of ripping out your jugular is something you and Wink have in common."

"He's much easier to get along with than people."

She considered this. At one point, she would've agreed. People were complicated and messy. "You know, I think we just have to find the right people, those who aren't energy vampires. Find people who give more than they take, and I think you'll find humans more tolerable."

She was staring at the paintings, her mind drifting, then the artwork came into focus. A stick figure stood by a four-legged animal. At first, she thought it a deer until she noticed the antlers were facing down, not up.

She drew closer. No, not antlers. Fangs. Ridiculously long incisors.

Suddenly, she knew exactly the story the paintings wove. Caveman Craig had painted Spot alongside Harold. The two faced off against two more stick figures: the Cro-Magnon himself, and that shape with what looked like a ball on his head would be the professor and his crazy, Einstein-frizzed hair. Arrows flew between the pairs. And if she squinted and tilted her head just right, that circle with sharp teeth in the middle of the standoff was redolent to a bear trap.

Goosebumps prickled her arms. Casually, she pointed at the jar in Harold's right hand, saying in an offhand tone, "That stuff still good?"

He held it up, swirling it like a fine wine. The distant lantern glow lit his hands, revealing red marks on his palms and the insides of his forearms. They were reminiscent of a similar injury she'd seen before, on Diego the not-pirate. Rope burns.

Everything fell into place. Ella took a hesitant step back, then another.

They were trapped with a killer.

CHAPTER TWENTY-NINE

"YOU OKAY? YOU look like you've seen a ghost." Harold sloshed the jar of peach juice around before guzzling the last of it. He chewed the fruit, a dribble of sticky liquid leaking from the corner of his mouth.

"Fine." Ella's shrill voice bounced around the cavern and came back to her ears. Biscuits and gravy, was that her voice sounding like a howler monkey?

Spot's head shot up, and she realized she'd edged too close to the sabertooth. "How'd he get that injury on his paw?"

Harold's face darkened, his fingers tightening on the empty jar. "Got caught in a bear trap."

Her eyes flitted to the limestone wall, below the paintings, to the gunfire marks. The plasma cannon was across the cavern, near the cave-in, resting against a rock cropping.

Their situation was dire. Not only were they trapped, low on food and water and bathrooms—save for the "potty corner" they'd designated earlier—but they were trapped with a murderer. Their survival depended on her reaction. She had to play it cool.

After rejoining Flo and Wink, they resumed the laborious task of relocating the rubble.

"El?" Wink asked when she saw her face. "You look pale."

Harold was nearby, stroking Spot's tan fur.

"That's the second time someone has remarked on my complexion. I just want to point out that we're coming out of winter—not that that's relevant in a town that jumps locations and seasons. Point is, I've been indoors quite a bit lately."

Wink's eyes narrowed, and Ella knew she was rambling, one of her signature nervous ticks, right up there with deflecting using humor. But she couldn't say anything with the farmer and his hellhound close by.

"Do you need more water?"

Ella shook her head, then stopped. "Wait, we have more water? That's an option? Because my tongue feels like sandpaper."

Small pebbles cascaded down the mountain of detritus as Harold scaled up the side. The moment he turned his back to pick up a large rock that could probably be classified as a boulder, she motioned at her friends, pointing at the man's back, then to her throat, making the universal gesture of death by slicing her finger across it.

Flo squinted. "I think the lack of oxygen's cracked her noodle."

Harold turned, hefting the boulder.

Ella's hands fell to her sides, and she glared at Flo. Coming from someone who wore tinfoil on her head like a party hat, the woman's quip was rich.

Climbing, she took up a position at the top of the rubble, handed off a jagged remnant of limestone to Wink, and dropped her voice to a whisper. "Harold's property has a well, right?"

"Yes, but what's that have to—" The confusion in Wink's face cleared, turning to alarm. She mouthed, *He sabotaged the water plant?*

Ella nodded. Wink's mouth turned down as she pondered this implication, and Ella knew she was trying to connect the dots to the professor's murder.

Off to the side, Harold stopped so abruptly, Ella dropped the rock she'd been holding in alarm. It hit her toes, sending pain shooting up her foot as she hopped up and down like a human pogo stick atop the hazardous mound of debris.

"Jelly-filled donuts! That hurts." After sliding down the pile, she continued her clog dance of pain while keeping one eye on the farmer. Her foot smarted so much she found further speech difficult, save for a few swear words.

Harold had stopped to mop his brow. "What about the cannon?" He aimed a thick finger at the weapon resting nearby. One of the lanterns chose that moment to flicker eerily, creating a menacing umbrage over his face. The kerosene was running low.

"What about it?" Wink's body stiffened.

Oblivious, Flo chewed a hangnail on her grimy hand. "It's nice, ain't it?"

"Nice isn't what I'd call it," Harold said. "But that's not what I meant. That contraption got us into this mess. Maybe it can get us outta it."

The pain in Ella's foot subsided enough to allow for speech again. "That's not a bad idea, actually." She gave the killer a thumbs up. "Good job, Harold. Flo? What do you think?" If Flo adjusted the settings just right, perhaps it could clear the rubble without creating more.

"Gotta dial the power up, but maybe...."

"I'm sorry, did you say dial the power *up?* As in, *increase* the dangerous ionized gas that can blast rock like dynamite?" Ella wiggled her fingers in her ears, certain she was hearing wrong. Hypoxia was probably setting in. "Yes, that seems like the smartest course of action. We can die, buried in our own tomb like our ancestors."

"You're always so dramatic. We gotta increase the range of the electro-something. With the power high enough, it can change the state of matter and melt rock."

"The 'electro-something'," Ella repeated. She was now certain the time had finally come when one of Will's inventions, in the hands of her insane friend, would kill her.

"Flo," Wink intoned, "do you have any idea how the cannon works?"

"Isn't it kind of late to be asking that?" Ella said.

The stubborn woman jutted out her chin. "I don't gotta understand the physics to know it works. William gave me a demonstration—melted his concrete bird fountain right there in his backyard."

So, *that's* what that blob of gray rock was. She'd just assumed he was into abstract garden decor.

Harold clapped his large calloused hands together. "Sounds like a plan." He made for the weapon, but Ella darted over, hoisting it up first.

"Someone who's handled it before should probably fire it." She gave him a sheepish grin. Behind him, Wink let out a breath, nodding in approval.

"I agree." Flo strode forward, nearly tripping over a large rock, and tried to rip The Hammer from Ella's grip.

"Someone who can *see*," Ella amended.

After arguing about who got to take the shot, with Ella pointing out that the boarder would be unable to see an elephant sitting on her face, they took refuge at the far end of the cavern behind a mineral formation the size of a stegosaurus.

Spot sat on his large haunches at Harold's feet, growling and baring his elongated teeth at them. They'd left one lantern near the entrance so Ella could see her target.

Flo had already calibrated the cannon to what they needed, or so she'd said. The doubt in her voice hadn't filled Ella with confidence.

The steel, a cold bite through her clothes, gleamed as she hefted the weapon to her shoulder. She closed one eye, training the sights just high of the center of the rocky mass.

She paused, glancing down the line of tense faces alongside her. "Flo, just out of curiosity, what're the chances this will cause *more* of a cave-in?"

The woman made a weighing motion with her hands. "I'd say fifty-fifty."

"Okay, good. For a moment there, I thought we were in real danger."

Air hissed out of her lungs as she steadied herself once again. She could do this. It wasn't like their lives depended on it or anything.

She focused and became acutely aware of her own breathing, the damp smell of the cave, Spot licking his mouth, and Flo's impatient fidgeting.

"I've been waiting for the right opportunity to say this.... It's Hammer time."

Her finger pulled the trigger.

The surrounding air *whooshed* as a plasma ball shot out. Every hair on her body stood at attention. The fillings in her teeth hummed, which was a new, disturbing side effect.

Just as she was wondering if she should be concerned about some sort of radiation and the ability to bear children, the magenta and royal blue ionized plasma ball expanded to fifteen feet across. All four of them sucked in a collective breath, Wink's backpack wiggled, and even Spot paused amid bathing his stomach to peer at the shiny ball of lightning.

It discharged against the rubble barricade.

Limestone pebbles and rock chips sailed through the air, but far less than expected, most of the pile remaining intact. Electric lines danced over the debris, bouncing around before dissipating.

"Huh." Ella rested the cannon upright against the mineral formation. "Well, that was anticlimactic."

Then she realized the cavern was growing brighter. The rubble began glowing a dim red, slowly flaring to a brilliant orange the color of fire.

An odd gurgling noise echoed around the chamber, and she ducked behind their cover again in case the barricade spontaneously exploded. When the light receded to a dim glow, she poked her head up.

The mountain of rubble had turned to molten rock, oozing and cascading out from the now-uncovered passage. It bubbled around the floor of the mouth like a volcanic welcome mat, glowing and radiating heat out in waves.

Flo let out a *whoop* and jumped—or rather, Ella guessed that's what the bunny hop was supposed to have been.

"You look disappointed, El." Wink raised from her crouched position, brushing off her trousers.

"No. Well, yeah. It's just… one of our plans worked. A plan involving one of Flo's experimental weapons, I might add. I'm kind of waiting for the other shoe to drop, you know?" Any minute now, something would explode. Or cave in. Or blind them. Or knock them out.

Nothing happened.

Wink was rushing towards the opening. "What do you say we don't wait around to find out, dear? Or as you'd say, 'Let's lick this popsicle stand.'"

"Yes. That's exactly what I'd say. *Lick*. Let's *lick* this popsicle stand."

With access to the main tunnel again, a new obstacle presented itself in the form of the lake of molten rock and how to span it. Judging by Flo's recent jumping display, Ella didn't have high hopes they could leap over it. So, they began the arduous task of relocating the rocks they'd cleared away from the cave-in, which hadn't melted, and stacked them, creating a bridge of sorts.

The moment they deemed the overpass "possibly stable enough to not burn to death," Wink grabbed Ella's and Flo's sleeves, dragging them towards the exit.

"But the lanterns—" Flo protested.

"Leave them," Wink hissed at Flo. The diner owner's pack bounced on her back at their rapid retreat.

"Have you gone off the rails? Leave a perfectly good lantern? How are we gonna see our way back?"

"Ella's rotary phone."

"I think you mean cell phone." At Wink's expression, Ella added, "But let's not split hairs." She just hoped she had enough battery power to light their way, since she hadn't been able to charge the device the night before, the cave lacking outlets and all.

Rushing to the foot of the bridge, the plasma cannon felt like the weight of the world on her exhausted back, and she Atlas. She was so tired.

They were partway across the bridge when Harold's voice stopped them.

"What's the rush?"

CHAPTER THIRTY

HAROLD'S TONE EDGED with menace. At a commanding whistle from him, Spot bounded forward. He crouched at the foot of their makeshift bridge, ready to spring across the rock and attack his prey.

Ella's brain performed haphazard calculations, and she realized that even if they sprinted at top speed, the saber-tooth would overtake them before they made it to the passage. And if by some miracle they did make it, the tunnel didn't offer much more safety.

Whatever they did, they needed to do it now. The pond of molten rock had begun to melt the bridge.

"The rush?" Ella kept her voice steady. "Oh, I don't know. Maybe because we've been trapped in a cave, missing for several hours, and haven't eaten or slept or—most importantly—haven't had our morning cup of joe. That's the rush."

"You think I don't know you figured it out?" He took a menacing step towards the bridge, and Spot let out a low growl that belonged in a made-for-TV horror movie.

The trio stood in a tight line halfway over the narrow bridge with nowhere to run.

"What're you jawing about?" Flo pushed her cracked glasses up her nose, squinting at him. "Figured what out?"

Subtly, Ella shifted her weight, hoping to bring the plasma cannon about in a way that didn't draw his attention. Glancing back, she raised her eyebrows at Wink and mouthed, *Stall*.

"He means," Wink said to Flo, "he knows we figured out he killed the professor."

Flo snorted, obviously thinking it a joke. When no one laughed, her head swung back and forth between the diner owner and the farmer. Meanwhile, Ella kept a wary eye on Spot, her fingers fumbling with the dial, buttons, and toggles on the cannon.

"Why would he kill the professor?" Flo asked.

"Because," Ella said, discreetly turning the dial further, "that's *his* water stash. Not Norm's. It's the real reason he was in the caves."

Wink called out to him, "You're the one who sabotaged the water plant, aren't you Harold?"

He grunted. One muddy boot reached the bridge, the rocks already having sunken an inch. Sweat tickled her back. The heat emanating from below wasn't unlike what she imagined falling into the sun to feel like.

"What's wrong with making a bit of money, hmm? It's amazing how much people are willing to give you when they're thirsty." He stole another bold step.

Without seeing the settings on the plasma weapon, Ella had to hope she'd dialed the power back enough not to make a melted puddle out of the man.

At her back, she could feel Flo spin around and say to Wink, "But how's the water connect to the professor?"

Ella answered for her. "Because Dr. Kaufman discovered Harold's stockpile and figured out what he was planning."

Her finger lingered on the trigger pull. "Isn't that right, Harold?"

His silence and enraged face betrayed his guilt.

Flo leaned over Ella's shoulder to make a *tsk-tsk* noise at the murderous farmer and shook her head in disapproval, her drooping hair wobbling about like a sad bobblehead.

"He shot at us," Harold snarled. The anger in his voice caused the sabertooth to tense, his ears twitching forward, pupils dilating. "Then he set that trap that injured Spot. If I hadn't found him in time, he could've died."

The bear trap, Spot's wounded paw, and the bullet ricochet marks in the cavern—all of it to keep the professor's new hiding place safe.

"I'm guessing Spot gave him a reason to think he was going to attack, and he was defending himself," she said.

"That don't give him the right." He spat, and the molten rock sizzled where his phlegm hit. "You know how many families he's ruined? Look at our town! I did us all a favor."

"So, because he threatened your wild pet, you killed the only man capable of getting us all back home?"

"If he could've fixed the time contraption, he would've done it by now. We've still got that inventor beau of yours."

"Huh? Oh, yes! Will. What I meant to say was, you killed the only man, *other than Will*, capable of getting us all back home." She whispered loudly to Wink and Flo, "Please don't tell him what I said."

Ignoring her, Flo tutted at him again. "Shouldn't have murdered him."

"That man tried to kill the only family I have left! I was just protecting what's mine. You all would've done the same." He glanced down affectionately at his prehistoric bodyguard.

Ella coughed. "Seriously? You're insane. That's a horrible reason to murder someone. Not that there's ever a good reason, but if there was, I'm telling you, him threatening your pet isn't it."

Now that she said it aloud, she reflected on her statement. Fluffy was family, but also still an animal. However, if someone threatened him, she'd rain hellfire down on that person. Still, murder seemed extreme.

Wink's voice came out subdued. "I get it."

Ella's head whipped around before she realized she'd turned her back on the killer.

"Really, I do. I'd do anything for Chester."

"Even kill?" Her voice echoed around the chamber.

"Well, no. Not that."

It was nice to know her boss toed the line somewhere.

Ella opened her mouth to continue questioning Harold, such as asking him where he'd procured cyanide. Or why he always wore overalls and did he not own another pair of clothing? Or did she look like she'd been working out and would he mind giving her biceps a squeeze?

In the end, she settled on making awkward popping noises with her lips and saying, "Welp, now that we got all that unpleasantness out of the way... Wink, Flo, let's lick this popsicle stand."

She kept the plasma cannon aimed at the farmer and brandished it in a way that warned him not to follow, telling the other two to go first. Then she considered Harold. If they ran, they would leave a killer on the loose, and they'd also have to be looking over their shoulders the entire way back.

"Once we're across, you're going to follow us from a safe distance. You got that?" She waved The Hammer in what was supposed to be a threatening manner but nearly sent her reeling into the bubbling lava.

One side of his mouth rose in a sneer. Down at his feet, unnoticed by Harold, Spot gave her the same sneer. They did say owners and pets began to look alike, and at this moment, the resemblance was uncanny.

Harold's eyes were alive, calculating, and she could practically see the conundrum behind them. Allow himself to be led out at cannon point, whereby he'd be arrested for the professor's murder? Or take out an annoying waitress and her two feisty, geriatric friends?

His eyes fell to the barrel of The Hammer which had drifted to the side while Ella had been waiting impatiently for a response.

"Oops." Squinting down the sights, she realigned it over his chest. "That's better."

The heat at her feet was nearly unbearable now, her clothes drenched in sweat. Her calves felt like those turkey legs at concession stands in theme parks that had been sitting under a heat lamp all day, just over-roasted meat on bones.

"What's it going to be, Old MacDonald? Oh, and if you're coming, grab one of the lanterns, will you?"

The cold, withering look he gave her made her mouth go dry. But after retrieving the nearest lantern, he took a ponderous step onto the bridge, defeated.

She let out an inaudible sigh of relief.

When she glimpsed behind her, she noticed Wink and Flo were waiting for her in the relative safety of the cool passage. Carefully walking backward, she joined them while Harold balanced on the narrow span, lantern swaying in his hand, followed by Spot. Wan light bled from the cavern into the tunnel, only illuminating a short distance in either direction.

Harold's boots hit the limestone a few yards in front of her. Her hands occupied with the cumbersome weapon, she said, "Flo, would you mind reaching into my sweatshirt pocket for my ph—"

Harold twitched his hand forward, and Spot leaped. The walls echoed with the beast's loud, blood-curdling scream.

Fangs.

She glimpsed massive, sharp teeth coming at her face as she squeezed the trigger. On her shoulder, the Hammer hummed. A plasma sphere shot out and hit Spot dead center of his furry chest, sending him flying back.

The sabertooth hit the wall and landed on his feet. He shook his head, appearing little more than stunned thanks to her blind adjustments to the power settings while in the chamber.

Another scream, this time from Harold. He barreled towards Ella, spitting like a deranged animal. She blindly thumbed the dial and mashed buttons.

At the same time, Flo's hand whipped up to her wilting bouffant. Something winked in the dim light before she flicked her wrist.

A throwing knife hissed past Harold's ear. With the woman's impaired vision, it was a wonder she'd managed to get that close to her target. Then again, she was standing five feet from the enraged psycho.

With a *thunk,* the handle of the blade hit Wink square in the forehead. She cried out, stumbling to the ground and clutching her head.

Harold collided with Ella like a freight train. Together, they crashed onto the cave floor. White-hot pain shot up her back as all the air escaped her lungs, which was unfortunate because the farmer wrapped his meaty hands around her throat.

In their tussle, the cannon had slid across the cold limestone, just out of reach. She flailed for it, gasping for air. Then she motioned for Flo to grab The Hammer, but the woman's attention was on their injured friend.

Wink's backpack had fallen beside her, and the flap wiggled open. Chester chose that moment to shoot out like a furry gray cannonball, apparently deciding he'd had enough of their shenanigans.

"Chester, no!" Still clutching her forehead, Wink bolted to her feet. She swayed in place, snatched up Harold's dropped lantern, then gave chase.

Spot growled and hissed before dashing after them, overtaking Wink in half a breath. Squirrel, sabertooth, and diner owner plunged around a bend, the light fading. From the depths, the sabertooth released another feral cry that reverberated through the passageway long after they were gone.

Harold's hands were still around Ella's throat. Darkness encroached at the edges of her vision, and her eyes felt like they'd pop out of her skull at any moment.

In a desperate attempt for air, she jabbed her thumbs in the farmer's eyes. It felt as gross as she'd expected.

He yelled, his grip seizing harder.

Lights, like fireflies, floated around the cave. Stars. She was on the verge of passing out.

Desperate, she scratched, punched, flailed, and kicked—all to no avail. Behind him, Flo hefted up The Hammer. The barrel exploded with a lightning ball that missed the man by a good ten feet. It floated down the tunnel, deeper under the mountain.

In a final attempt to thwart the man, Ella did what she always yelled at victims on TV to do when in similar situations: she played dead.

Her survival instinct reared up, making it difficult. The last thing her body wanted to do was go slack, but she did. Her eyelids fluttered shut, her hands stopped grappling, and she didn't move.

Harold's thick fingers fell away, and it took all of her willpower not to gasp for air. Incrementally, she expanded her lungs at a painstaking pace. It wasn't enough. Her body was still starved for oxygen.

"Ella?" Flo's frantic voice cut at her like a knife. She couldn't remember the last time the boarder had used her real name.

"What d'you do?! You killed her!"

Harold rolled off her, and it felt as if the weight of the entire rocky mountain above had lifted from her chest. She couldn't take it anymore, and she inhaled deeply, sucking damp oxygen like she sucked Bavarian cream filling from a donut.

Her eyes shot open in time to see Harold, hands raised, make a dive for Flo. At that short of a distance, even Flo couldn't miss.

Another ball of plasma shot out of the cannon, the color of a pre-dawn horizon, zapping and hissing in the air. The sphere grew, expanding like a bubble. It engulfed Harold and rendered him flat on his back where his head hit the cave floor with a loud *crack*. He lay still.

The plasma bubble continued to inflate.

"Uh-oh." Flo shuffled back rapidly.

"Uh-oh, what?" Ella croaked, sitting up, coughing and massaging her throat.

Flo's face flickered with relief upon seeing Ella alive before being displaced by fear. "Move it!"

Ella jumped to her feet. "That's it? No 'I'm glad you're alive, Ella. I sure was worried about you—'"

Flo gave a hard shove, and they ran from the expanding lightning. She was half a step behind the crazy woman when the plasma enveloped her.

Shades of blue crackled around her. If it was possible to *become* a disco ball, she imagined this was how it felt.

Tingles of electricity zapped up and down her body like that time when she was eight and stuck her finger in a receptacle to "see how it felt." Yet, somehow, it felt different from being electrocuted. The fillings in her teeth tried to escape, and she was pretty sure every hair on her body stood straight up, including the hair on her toes.

At one point—she wasn't certain when or how—she ended up on her back again. Colors shimmered overhead, opalescent greens and blues, in a miniature aurora borealis.

"Oh, shiny," she murmured.

It wasn't until she turned her head to see how Flo, who'd also been knocked out by the blast, was faring that she realized the light show was in her vision and not a new feature of the cave.

Well, that's concerning.

Flo groaned beside her, somewhere beyond the technicolor lights. "You adjusted the settings, didn't you?"

"What? No, of course not."

"What d'you put it to?"

Ella thought for a moment. "Is there a unicorn setting? I feel like I used the unicorn setting. All I know is, I turned the dial and pushed a button and toggled a doohickey."

"What have I told you about pressing buttons?"

"You've literally never said anything to me about buttons."

A shadow that was in the general shape of Flo's hair indicated she was sitting up.

Ella blinked several times until she could make out Harold's unconscious form. "Messy underwear aside, my settings got the job done. Dignified? No. But definitely effective."

"You soiled your bloomers, Poodle Head?"

"It's an exaggeration."

Flo sniffed. "I don't think it is." Shuffling over to Harold, she nudged the farmer's boot. "Look who got Hammered."

"Still no." Ella slowly climbed to her feet, feeling like she'd just fought several rounds in a boxing ring. "What do you say we tie this killer up and go rescue Wink before she's mauled to death? I'm pretty sure I saw rope at the professor's camp." She took a step and stopped. "Actually, how about you go first? You may want to walk upwind of me."

CHAPTER THIRTY-ONE

THE SOUND OF their footsteps echoed around the hospital's empty hallway. The entire building was roughly the size of one of the many clinics in Ella's hometown, but in Keystone Village, it was all they had.

Six hours after her encounter with The Hammer, her teeth still felt like they wanted to jump from her mouth, and when she'd last glanced at her reflection, her hair had resembled Medusa's head. Plasma and curly hair did not mix.

"You did, too," she retorted to a comment Flo had made when they'd first stepped into the building. "You thought I was dead." She said in a loud stage whisper to Wink, "You should have heard her. Tears. Real tears. She was bawling—"

"Was not."

"It's okay." Ella draped her arm around Flo's shoulders, which made walking difficult. "Now I know how you really feel about me."

The woman growled and shrugged out of reach. Ella felt too exhausted to go after her. Spending most of the night being chased by a saber-toothed tiger, moving large rocks alongside a killer, and getting jolted by a ball of ionized whatever-the-heck-that-was from the cannon had drained every ounce of energy she had. Even the thermos of Wink's stout coffee in her hand was barely keeping her from passing out. But she couldn't go home and sleep quite yet.

From an open doorway ahead, Chapman's gravelly drawl drifted out, and they slowed their pace. They'd come to speak with Harold, hoping to get more answers from him before Chapman and Jimmy locked him up.

The sheriff's words were too muffled to make out, and as the Keystone Gators edged closer, Pauline popped out of another room across the hall. It was rare to have more than one or two patients at a time, but the town's lack of water had resulted in a few cases of dehydration.

As one, the trio circled up. Wink and Flo adopted casual postures, chatting about how the weather was affecting their arthritis, while Ella pressed herself against the wall and froze.

"You realize I can see you, right?" Pauline frowned at Ella as she waddled past, continuing on, too preoccupied and harried to care why they were there.

Ella let out a breath the moment the doctor was out of sight. "I don't think she saw me."

Wink blinked, shook her head, then tiptoed to the door, making sure to remain hidden from the occupants in the room.

Some jostling and one crushed foot later, they practically stood on top of each other to eavesdrop on Harold's conversation with the lawmen.

"… was gonna turn me in. Said so himself. He knew the whole town hated him. He thought if he told you what I did and you arrested me, that he'd be some sort of hero," Harold was saying.

A metallic clanking noise Ella couldn't readily identify accompanied his speech. Then she placed the sound as handcuffs—most likely Chapman's ancient manacles that required a tetanus shot when used. The farmer must be strapped to the hospital bed.

"He was delusional. Like folks would ever forget what he'd done. He's doomed us forever."

"You don't know that," came Jimmy's voice.

"I do. I know Will said in the paper he thought he could fix the machine, but I saw his face at that meeting. He ain't close."

Ella's throat tightened, and she found it difficult to swallow.

"When did you start hoarding water?" Chapman asked.

"'Bout three months back." There was no shame in Harold's voice, no remorse, and Ella got the impression he was mostly upset that he'd been caught.

"How'd you get access to the water facility?"

Harold mumbled something.

"Speak up, son," Chapman groused. "Open that bone box of yours wider."

Flo's face scrunched, and Ella whispered an interpretation, explaining that a "bone box" meant "mouth."

Harold's voice rose as he repeated what he'd said. "I used my truck. The fuel went bad in it years back, but I hitched the cab to some horses I borrowed from the Fitzes. Anyway, I parked it under that window by the door, used a ladder in the bed to climb up, then used a rope on the inside." His pronunciation of "window" had an "r" sound at the end.

Wink glanced at Ella, her penciled eyebrows rising in appreciation that her theory had been correct.

"Then when I left, I broke down my ladder and pulled the rope out before ridin' off."

"Just to be sure I got this straight," Jimmy began, pausing, probably to consult his notes, "you killed Dr. Kaufman because he was going to tattle on you to Chapman?"

Harold let out a heavy sigh. "Not just 'cause of that."

"Oh? You killed him for another reason?"

Ella held her breath. Here it comes.

"He tried to kill my pet."

"Pardon?" Jimmy said.

At that moment, Ella cursed the fact that she didn't have superpowers and the ability to see through walls. She was sure both lawmen's expressions were priceless.

"He caught him in a bear trap, injuring poor Spot. Then he shot at him when all Spot was doin' was minding his own business. 'Course, he claimed Spot tried to attack him, but what d'you expect when you've got weeks' worth of food stashed in a cave?"

Several seconds passed before Chapman said, "That's the worst fimble-famble I've ever heard in all my years wearing the badge."

"Harold," Jimmy said, the hint of a smile in his voice as if he were fighting off laugher, "where did you get the poison?"

Ella leaned forward. This was the reason she'd come, the question she was going to ask.

Flo's breath, once again, was tickling her ear. When she jabbed her elbow into the woman to give her space, she lost her balance and landed with a *splat* on the tiled floor—right in plain view of the doorway.

Both Chapman and Jimmy turned. Neither seemed surprised to see her. Wink and Flo snickered behind her, still hidden.

"Hey, all. I was just looking for…" She grabbed the nearest thing she could find. "… this dust bunny?" Picking it up, she hoisted herself to her feet. "Yep, this dust bunny. And would you look at that? I found it."

With delicate fingers, handling the dirt puff like it was a baby bird, she placed the dust bunny in her jeans pocket and patted the outside. After a parting nod, she spun on her heel.

Two steps later, Chapman called out, "Ms. Barton, come here, please."

She stopped short, her shoulders slumping in defeat as both Wink's and Flo's eyebrows wiggled in mockery.

"And tell those two monkeys hiding in the hall that they may as well join us."

"Who's he calling monkeys?" Flo whispered.

"I know, right?" Ella said. "Apes would be more fitting. Or those baboons with the red butts."

When all three had crowded into the small room, Flo asked, "How d'you know we were here?"

"Because wherever one of you is, the other two aren't far behind." Chapman cut a formidable shape in the corner of the room, towering, his derby hat tilted back as he inspected them. "Not a word outta you three. Jimmy?"

"Sheriff?" The deputy's head inclined towards Ella and gang.

"I'd rather have 'em where I can see 'em, so I know they won't be causing a ruckus."

"And also because we were the ones who figured out who killed the professor," Ella added helpfully, a comment that earned her a glare from Harold. "Does this mean you'll let us observe all your interviews?"

"No."

"Maybe you should think—"

"No. And I just changed my mind. You can wait in the hall."

Ella made a motion of zipping her lips and remained in place.

On the bed, Harold let out a long-suffering sigh. This close, she could see the damage from the plasma blast. Broken capillaries, like branches, painted his skin. She had similar markings, although far less pronounced. The subsequent irregular heartbeat and the blow to his head when he'd fallen were the reasons for his medical observation.

"Harold," Jimmy prompted, "the cyanide? Where did you get it?"

The farmer's jaw twitched, and he looked from Jimmy to Chapman to the women. "I got it from a guy."

"Well, that answers everything," Wink murmured.

"A guy?" Jimmy didn't even bother writing that in his notebook. "Could you tell us about this man?"

He shook his head softly. "Don't know nothing about him. He showed up at my house one night. I heard this noise outside, and when I went to go look, he was there in the shadows. When I told him to scram, he said he could help me. Said he knew about my problem."

"Problem?" Chapman asked.

"'Bout Spot no longer being safe."

Jimmy's pencil scratched over his notepad. "What did he look like?"

"I told you, it was night. It was too dark to see more than a shape."

Jimmy waited patiently for more.

Harold tugged on the shackles chaining him to his bed, filling the room with their metallic dirge.

"I couldn't make out his face, but he was about your height, Deputy, and wore a trench coat."

An uneasy feeling came over Ella.

"Anything else?" Jimmy asked, jotting down the description.

Harold squinted, staring off into the middle distance. "Yeah, he wore a hat."

"What kind?" Ella asked before she could stop herself.

"Fedora."

She felt sick. The description matched the man in the professor's basement, the Shadow in the Hat. Dr. Kaufman's dying words *he found me* played on a loop in her head.

Chapman's expression didn't so much as flicker with recognition at the description of Will's attacker. She admired his poker face as he studied Harold a long while before he asked, "How'd he give you the poison?"

"Had it right there in his pocket. Reached in, opened his palm, and gave me a pill."

A pill? That took her by surprise.

Jimmy looked up from his notepad. "A pill? Just one?"

"One pill. It was weird, though."

"What was?" Chapman asked.

"The pill. I don't know what else to call it. Capsule, maybe? Vial? Whatever it was, it was made of glass."

"Glass?" Jimmy and Ella said at the same time.

After this, Chapman and Jimmy continued to question Harold, who explained how he'd sneaked into the cave, waited for the professor to leave (probably when he went to talk to Lou or Sal), then broke open the tiny capsule and emptied the contents into the strawberry jam. Ella half-listened, her mind still focused on the delivery method of the poison. Something tickled the back of her brain, a tidbit of random trivia that wouldn't quite surface.

Internally shrugging it off, she waited for a lull in the interview to slip in a question. "Why hit the professor on the back of the head, then?"

"That wasn't me. I never hit him."

When Chapman and Jimmy had finished questioning the man, they left Harold to pick at some turkey and cheese stacked between two slices of what looked like cardboard in the saddest sandwich Ella had ever seen. As a group, they ambled out of the hospital into the bright light of a beautiful day.

"Sheriff," Ella said, "the cyanide Pauline found in Dr. Kaufman's food, did she say if it was the pure chemical compound of hydrogen cyanide itself or the precursor amygdalin?"

"Should I be concerned you know so much about cyanide?"

"Only if Flo winds up dead under suspicious circumstances."

"I suppose there isn't harm in telling you... the doc said it was straight cyanide, not the amyg—what you said one."

Ella fell silent as the implication sunk in, and she stared past him. A few feet away, hitched to a light pole, Horse stood munching on the hospital's landscaping, his tail flicking.

How did a person obtain pure cyanide? *Who* would even have that?

"So somewhere in our town is a very dangerous person in possession of hydrogen cyanide—assuming there's more where that capsule came from—and with no qualms about murder." Ice settled over her chest. The same person who'd attacked Will and told him to fix the time device could poison him. "He's out there, somewhere, hiding."

"Hiding in plain sight," Wink added quietly.

Chapman swung up into Horse's saddle. "Not in my town, he won't. I'll find him." He leaned forward, resting one arm on the horn of his saddle. "I'll see you three tomorrow at Pauline's office."

Ella blinked at him. "What? Why?"

"You're going to scrub her place down until it shines, then you'll repaint it if that's what she fancies. After that, you'll help me hang her a new door."

Flo began to protest, but he held up a calloused hand. "You'll do all that without a lick of complaining if you don't want me arresting you." With that, he brushed his derby hat before trotting off, and the clop of shod hooves over cracked pavement faded.

"How'd he know it was us?" Flo looked at the others, earning a patronizing pat on the back from Wink and a pitying expression.

Ella supposed the crime fit the punishment and, all things considered, was more than fair recompense for blowing up the woman's lab. But did it have to be on her day off?

Jimmy strolled with them to Wink's car. Although he still wore a badge that glinted in the sunlight, his posture and gait shifted, changing from a deputy to their friend.

Ella stopped short, gasping, her hand flying to the nearest person, who happened to be Wink. "Nazis!"

"Excuse me?" Wink recoiled.

That single word had an immediate effect on her audience, as if she'd shouted the dirtiest, most vulgar word right in the middle of church. For them, World War II hadn't been that long ago, an ugly travesty still visible in their rearview mirror, the wounds still very fresh.

"That's where I've seen that type of cyanide capsule before. It was in a documentary about Nazis and their preferred method of suicide when allied forces were closing in."

Jimmy tilted his head. "But how did a cyanide capsule make its way here to Keystone? All the Nazi spies were rounded up towards the end of the war. I suppose it's possible one went amiss..." He pondered it a moment before shaking his head. "Sorry, but that's a bit outlandish."

"More outlandish than time travel?"

"You've got me there. Still... I think we'd know if a sleeper Nazi spy lived in Keystone Village. After this last decade jumping from place to place, they would've made themselves known."

Tempted to point out that that was the point with a sleeper spy, to go unnoticed, she instead opened the passenger-side door to Wink's blue Oldsmobile but didn't get in.

"Also, why would a Nazi hide *here*, of all places?" Jimmy added, more to himself.

His thinning scalp shone under the sun, and tired lines cracked the corners of his eyes. He hadn't made the connection yet between a possible spy and the professor.

She didn't blame him. Even she had to admit it was conjecture at this point, but there was that book she'd found in Dr. Kaufman's home about Nazi spies, and the diagrams of alternative timelines he'd been working on.

From what she could infer from pieces of scattered conversations, he'd been conscripted by his country to work on top-secret projects as a physicist in Germany during the war. How deep his convictions had gone, she couldn't guess. He'd been designing a machine that could manipulate space-time when the United States government covertly brought him to America. It wasn't such a leap to consider that the Nazi party had sent an agent after Dr. Kaufman to retrieve the machine.

His method of death was yet another coincidence that didn't sit quite right with her. Out of all the poisons to pick... was someone making a statement? Someone bitter over their predicament, who'd chosen to take their wrath out on the man responsible, using the very method by which Hitler had chosen to kill himself?

But all this untangling of conspiracies required more brainpower than she commanded at the moment. When she turned to get into the car, she discovered Flo sitting in her seat. The woman had managed to slip behind her unnoticed, no easy feat considering the boarder moved with the grace and rapidity of a drunken elephant.

"Out."

Flo produced an emery board from her hair and began scratching her nails across it, ignoring Ella. Too exhausted to pull a senior citizen from a car, she joined Jimmy in the back seat.

Riding through town, she let the breeze from the open window whip around her already tousled hair. They'd put another murderer away, but this time, it rang hollow. There were still so many loose ends. The Shadow in the Hat had supplied the poison that killed the professor, and if her hunch was right, he was something darker, viler, than anyone she'd faced thus far. Perhaps Wink was right, and this dangerous man was hiding in plain sight.

Her eyes drifted over to Jimmy before she instantly dismissed the thought. But what if it was someone they knew? Someone close to them? Someone who wanted to fix the machine, so he could re-write history?

Whatever it took, she needed to unmask this man before he killed again, before he took someone close to her.

CHAPTER THIRTY-TWO

ABOUT THREE HOURS of the rest of Ella's Saturday consisted of a long, sorely needed nap once she returned home from their visit to the hospital. Wink decided to close Grandma's Kitchen for the day, giving them and Horatio a much-needed break.

Sunday was spent—as demanded by Chapman—scouring the cold storage room of smoke and blast damage. Tired and sweaty, they helped the sheriff affix the new door in time to run home, change, and make it to the town hall meeting. It was full of the usual town disputes that devolved into bickering and threats and one of Flo's photon bombs that blinded them all for thirty minutes.

The next few days drifted by like the passing clouds overhead, punctuated by the cleaning of Sal's barbershop as recompense for the window they'd busted. He'd already had the window replaced with a dusty, low-quality glass one, so sweeping the floor, polishing metal fixtures, and trimming his hedge out back was their punishment.

They'd offered up the work in exchange for him not telling Chapman what they'd done. Despite the bitter blood between Sal and Wink, the man had moments when he was tolerable.

Along with the obvious charge of first-degree murder, Harold had been charged with vandalism for the water treatment facility. A week later, Craig the caveman was relocated back to the cave system, much to his delight, after placing him in various lodgings had resulted in ruined furniture and unwanted wall murals.

When back in his old digs, Ella took a plate of bacon to him, which he promptly devoured, and she managed to capture more of his language for analysis while asking him about the blow to the back of the professor's head. He pantomimed hitting him, uttering a string of words she recorded. From what she could piece together, the two roommates had a falling out over some food—probably the jam and bread—and Craig had hit him. Unbeknownst to the caveman, the doc had just ingested cyanide moments before. Talk about horrible timing.

Sometime Wednesday of the following week, the water treatment facility was up and running again, and the unrest that had been building in the village like the pressure in a volcano died considerably. As a bonus, people began smelling markedly better—especially Flo.

"Well? Say something?" Wink, her elbows resting on the lunch counter, stared expectantly at Ella.

Ella pulled another hunk of bread from the slice on the plate and let it dissolve in her mouth, her eyes sliding shut. "This is the one, the winning recipe. It's perfect, Wink."

The gingerbread was the taste of Christmas with her family, a flash of her mother's smile as she spilled flour all over the floor, and warm evenings wrapped in a blanket beside a roaring fire. Her eyes stung, and she looked away, blinking.

"Your turn." She slid a silver malt container across the counter, the questionable-looking contents of the smoothie sloshing around inside.

Wink's nose wrinkled. "Why's it purple?"

"You know, I'm actually not sure."

"Maybe you should try it first."

"Fine, I will." Ella brought the drink as far as her lips before the odor knocked into her like a stiff breeze off a garbage dump. Clearing her throat, she placed the smoothie back on the counter. "Hey, what do you say we see what Horatio's up to? It's been a while since we've made fun of his hair. Let's do that."

Wink smiled.

Later, during one of her breaks, Ella sat in the corner booth, flipping through photos on her phone. A partially deconstructed cheeseburger lay demolished on her plate. Her thumb slid over the screen, rapidly flitting through images of Craig's jail cell paintings she'd taken the previous week when she first began communicating with him.

She stopped.

Bringing her phone to her face, she zoomed in. Just like his cave paintings, these had stick figures representing the caveman, himself, and the professor standing off against Harold and Spot. At the time she took the photo, she'd mistaken Craig's accompanying yells and nonsensical gesticulations as being freaked out at the sight of her phone, but now she realized he'd been reenacting a confrontation between the professor and his would-be murderer.

A fourth figure hovered at the periphery, one with a strange head. She squinted. No, not an oddly shaped head, but a *hat*, one that resembled a fedora.

Her head shot up. The Shadow in the Hat had visited Craig's cave. Had he confronted the professor? If so, why not just kill him there and then rather than use a proxy?

Endless questions rolled around her mind like a turbulent sea, then an island of hope emerged. If the dangerous man, the possible Nazi spy, had visited the cave, then perhaps Craig could identify him. It was worth a shot, at least.

Don't fix the device. He'll use it and change everything.

Ella stood before a Victorian-style house on the outskirts of Keystone Village. Emerald green grass reflected morning dew, diamonds of a waking sun.

The man who answered the door was around Jimmy's age and smiled at her, a question in his eyes.

"You're that Ella Barton woman, aren't you? The one from the future."

"I am. Is Judy here?"

He gave a nod, the curiosity in his eyes deepening as he stepped aside. "In the backyard."

As they passed through the kitchen, Judy's mother rose from the table, a fresh stack of pancakes steaming in the middle. She wore a pressed apron with nary a stain on it. Her hand reached for the percolator, but Ella waved her off.

Ella stepped into the cold shade of the patio where she could see Judy's parents watching from the kitchen window. She plunged into the damp grass. When she'd asked how the little girl was faring after her ordeal in the cave, seeing the professor's body, they'd said she'd been quiet, withdrawn, and she'd stopped playing with her dolls.

In the middle of the yard, a large wooden spool sat on its side, creating a makeshift table for a tea party set. Dolls sat in chairs around the perimeter, and Judy sat with them, still as the nearby apple tree. Copper braids fell around her shoulders, and her face angled towards the horizon, staring.

She didn't move or play or pour tea.

"Mind if I sit?"

Judy blinked, the only acknowledgment she'd heard her.

Ella took that as consent and picked up a stuffed bear that could've used a spa day in the washing machine. Resting the bear in her lap, she poured herself invisible tea. "I hope you don't mind. Does this have caffeine? I ask because I've already had three cups of coffee this morning. Also, I was going to offer some to Mr. Bear here, but I'm not sure it's safe for his kind."

Judy's eyes found hers. "Mr. Bumbles." Her voice came out soft, haunted.

Ella inspected the bear. "Mr. Bumbles, you say? Did he get stung by a bumblebee to get that name?"

A ghost of a smile flickered on the girl's face. "No. He just bumbles around a lot."

"Yes, they do say bears are clumsy." Holding Mr. Bumble's by the back, she dipped his face in her teacup. "Mr. Bumbles, that's not very nice." She slurped loudly out of the corner of her mouth. "Really, that's quite rude now. Who taught you to drink like that?"

It was no longer a hint of a smile, but a grin.

Ella released the bear so that he flopped his head onto the table beside the cup. She whispered loudly, "I think he might've had too much to drink." She let out a small burp, and Judy giggled.

Their tea party continued for another fifteen minutes until they'd drunk all the invisible tea and eaten all the invisible finger sandwiches.

"I brought you something." Ella pulled out a small jewelry box from her sweatshirt, set it down, and slid it over to the little girl.

"You brought me a present?" Her small hands popped the lid open before Ella could respond. Her face lit up, the smile stretching from ear to ear.

"Do you know what that is?" Ella asked.

"Polaris, the North Star."

She blinked. "Right. I forgot you're a Firefly and know things. Anyway, it made me think of you because it represents a guide, something that can always point you home.

"Sometimes, when bad things happen in the world around us, we need that beacon of light to remind us who we are. Never forget: you are strong, you are resilient, and there is nothing you can't get past." They were simple words, but they were the best she had to offer.

The morning sun lit the girl's hair like fire, her face radiant. It was a beautiful moment that scored Ella's heart, and she tucked it away in her memory to keep with her always.

Judy's small chair tumbled into the grass as she bolted to her feet and ran into her house. The door was left open, and her words gushed out as she told her mother about the new charm for her bracelet.

Blinking, Ella rose and retreated across the lawn, using the side gate to leave. There was one more stop she needed to make, one that required fortitude.

The door to Lou's auto shop stood open, letting the clamor of tools and cursing spill out into the pleasant morning. From the sidewalk, she watched him work, then realized she probably looked like a creeper. That was fine. This would only take a moment.

All that she'd lost—everything—had become a source of gut-wrenching pain, and this man was the cause. Standing there, she realized she couldn't fully forgive him. Not yet.

Her mother had once told her forgiveness wasn't a one and done decision, but a choice made every day until sometime in the future, you looked back, and it was complete. Today would be her first step of unknown, countless ones, and tomorrow she would have to choose again. And again. And for every day after until the anger was gone.

She breathed deeply as a single tear rolled down her cheek.

"I choose to forgive you," she whispered to the open air.

"Will, hurry!" Ella sprinted through the park. When she looked back, she arranged her expression into panic. "It's behind us!"

Will's hat flew off.

"Leave it!"

"What is it?" He gasped for air.

"I don't know, but it's big. And has sharp teeth."

He caught up, his chest heaving, as they continued running, their shoes pounding the grass in the park. "Is it a T. rex?"

"It's not that big."

His pace slowed as he peered back. "I don't see anything."

"You sure? I swear it was right behind us. Better keep moving."

"I thought all the dinosaurs were gone."

She fell into a rhythm and, instead of aiming for the safety of the forest, rounded the lake. Soon, they were running along the trail.

Will twisted, looking back again, and stopped.

"What are you doing? Hurry! Keep moving, old man."

"El, there's nothing there."

"Sure, there is." Her shoes scuffed concrete as the trail became sidewalk, the scent of the lake heavy in the air. Turning, she retraced her steps to where he'd stopped, then jogged in place.

He frowned at her. "What're you doing?"

"Hmm?"

"You're looking at your watch... Aha! There's no dinosaur chasing us, is there? You're trying to trick me to go on another one of your jogs!"

"I've no idea what you're talking about," she said in a flat tone, glancing at her watch again. "But if we don't pick up the pace, I'm going to have one of the slowest times since arriving here."

After much cajoling, they finished the large lap around the body of water, mostly because she dragged him by his wrist. He grumbled the entire way, ending with, "What if I *like* having high blood pressure?"

An hour later, under the shade of budding oak leaves, Ella sipped lemonade, watching a fisherman on the water. He'd been out there for some time and seemed to be doing more drinking than fishing.

Beside her, Will lounged on a matching lawn chair, his hat covering his eyes, exhausted. Ice clinked in her glass as she took another sip. The smell of chicken on the inn's grill on the terrace wafted over as Rose and Jimmy quarreled about whether the meat was done cooking.

When she hollered an offer to check for them, they shouted, "No!" almost immediately. One dish of undercooked chicken at a potluck and suddenly she can't come within ten feet of raw poultry. Of course, no one had gone to the bathroom right for a week afterward, but how was that her fault?

The hair on her arms rose, and she felt a familiar tingle that wasn't unlike the effects of the plasma cannon just before it fired. Above, an azure sky crackled with fuchsia and pink lightning, creating a dome, building until the flashes coalesced. She closed her eyes a moment before the now-familiar flash of blinding light like that of a nuclear bomb.

It took a few moments of blinking for the after image to clear and to see again. When the blindness faded, her mouth fell open.

"Will." Without looking, she reached over and nudged him, hitting his fedora-covered face. "Will, wake up."

Words failed her. Looming just beyond the forest, blotting out most of the sky, were three pyramids. "Large" didn't come close to describing their magnitude. Judging by the state of them, they were within spitting range of when they'd been erected. They had that shiny, recently built pyramid look to them.

She'd never had the pleasure—or capital—to visit any in person, but she'd seen photographs. Pyramids were found around the globe, but these were distinct, instantly recogniz-able. Somewhere at their bases would be smaller imitations, as well as a sphinx, obscured at that moment by the Key-stone Forest.

The pyramids of Giza. They'd jumped to ancient Egypt.

TRAVELING TOWN MYSTERIES

#1 Pancakes and Poison

#2 The Body in the Boat

#3 Christmas Corpse

#4 Phantoms and Phonographs

#5 Perils and Plunder

#6 Ghastly Glitch

#7 Campfire Catastrophe

PET POTIONS MYSTERIES

#1 Potent Potions

#2 Ghostly Garlic

#3 Brutal Brew

Made in the USA
Monee, IL
26 September 2020